Barbed Wire

**Fear, romance and betrayal
in Occupied Guernsey**

Theresa Le Flem

Theresa Le Flem © Copyright 2024

The moral right of Theresa Le Flem to be identified as the author of this work has been asserted in accordance with the Copyright, Design and Patents Act 1988.

All rights reserved. No part of this publication may be reproduced, stored in a retrieval system, or transmitted in any form or by any means without the prior permission in writing of the author. Nor may it be otherwise circulated in any form of binding or cover other than that in which it is published.

This book is a work of fiction. All characters and events, other than those clearly in the public domain, are fictitious. Any resemblance to real persons, living or dead, is entirely coincidental and not intended by the author.

A CIP catalogue record of this book is available from the British Library.

Cover photography and design by the author.

ISBN – 13 979-8883971104

Ebook ASIN B0CW7V3WZ4

For all those in the Channel Islands who lost their lives
during the German Occupation
1940 – 1945.
May they rest in peace.

Prologue

Guernsey, June 1940

Thirty miles off the coast of France, the island of Guernsey had enjoyed a relatively peaceful existence until a year into the Second World War when the German advance across Europe left the islanders uneasy. How long would it be before Hitler set his sights across the small stretch of water from St. Malo and Cherbourg to the tiny Channel Islands which were under the jurisdiction of the British Crown? However, Prime Minister Winston Churchill, believing Hitler would have little interest in them as they were so small, declared that he was unable to spare the military to defend them. He ordered the troops who were stationed there to be withdrawn and that the islands should be left undefended. As a precaution, he advised that the population should evacuate to England. The people of Guernsey, on hearing this, understandably felt vulnerable and panic ensued. They had the choice whether to stay or to leave and with ships soon arriving from England, they had just twenty-four hours to decide. Allowed to carry just one suitcase, sandwiches and one change of clothes, evacuees were told to gather on the harbour ready to leave.

As a result, many families were separated. Some of the schoolchildren, accompanied by their teachers, boarded the boats in tears. Others were excited because they had never been off the island before and believed it was like a holiday. But many women, often with babies in their arms, kissed their menfolk goodbye without knowing when they would see them again. In their haste, many islanders abandoned their vehicles by the harbour, while departing farmers humanely slaughtered or turned loose their livestock and these joined the cattle and sheep arriving in Guernsey from the small island of Alderney. Most civilians had no option but to have their pets put to sleep. Having had to leave their homes with barely time to prepare, those who chose to stay described how they found their neighbour's houses empty, eerily quiet, with meals left half-eaten on the table and fires still smouldering in the grate.

For those who remained, the future was uncertain. Then, for a day or two, an uncanny calm prevailed. There were no children's voices playing in the streets, and none of the usual comings and goings of a busy town. Allied planes could be heard overhead, thrumming their way across the channel on bombing missions, darkening the sky and producing clouds of smoke on the French coast. It was the lull before the storm, however. The Channel Islands' strategic position, situated less than fifty miles from France, unfortunately gave Hitler every reason to claim them for himself. To gain a foothold on British soil was his prize. Several Luftwaffe planes circled the islands like vultures above the calm blue sea. A day later they returned with dire consequences.

It was the end of a hot summer's day. Growers were loading their crates of tomatoes and flowers onto boats ready for export when three German Luftwaffe planes were again seen approaching. However, this time without warning they attacked. They machine-gunned the harbour, dropping bombs on the queuing tomato lorries and causing bloodshed and devastation for almost an hour. Men who were sitting in their cabs waiting to unload their produce dived under their lorries for shelter only to be crushed or burnt as their vehicles erupted in flames. Almost forty people, including farmers, lorry drivers, dockworkers and ambulance men were killed. Hitler's invasion of the Channel Islands had begun. A scene of carnage unfolded on White Rock harbour that day and sadly it proved Churchill's judgement tragically wrong.

Also by Theresa Le Flem

Novels

The Sea Inside His Head
The Forgiving Sand
The Gypsy's Son
Dreamcatcher Girl

Anthology of Poetry

Meet Me at Low Tide: Poems and Drawings

Chapter 1

Guernsey, October 1942

As Ellen walked to work at the bakery she felt uneasy. Dawn was breaking, and the neighbouring islands of Sark, Herm and Jethou were looming out of the sea mist on the horizon. Seagulls soared overhead, sending their raucous cries across the rooftops. The air was cool, pungent with the scent of falling leaves and the salty tang of seaweed. Her journey to the bakery took her away from the bustling town, with its rickety roofs and helter-skelter alleyways, towards the quieter parish of St. Martin. All appeared normal, peaceful even, but she knew the whole island was holding its breath. The cobbled streets of St. Peter Port would soon be ringing with the daily march of German soldiers' jackboots.

Behind her she suddenly heard the rattling of an army truck approaching. As it came up and passed by, she caught sight of the gaunt faces of several prisoners staring out at her. She swallowed hard; their plight was more than she could bear. Stories of their maltreatment were on everyone's lips but any attempt to intervene would lead to imprisonment themselves and few dared even to try. The vehicle hurtled on and was soon out of sight. Ellen breathed deeply, dreaming of the day when they would all be free from the tyranny of occupation. As she approached the gates, the sight of her friend Lucy coming up towards her on her bicycle cheered her up. They greeted each other, exchanging the latest gossip in hushed tones, and after storing the bicycle away they entered the bakery together. Wrapped in the warmth of baking bread and its delicious fragrance, and hearing Lucy chatter away about her latest escapade, Ellen's spirits lifted. They went to hang up their coats and put on their overalls. Another day had begun.

But now, along that same road, slave workers were being marched to face another day of hard labour under their German guards. Lukasz, a young Polish prisoner-of-war, stared longingly at the open fields on either side as he passed. He sensed the peace out there, it was so tangible, freedom from his captors so temptingly close. One of fifteen already exhausted men, he was being kept in line by the ruthless guards of the Nazi Organization Todt. As a distraction from their whips and curses, he pictured in his mind's eye the family farm in Poland where he used to work with his father. But suddenly he stumbled. A guard yelled at him, his whip catching Lukasz viciously across the face.

   Then he heard a familiar sound which brought more memories of home. A horse and cart was approaching them; the horse being led by an old man on foot. The animal was so thin, it was obviously incapable of pulling such a heavy load. As it sank down on its haunches, the guards were enraged as it blocked the road. Desperately the man tried to coax his horse back on its feet. While the guards shouted and threatened, the prisoners glanced at each other, grateful for the opportunity to rest. But anger and pity surged through Lukasz at the plight of the horse. One of the German guards was becoming increasingly impatient. Finally, he stepped away from Lukasz and went to sort the situation out. While the guard's attention was diverted, Lukasz withdrew. Still facing forward, he shuffled back and back until he felt the prickle of shrubbery against his legs. As the confrontation became louder, charged with a new-found energy, he ducked down and disappeared quickly out of sight behind the hedge.

A shot rang out. Peering through the hedge, Lukasz saw them drag the horse to the side of the road. Several prisoners were ordered to shoulder the cart. It was heaved out of the way, its contents searched briefly and evidently of no interest, the march of prisoners' feet resumed, and the party moved on.

As if waking from a nightmare, Lukasz found himself alone. He looked around him. Birdsong filled the air. All that remained of the drama was the man who knelt by the body of his horse. A robin swooped down and began pecking grass seeds on the path nearby. Lukasz watched the bird incredulously, marvelling at it. After a few minutes he emerged from the hedge and looked up and down the road. Over the crest of the hill, he saw a valley and beyond that a calm sapphire sea with waves lapping onto the beach. It was as serene as a watercolour painting. His attention turned back to the old man. Gently he moved his feet in the dirt to make his presence known. The man cowered, perhaps expecting more heavy blows. Lukasz went to the horse. Crouching down quickly he felt for a pulse, his experienced hands following the curve of the neck and the deep chest. Then he saw the blankness that death brings so rapidly to the eye. Murmuring softly, he looked round at the old man and gazed at him in sympathy. He could do nothing. 'I sorry,' he said, in his broken English.

The old man nodded and grunted, raising his shoulders to reflect his despair. But the danger became too great for Lukasz. Making a quick decision, he stood up and set off to follow the hedgerow that bordered the field behind him; hopefully it would shield him from sight. His only chance was to find somewhere sheltered so he could think what to do next. Like a fox with the hounds on his scent, he made off as fast as his strength would carry him. He scoured the landscape, searching for a barn or an outbuilding – somewhere where he could hide. In the far distance there was a group of houses with smoke rising from the chimneys. Keeping well away from the road, he made off, savouring the taste of freedom like sweet white wine. If the Germans saw him and shot him at least he would have regained a tiny part of himself again before he died. All he needed were a few precious hours, just to think, to remember who he was.

Chapter 2

It was almost dark in the sitting-room as it was late in the evening, well after blackout, but there were still candles alight when Ellen came downstairs from her bedroom for a glass of water. She was surprised to see her parents were still up. Her father, however, looked as though he had fallen asleep in his chair. Albert de la Mare was a pharmacist, and as medical supplies were scarce, his job had become increasingly difficult.

'Mum, what on earth are you doing?'

Meg was kneeling on the floor and spread out before her was a long white dress. 'I went up in the attic this afternoon, looking for things we might be able to put up for sale in Dora's shop. You know, I'd almost forgotten it was there.'

'It's beautiful, Mum! But it's your wedding dress! You don't want to part with that, do you?'

'No, I don't, but any young bride in Guernsey will be struggling to buy a new dress these days. I was thinking of keeping it for you, Ellie, because one day, you know…'

'But I haven't even –'

'I know, Ellie. And it's no use hoarding things up when folks are needing them right now. We have to share what we have. I've probably got a few other things stored away I'll never use again.'

Ellen's gaze fell on the photograph of her parents on their wedding day. Her mother looking blissfully happy, wearing the dress that was now crumpled on the floor.

Meg sat back on her heels and reminisced for a moment. 'You know, I wore it all day long, even when I was dancing with your father! Do you remember our wedding day, Bert?'

There was no reply. She tried again, but louder. 'Bert!'

Albert stirred from his doze and cleared his throat. 'Eh? Of course, I do, dear.'

Meg smiled, winking at her daughter as she began folding up her wedding dress and putting it back in its box. At that moment there was a loud scuffling at the back door.

'Bother!' said Meg. 'That must be our neighbour's cat again. We can't spare any food for him tonight. It's hard enough finding anything for ourselves these days. It's wet outside too, the poor creature. I'll see if I can find him a little milk.' So in spite of her complaining, she got up and taking one of the candles with her, went to let the old cat in.

Ellen caught her father's eye as he tossed his head and chuckled. 'There she goes, your mother, she can't help it. She's a real softie at heart.'

They heard her kind cajoling voice: 'Come on in, then!' and then: 'Oh!' There was a startled cry.

'What's the matter? Is everything alright, Meg?' Ellen and her father rushed into the kitchen. What they saw was a tall stranger in the doorway. He was dirty and bloodied, his clothes in rags and smeared in mud. The rank smell of him filled the kitchen. One of his eyes was closed under a huge purple swelling but the one eye that remained open darted about, desperate as a hunted animal.

'Look here, what do you want?' demanded Albert, wielding his newspaper which he had rolled up like some kind of weapon. 'Wherever you've come from, you can't stop here! Get out!'

'Dad, wait!' Ellen stepped towards the man and saw how blood was oozing from a deep gash in his forehead.

'We won't hurt you, don't worry,' she said gently. 'What do you want? Are you being chased?' He began attempting to answer her and seemed to be speaking in a foreign language. Albert intervened, squinting at the man as if he was about to take a swing at him.

'I'm sorry young man! It's no use pleading with us, we can't understand you. Be on your way.' He was speaking in his most commanding voice and had puffed himself up to his full height to challenge the intruder. But Lukasz was gasping for breath, holding onto the door frame to support himself. Words that were barely comprehensible fell from his lips.

'Are the Germans after you?' cried Ellen.

'Please,' he breathed. 'Please help me!'

'Be off with you!' Albert was shouting now and turning red in the face.

'Dad, don't! Can't you see how frightened he is?'

'Bert, wait a minute, dear. Just look at him!' Meg restrained her husband by laying a hand on his arm. 'He must have escaped from the guards, the poor man!'

'Well, he can't stay here, I won't have it. And he stinks. Look at the filth on him!'

'Please Dad, let me talk to him.' Ellen began again in a calm cajoling voice. 'Who are you? We want to help you, but tell us, are the soldiers after you?' She was afraid that at any minute German soldiers with vicious dogs could be chasing him and could come rampaging up the path into the house. She just wanted to bring him safely inside and close the door as quickly as possible.

Gazing from one face to another, the stranger turned his gaze back to Ellen and stretched out a hand towards her, pleading: 'Irena! You help me, Irena! Need water! Need water …'

'What did he call me?' cried Ellen. 'We've got to help him, Dad! We can't turn him away, look at him.'

Meg was staring from Albert to her daughter in dismay. 'Ellen,' she said soberly. 'Listen. You know what could happen if we take him in. If they find out, we'll be arrested, we would all be shot.'

Albert sighed. 'Your mother's right, love. If he's discovered, well, it'll be the end for all of us.' He faced the man again. 'I'm sorry, we would if we could, but we can't help you. Off you go, now young man. Be on your way and good luck to you.'

'No!' argued Ellen. 'Let him stay, please, Dad. You wouldn't turn away an injured animal looking like that, let alone a fellow human being.' Saying that, Ellen went to the sink, drew a glass of water and held it out to the man. He grasped it shakily and drank as if his life depended on it, groaning as he did so, sucking at the water noisily. Some of it was running down his chin onto his beard and bloodstained shirt. Having drained the glass, he staggered forward into the kitchen a few steps more. Faintness appeared to overcome him then

A Sea of Barbed Wire

and he sank down and collapsed. They all rushed to support him and between them they managed to get him up onto a chair. Ellen turned, closed and locked the back door. She swung round and stared at her parents defiantly, 'He's staying, eh? Mum? Dad?'

Albert nodded and looked at his wife. Without saying anything, Meg turned away, took a basin from the kitchen cupboard, poured water still warm from the kettle and having no disinfectant, added a little of their precious salt. With a clean rag, she approached him cautiously.

'I'll just clean this up for you a bit, okay? I'll try not to hurt you.' He eyed her as she began dabbing at the blood on his forehead. He winced and gasped but didn't resist. Albert retreated, taking his newspaper with him and grumbling to himself. As he did so he sent a stern warning.

'Not a word, Ellen, understand? Don't breathe a word about this to a single soul. Do you hear me?'

'Yes, Dad, and thank you.'

Yes, she thought to herself, sometimes life just comes and hits you in the face and there's not much you can do about it. You have to go with it, follow your heart and do what you think is right, if you want to be able to live with yourself, that is.

It was almost midnight when Ellen and her mother managed to get the young man settled and hidden for the night. Having made a bed up for him in the attic, a simple horsehair mattress with several blankets to cover him, they doubted he would have the strength to climb up there. However, after a little bread and milk, and much coaxing and encouragement, he managed it. Possibly desperation alone gave him that final essential boost. Leaving him a jug of water and a bucket "for the necessary" as Meg put it, they closed the trapdoor behind them and retreated down the stepladder. At the foot of the stairs, they stood and hugged each other before each going to bed themselves. Whatever they had let themselves in for, there was no going back now.

Chapter 3

Lukasz lay back on the pillows and sighed in relief. He was exhausted and overwhelmed. Such kindness he hadn't experienced for a very long time. Such darkness he hadn't known since he had travelled in the hold of the ship with other prisoners for what seemed like weeks on end. On the ship, the heaving, rolling motion of the sea, and the stink of diesel fumes and sweat had caused the men to vomit. He had vowed to himself that one day he would get home to Poland again. One day he would find his mother and his poor sister, look after them and take them somewhere safe.

Wherever it was he was being shipped to with other prisoners, he expected it to be as bad if not worse than before. Weeks, months, it could be years had passed since his father had been murdered on their farm at home in Poland. When the ship eventually docked and Lukasz, along with the other prisoners, were driven down the ramp like cattle, he had no idea where he was. It looked to him as if he had arrived in heaven. It was a land of peaceful fields, country roads, beautiful scenes and a blue sapphire sea. He remembered blinking, blinded by the sudden harsh sunlight. Everything was now so disconnected from his previous life that it became impossible for him to keep track. All Lukasz remembered of the journey by ship was the darkness, the moaning and sickness. But now, as he lay on the mattress enveloped by the comforting weight of blankets, he felt safe, wrapped in a cocoon of warmth.

However, whenever he dropped off to sleep, the nightmares returned. He couldn't convince himself that at any moment a guard might not bear down on him again. As soon as he drifted off, he would jolt awake again and cry out in fear. He listened, panting, afraid that someone might have heard him. Far off, the distant sounds of the night gave him reassurance: the revving of a vehicle, the odd shout, the whine of a dog. His thoughts turned to the inhabitants of the house itself. The girl. Who was she? He remembered how, in his confusion, he had mistaken her for his sister, Irena. He knew that his mind was playing tricks on him. Before he could fathom out what had happened, how he had managed to be where he was now, feeling safe at last, he succumbed to exhaustion and fell into a deep sleep.

After the events of the previous night, Ellen had hardly slept. Distressed by what had happened, and disturbed time and again by a groan, or a sudden cry from the attic above her head, she couldn't help but keep listening out for any more sounds. By the time her alarm went off she felt ill with lack of sleep. There was no alternative but to get dressed and go to work. If she behaved any differently and didn't stick to her normal routine, suspicions could be aroused. She had to act normally even if she didn't feel it. So as usual she left the house soon after dawn; work at the bakery had to be well underway before the grocery shops opened so their boss could deliver the bread on time.

A Sea of Barbed Wire

Not long after she had set off to work on foot, she saw a group of prisoners and the forced slave labourers of the Nazi Organization Todt. The poor men looked desperately unhappy and dirty. The sight of the ragged, half-starved men filled her with pity. She thought of the man they had hidden and breathed a sigh of relief as she saw some of them wore no shoes and their feet were bleeding and bound with strips of dirty cloth. One man had pulled a cement sack over his head and was wearing it to keep out the cold. Pitiful as he looked, still the guards swore at him and shoved him onwards with their rifle butts. She couldn't bear to walk too close to them and she held back, waiting for them to go ahead. The rising sun glittered on the sea in the distance, greeting the new day with a drift of warmth and healing. That so much beauty could exist alongside such evil cruelty brought tears to her eyes. It couldn't be possible, not on their beautiful island.

Turning a corner, she found herself alone again with only the sound of seagulls wheeling overhead. If only people could be as free as the seagulls, she thought, like we used to be. If they could only save one poor man, and give him his freedom back, it would be worth it. Just as she mulled this over, a German armed vehicle came roaring round the corner towards her, and she had to jump out of the way to get out of its path. One soldier sitting next to the driver leant out of the window and gave her a piercing wolf whistle. She pretended not to notice.

On reaching the bakery Ellen was drawn into the warm busy atmosphere of breadmaking and she joined her friend with relief. Lucy was already working, sleeves rolled up, plump arms plunged into a huge bowl of flour. After half an hour or so of mixing, kneading and weighing out, she was surprised by Lucy suddenly saying:

'Okay, so come on, Ellie, what's up with you today?' She had stopped work to hitch up her skirt, leaving a dusting of white flour on her overall.

'I'm fine, Lucy, I'm tired that's all, didn't sleep too well. Let's get this lot done and we can have our tea break.'

When the two girls had finished work that day, they walked out of the gates together to collect Lucy's bicycle from the outhouse. Ellen was studying the road ahead where a group of German soldiers were gathered, smoking and chatting on the corner. She knew she would have to walk past them to get home. 'Honestly, Lucy, I wonder if we'll ever get our island back. With nearly all the beaches mined, and the coast surrounded by guards, it's like a prison. I went to walk on the beach the other day and it was just a sea of barbed wire. We can't even swim in the sea anymore. Don't you feel trapped?'

'No, not really. At least the war's flyin' over our heads and they're leavin' us in peace, even if they are watchin' us all the time.' She giggled. 'Anyway, some of them are rather alright! I don't mind em' lookin' at me! I'd better go, I'll have the mother-in-law on my back again. See you tomorrow!' Lucy flicked her blonde hair, climbed on her bicycle and waving cheerfully, she peddled off.

Ellen walked on alone, avoiding the gaze of the soldiers who stood there eyeing her. She felt excited about the man they were hiding and her pulse raced.

When she arrived home her cheeks were flushed as the wind was fresh, bearing the chill of Autumn approaching. As soon as she got in the door she couldn't wait to ask:

'How is he, Mum?'

'He's alright, love. He seems to be sleeping all the time, exhausted probably.'

'I'm not surprised. I bet he's just glad to be alive.' Hanging her coat on the nail inside the door she added, 'Oh, I got a wolf whistle this morning!'

'At seven o'clock in the morning? Who from?' Her mother raised her eyebrows.

'One of those German soldiers of course. He was just driving past or I would've told him to get lost.'

Her father overheard and lowered his newspaper. 'You be careful, love. Don't go giving them any of your cheek, you could find yourself being arrested.'

Ellen laughed. 'I don't think he wanted to arrest me, Dad. I think he had something a lot more friendly in mind!'

Meg smiled. 'Take no notice of your father, love. He's showing his age. He's forgotten what it's like to flatter a pretty girl.'

Albert huffed. 'Just be careful, that's all I'm saying, they're not to be trusted, none of them.'

'Our daughter's a sensible young woman, Bert.'

'I'm just saying. I've heard enough stories of girls getting themselves into trouble, so steer well clear.'

'I'm sure they're not all bad, they're just young men doing their job and following orders.'

'Just doing their job? Have you forgotten how that soldier hit your poor father and gave him a heart attack? You can't trust those Jerries an inch, none of us can.' Retreating into his newspaper, he kept on mumbling to himself. He didn't like being beaten by a woman any more than he did by the Germans.

Fortunately, their conversation was brought to a close by the sound of a horse and cart rattling to a halt outside. Seconds later there was a thump on the door and Meg stood up quickly. 'That'll be your nan with the delivery, bless her. I don't think I'd have half her determination, carrying on the way she does.'

Joan's head appeared around the door. 'Here's your potatoes, Meg and I've got your logs on the cart. Come and give me a hand, would you Bert?' She had her usual commanding tone and stopped to stare at him until he put aside his newspaper before disappearing again.

Albert dragged himself out of his armchair. 'How that woman keeps going with her husband still warm in his grave is beyond me.'

'Just be thankful she does, or we'd be going to bed hungrier than we do already.'

When they had finished unloading, Joan tied her old mare to the gate post and gave her a bag of oats. Coming in, she sat down with a huge sigh. 'It's all go! I've been on my feet since five this morning. Max used to bring me a cuppa before he went off to start work and it set me up for the day. No chance of that now.'

'He was a good man,' agreed Albert. 'I never knew a more helpful chap.'

'Poor Gran'pa. I miss him too, Nan.' Ellen was sitting on the window seat, while Joan settled into the armchair more comfortably and sighed. Filling the kettle, Meg regarded her with concern. 'You ought to be taking it easy now, Mother. Perhaps you're overdoing it.'

'Huh! Can't be doing with idleness, never could.' As if to emphasise her point, Joan looked around the room keenly. 'My goodness, Bert, where's that sideboard gone? You know, the one Max and I gave you that stood by the fireplace there.'

Meg pulled a face and looked a little guiltily at her husband. 'I'm afraid Bert had to chop it up for firewood. We ran out of fuel for the fire and it was -'

'But you could've asked me for some! I've still got plenty in the outhouse!'

'We didn't want to trouble you, Mother, so soon after, well - you know. And with you coping on your own now. You do enough for us as it is.'

'I'm not afraid of hard work, never have been. Max wouldn't be very impressed if he was looking down on me now and seeing you'd got no logs and were chopping up decent furniture to burn.'

Ellen, quietly sewing up the hem on her overall, was reflecting on the loss of her grandad. Her grandparents' home had played a huge part in her childhood, with the farm, the large vegetable garden, the outbuildings, and the orchard where chickens pecked about under the trees. Her grandparents' relationship was one of real co-operation, each sharing the load and working from morning until night. Theirs was an idyllic country life. But all that was before the Germans came.

The family sat and talked for a while but before she got too comfortable, Joan declared that she ought to move on and make the rest of her deliveries before it got too late.

'I daren't leave the old horse out there unattended for too long, she could disappear. They'd have the knackers to her and be carting her off to the kitchen.' Minutes later, as Ellen watched her nan climb back on the cart and heard the clip clop of her horse's hooves ring on the cobbles, she felt the burden of her secret lift.

'So when do we tell Nan about… you know?'

Meg shrugged and gave a quick shake of the head, but her father was more direct. 'We don't. Not unless she needs to know. The less folks know the less they have to say, right? Whoever knows about him puts them in danger of arrest – and we all know what that leads to, don't we. Your nan's got enough to worry about, so we'll let her be.'

Ellen and her mother exchanged worried glances, but they said nothing.

Chapter 4

After their tea-break the next day, the girls set about mixing a new batch of dough. 'Look at this!' Ellen had just opened a sack of flour and her heart sank. Running her fingers through it, she could feel the sharp husks that they knew irritate the stomach. 'Look how grey and horrible this is. How are we supposed to bake bread with this stuff?'

Lucy took a scoopful and wrinkled her nose. 'Is it mouldy? I wonder if George knows how bad it's got. I'll go and tell him, I bet he don't do nothin' though. Those Germans always pinch the best quality flour for themselves.'

Ellen watched her friend march off, flicking her blonde hair and swinging her hips. As she went, Lucy glanced back over her shoulder with a cheeky smile. Nothing seemed to phase her. Ellen wished she had some of her optimism and watched from a distance as Lucy stood talking to George. After a few minutes she returned empty handed. 'He said that's all they've sent us, so we've got to put up with it and it's better than nothin'.'

'Well done for trying, Lucy. Come on, let's put the next lot in the oven. It's not his fault. If we dared to complain about it, we'd probably find that would be the last of the flour we got. No meat, no potatoes and hardly any coal to buy now either. I don't know how we're going to cope in the winter, it's cold enough at night now.'

'We'll manage! You'll just have to go to bed earlier. How's it goin' with that new boyfriend of yours? Canoodlin' isn't rationed, not yet anyway! He might keep you warm!'

Ellen laughed off that remark and another hour passed by while they were mixing dough, dividing up and leaving loaves to rise in the warm kitchen. It was hard work kneading the dough by hand and they spoke little. Finally, they could have a break and make some tea. It wasn't tea as such, but an infusion of dried blackberry and hawthorn leaves and it tasted bitter, especially when there was no sugar to be had.

'Don't you ever feel like rebelling, Lucy? You know, when you've been standing in a queue for three-quarters of an hour and then a big-headed German officer comes pushing his way to the front and starts buying all the stock up so there's not a crumb left for anyone else. Don't you feel like telling him to wait his turn?'

'I wouldn't have the cheek! They're quite handsome though, aren't they, them soldiers! I wouldn't want to get on the wrong side of them. Imagine that!!' She chuckled, raising her eyebrows.

Ellen fought for a serious conversation. 'But that's how they always win though, how they get all the best stuff. Sometimes I've been queuing for over an hour and then find a German's been in and taken the lot.'

Lucy just giggled, saying, 'Naughty Germans!'

A Sea of Barbed Wire

The girls finished another day at the bakery, and it was about three thirty when they were on their way home. Lucy retrieved her bicycle from where it was hidden in the outhouse at the back of the bakery, out of the way of the roving eyes of the Germans, or anyone else who might take a fancy to it.

'I'll see you tomorrow then, eh?'

Lucy was tucking a small loaf of bread in her saddlebag. 'I bet my mother-in-law's been spoiling Charlie again. Honestly, she goes without herself, saves up all her sugar rations an' then makes him sticky sweets. He hasn't got many teeth comin' through yet an' what he has got will be rotten soon at this rate.' She pushed her bike out of the shed and began tucking up her skirt in readiness to ride. 'Hey, before you go.' Lowering her voice and casting her eyes about for any onlookers, she gestured for Ellen to come closer. 'Now we're alone. I've got something to tell you. but keep it to yourself, mind! I'll be shot if anyone finds out.'

Ellen glanced towards the bakery to make sure the boss wasn't about. 'What's up?'

Lucy's face flushed and her eyes opened wide in excitement. 'Now you won't say anythin', promise? The thing is, I'm seein' someone, a German soldier. He's gorgeous! It's not bad of me, is it? I mean he hates the war as much as I do, an' he hates Hitler, I know he does. He feels sorry for me an' my littlun, havin' to do without all the time. He brings me lots of nice things, extra butter, cheese and chocolate, and lovely soap and ...'

'Oh Lucy, what about your husband?'

Lucy stepped back and her face became guarded.

'Franz is much kinder to me than Pete ever was. He treats me like a proper lady. He's not horrible like some of the others, honestly. He's ever so sweet and he adores my little boy.'

A million thoughts flashed through Ellen's mind. The rumours she had heard about those so-called 'Jerry bags' – women who were sleeping with the enemy – were cruel. Talk was often about what people would like to do to them.

But seeing her friend, with her eyes now brimming with tears, Ellen couldn't help but sympathise. Lucy was her best friend after all. How could she not feel happy for her? She was always alone at home with her son with no-one to keep her company at night after curfew and blackout. Since her husband Peter had joined up, she had no-one to share her worries about finding enough food for him or how to keep him warm. Putting an arm around her shoulders, Ellen hugged her.

'I'm sorry. It must be so tough for you, coping with little Charlie and Peter away fighting. I won't tell a soul, I promise.'

At these words Lucy's smile broke through her tears. 'Thanks, I don't know what I'd do without you.' Having said this, she set off, waving happily.

Ellen was walking on home to the Rohais when she saw a troop of German soldiers marching towards her, blocking the road. It was impossible for her to avoid them. With their fast, military high goose-step, they marched while singing a German song loudly in unison. They were so serious about it, the way they moved together so smartly and proudly, they were almost like clockwork toys. She had to smile to herself. Standing

A Sea of Barbed Wire

aside, she pressed her back against the wall to let them pass, keeping her eyes averted. But close up, she noticed they weren't looking as fresh and confident as when they had first arrived in Guernsey.

To avoid the soldiers, she popped into the local shop. When she opened the door, the bell tinkled and she saw Dora, the shopkeeper's wife, standing by the window. It seemed she had been watching the soldiers pass by, their shadow darkening her little shop. The shop was a grocery store that sold everyday food requirements, or rather used to. Now a lot of the shelves were empty or displayed second-hand oddments which were open to offers for swapping or purchasing. Among the tins of food were children's toys, various bric-a-brac items, clothes and even shoes which had been outgrown. Dora and her husband stocked whatever they could get, whatever people were in need of, basically. The exchanges offered were, in some cases, very bizarre. Local advertisements were equally eccentric. In the Guernsey Evening Press, the Classified ads listed items open for bartering, for example, *"Four ounces of pipe tobacco, willing to swap for men's shoes, size nine."*

'Hello, dear! Sorry to hear about your gran'pa. What a dreadful business. He was such a nice man.'

'Thanks, Dora. Yes, I miss him so much. They were so harsh, hitting him for no reason, just because he couldn't find his identity papers.'

'Goodness, you wouldn't believe it would you, picking on an innocent man like that.'

'It's only because he was a little late getting home. He missed the curfew by just a few minutes, but he would have been okay.'

'How's your poor nan taking it?'

'She's coping and she'll manage, I'm sure. She's a tough sort.'

'Yes, she is and your mother takes after her, bless her. It's hard for your mum, though, losing her father suddenly at a time like this. 'Anyway, what can I get you, dear?'

Ellen mentioned a few things which she hoped might be available: butter, porridge oats and a tin of spam. But what she had to settle for was lard, rice, and a tin of sardines. She paid and was about to leave when Dora, after taking a sideways glance at the shop door, reached down under the counter.

'Wait a minute, dear. I keep some things back for my special customers.' Giving her a wink, she brought out a bar of perfumed toilet soap. It was brand new and wrapped in pink paper.

'Oh, what a luxury! I bet I can't afford it though, Dora. How much is it?'

'Nothing! It's a gift for you, my dear. A little present since you've lost your poor gran'pa. Sometimes we women need a little comfort, eh?' Ellen felt overwhelmed and was about to hug her, but judging by Dora's expression she hastily popped it in her bag as the shop door opened and a tall German officer walked in. She hurried outside, breathing a sigh of relief. That was close!'

Chapter 5

When Ellen got home, she dumped her shopping in the kitchen and greeted her father who, surprisingly, was already there sitting in his chair.

'You're back early, no more work today?'

'I took the afternoon off, love. We're short of basic supplies but I'm hoping to get a delivery of medicines tomorrow so, all being well, I can put a few extra hours in then. The Pharmacy's running on half-empty now though. Folks don't realise, if I haven't got the tablets, I can't dispense them. It's as simple as that.' He was shaking his head. 'It's a sad day when I know I'm depriving my patients, especially when their drugs are needed so urgently. We're short of insulin now. It'll be a matter of life or death soon if we can't get any.'

'It's not your fault Dad,' she said. 'Try not to worry.' She remembered the soap and trying to cheer him up she added, 'Look what Dora gave me!' She held the pretty package out to show him.

'Huh, and where did the woman get hold of that I wonder?'

'I didn't ask. It was kind of her though, wasn't it. And guess what, just as I was leaving, a German officer came in so I made sure I got out of the shop quickly.

Albert looked glum. 'Well, girl, we've got ourselves into a bit of a mess with our chap upstairs, eh? What do we do if they come knocking on our door and want to search the house?'

'I don't know, we have to hope they don't, that's all.' She pulled a face. 'How is he today? Have you been up to see him?'

'No, but your mother's been up and down a hundred times, taking him food, hot water, bandages, and I don't know what else. She said he's very weak but seems glad to be here. I should think he bloody well is.'

Her father hardly ever swore, and she looked at him twice. 'He was in a state though, wasn't he, Dad. You do feel sorry for him, don't you?'

'I feel sorry for the trouble we've got ourselves into, that's what I feel.'

'Don't you think us locals ought to show a bit of bravery though? We ought to try to help those poor prisoners and stand up to the Germans; they're so cruel and heartless.'

Her father shook his head. 'Oh, the dreams of the young and foolish!' And sighing, he picked up his newspaper, dismissing her.

But his comment gave Ellen a twinge of conscience. When she had given the poor man a glass of water, closed and locked the door behind him that night, she had defied her father and made the decision for them. Now they were all in it together, all of them at risk. She bit her lip. 'Dad, I will be careful, honestly. Do you know what his name is, or where he comes from?'

'Your mother asked him and he wrote his name down, it's over there.' Albert nodded to the table where a scrap of paper lay with jagged but clear handwriting in

A Sea of Barbed Wire

pencil. 'At least he can read and write even if he doesn't say much. That had better go on the fire - soon as I've lit it.'

She picked it up and reading it aloud, spelled the name: 'L U K A S Z. His name's Lukasz? That's a funny name, I wonder where he's from.'

'Poland, apparently.'

Before all this had happened, she had invited her new boyfriend, Robert, to come for supper after he had finished work. To cancel his visit without a genuine reason could have looked suspicious but admitting that they had taken in an escaped prisoner and hidden him in the attic was difficult to say the least. The subject of resistance in some way against the Occupying Forces had been raised before in discussion but this was resistance on a grand scale. Robert was a bank clerk and he had mentioned about the Germans' bullying attitude in the bank several times.

That the Germans should dictate how they should live, when they were allowed to go out, and what they could eat had got under Ellen's skin. Most locals managed on the limited supply of food and fuel, even though some underhand dealings were going on through the black market. But many now were falling sick and cases of malnutrition were occurring. On the whole though, people shared their limited supply of food and took on the hardship with their usual good humour. However, when Ellen saw her father's pale face and thought about the prospect of what to do, she began to feel very uneasy.

'Dad, you don't regret us helping Lukasz, do you?'

'I'd be stupid not to, Ellie.' He looked up at her. 'You realise what it means, don't you love? That if someone gives us away, we'll be treated no better than the worst of criminals. Imagine your poor mother being hauled away by the German police, tried in a German court, thrown in prison or deported to a prison camp in Germany. We could all be shot for what we've done.' He was shaking his head from side to side. 'Why did he have to choose our house? Of all the doors he could've knocked on, it had to be ours!'

'But Dad, we shouldn't allow the Germans to walk all over us. Everyone is too scared to do anything to cross them. Men and women all over Europe are defending us, fighting for their lives, fighting for our freedom. If everyone acted like we do in Guernsey, the Germans would already have won the war. Over here they seem to accept that whatever the Germans want they get. They can live alongside us, issue their orders, tell us what to do and everyone obeys. No-one threatens them or does anything.'

'Well, you've made your contribution to our war effort, Ellie. He's upstairs. So you can't say you haven't done anything.'

She glanced at him uncertainly, a little frown creasing her brow. 'We'll be alright though, won't we, Dad?'

'Time will tell, love, time will tell.'

*

Meg made up her mind to have another go at repairing the wedding dress to make it presentable to display in Dora's shop. It was a damp afternoon, the view across

A Sea of Barbed Wire

the sea to the islands of Herm and Sark was obscured by a heavy sea mist that had just come down. Determined to make some progress, she laid it out on the carpet before her. With pins beside her in a small tin, she worked her way around the frayed hem, pinning up the fabric. However, pushing the pins through the satin, she noticed to her dismay that they were marking it with rust. She stopped what she was doing and covered her face with her hands. Hardly any thread left to stitch with, no new ribbons or silk flowers available in the shops and now her pins were useless. Wiping a tear from her eye she gathered up the dress and put it back in its box. Her heart had gone out of it. She longed for the war to be over, for the shops to spring back to life, the shelves to be stocked full of new clothes, and to have joy and excitement back in their lives.

Footsteps were heard on the stairs and Ellen came hurrying down. 'Is it still raining, Mum? I'm meeting Lucy in town. Anything you want?'

'Just the usual, if you see anything worth having.' Meg went to the window. 'It's leaving off, love, but take my umbrella. Hang on a few minutes though, till that lot have gone past.'

Coming to the window, Ellen peered over her shoulder to see prisoners being marched to work. 'Oh, those poor men, Mum, look at them; their clothes are just rags! I wish there was something we could do.'

Meg looked at her. 'We're doing our bit looking after Lukasz, we can't do any more.'

'You'd think they'd realise men have to be fed and clothed to work hard though, honestly!'

Her mother gave her a rueful smile. 'Huh! There are plenty more men where they came from. I suppose they can afford to lose a few. Lives are cheap in their eyes.'

'It's horrible! They should be reported, Mum.'

'Reported to who?' Meg chuckled. 'They're the ones making the laws remember. This is Hitler's doing, Nothing's fair. By the way, just so you know…' She lowered her voice. 'I've heard a local woman's been caught trying to pass them a few crusts of bread. They were so starving they fought over it. Now she's being sent to Biberach in Germany.'

'For giving them a crust of bread?!'

'Yes, I'm afraid so. Look, they're going up the road, so if you're heading into town, be quick and you'll be alright if you leave now.' Then she added, 'See if you can buy something to help towards making a dinner, anything will do. Thanks love.'

When Ellen reached the town, Lucy, it seemed, was in no mood for waiting around.

'Where have you been? I've got nearly all I wanted already 'cos I got a lift into town early.'

'Lucky you.' Ellen shook out her umbrella and folded it up. 'Seems to have stopped raining at least. Who did you get a lift with then, your neighbour?'

'No, just someone I know. I'm going out to a dance tonight, but I don't need to worry about stockings now!' She dived into her bag and waved a brand-new pack.

'Where can you get stockings from these days? It's the first I've heard of it.'

'A friend of mine gave me some. I'll see if he can get you some too if you like.'

A Sea of Barbed Wire

'He? No, don't bother. They'll be more than I can afford anyway. You go and enjoy yourself. I've got a few things to get for my mum.'

Lucy's enthusiasm wasn't dimmed, and she toddled off in her high heels, leaving Ellen to wonder who it was managed to get hold of such a rare commodity.

Clutching her ration book, Ellen was expecting to have to queue for a while and her heart sank when she saw the length of the queue in the High Street. Taking her place behind the others, she was soon involved in the conversation that was going on. People were discussing the fate of what was apparently a prisoner who had escaped from a working party a couple of days ago. There were various guesses going on about who would dare shelter someone and where the fugitive might be hiding. Various houses had been searched already, she heard, and had their homes ransacked.

'Have they been an' searched your place yet, dear?' asked one elderly lady, fixing her sharp eyes on her.

Ellen shook her head. 'No, why? Why would they search us?'

'You know one of them prisoners escaped, eh? Rather him than me when they find him. Most likely tear him to pieces like dogs at a rabbit.'

Ellen began delving into her handbag, pretending to search for her purse. Her cheeks were burning. The queue shuffled up a bit and the discussion changed to the shortage of bread. At least here she was on safe ground. She began to tell her eager listeners about her job. Launching into it, she started describing the poor quality of the flour, telling them she suspected the Germans were adding stuff to it before they gave it to them to make it go further: coarse husks of wheat and oats, potato flour and even sawdust. They all nodded in disgust, clicking their tongues. All the time she was thinking: What would her mother do if they came to search the house? Her heart raced. Torn between remaining in the queue and rushing back home, she began to tell them about the time the Germans blundered into the bakery and demanded their whole morning's work for themselves.

'They grabbed all the fresh bread and stuffed the loaves into sacks, some of them were still hot from the oven too, honestly!'

Her audience were all ears. She enjoyed embellishing the story a bit. But they soon grew from being incredulous to disgusted. Hunger turns so swiftly into anger. It was half an hour before Ellen reached the counter and handed over her ration book. Her eyes stung when she saw what a pitiful amount was left. The shelves were virtually empty. Thinking of her mother at home waiting gave her an overwhelming sense of sadness. The responsibility of hiding Lukasz and keeping him fed in addition to themselves scared her, but there was no going back.

She left the shop with a swede, a cabbage and two eggs. It could have been worse. She hurried home, but before she could get back to warn her mother about the search, she saw the soldiers had already reached their street. As soon as she got to the house, Ellen flew in the door.

A Sea of Barbed Wire

'Mum, they're searching the houses! I just saw them up the road and heard a crash as if they were breaking a door down. What shall we do?'

'God help us if they come here, Ellie. Why are we risking our lives for him, love? A man we don't even know!'

'We had to, Mum. You know we did.'

She didn't reply. Her eyes were glued to the window.

There was some splintering of glass outside, and then she heard their voices. Meg gave a sharp intake of breath. 'Sounds like they're at Hilda's, the poor old soul! Stay here, love. I'll warn Lukasz.'

'Mum, don't go! He can hardly do anything about it!'

But she was gone.

To get into the attic, they kept a small stepladder stored under the double bed. Meg, to save time, took a chair from beside the bed and placed it on the landing under the hatch. Climbing up quickly she opened the hatch to the attic just an inch or two:

'Lukasz! The soldiers are coming. Hide yourself, now! Remember, the way I told you? Quickly!'

A few more words were exchanged and all that could be heard was Lukasz scrambling and shuffling about, the ceiling boards creaking and groaning as he moved. Meg closed the hatch, returned the chair and coming back down, she told Ellen to join her in the kitchen. There was nothing they could do now except hope and carry on as if nothing had happened.

'What's Lukasz doing, Mum?'

'I showed him the other day how to climb in the water tank and hide if the soldiers come.'

'Did he understand you?'

She shrugged. 'I hope so.'

Ellen sighed and pulled a face. 'In the cold-water tank, poor man.'

'It's just as well your father isn't at home. He said our lives are more precious to him than that man's up there and we shouldn't be taking these risks at all.'

'I know, Mum, but –'

'Ssh, hear that? I think they're here. Try to distract them with your pretty face, so smile nicely but be careful. We don't want you attracting too much attention from a soldier, however handsome he might be.'

Ellen looked at her mother quickly. Had she actually told her to flirt? Amazing!

A terrific banging came on their front door. Meg went to open the door. 'Good afternoon, gentlemen. What can I do for you?' She stood facing them with a polite smile.

'Schönen Nachmittag, Madame. Bitte treten Sie zur Seite!'

Without waiting for her reply, the two soldiers barged past her. They were as eager as dogs on the hunt. One stopped in front of Ellen momentarily and looked her up and down, his blue eyes lingering on her body before he moved on. The two women stood petrified as they followed the sounds of the soldiers' progress through the house. They heard cupboard doors banging, drawers flung open, things overturned. Their footsteps progressed up the stairs, stomp, stomp, stomp. Suddenly a shout from above sent them both rushing to the foot of the stairs. One of the soldiers was demanding something, and, not understanding what they wanted, Meg began to ascend the stairs after them. He was hammering his rifle butt on the attic door above his head. She took the steps from under the bed, feeling sick with fear and muttering what a nuisance they were and how busy she was.

The soldier leapt up on the steps and using the strength of his arms alone he flung open the hatch door and swung his body up through the opening. A cold blast of air rushed down from the roof. The draught reached Ellen who stood at the bottom of the stairs. It set goosepimples prickling up her arms. She was forcing herself to remain calm, picturing the broad sweep of the beach at Cobo and the gentle waves lapping where she used to bathe. Heavy footsteps thundered over their heads, and the ceiling joists of the old house were complaining with the extra weight. At the top of the stairs, the second soldier stood guard, his ice blue eyes fixed on Ellen who stood at the foot of the staircase.

There was a clambering sound as the soldier's legs reappeared. He landed with a thundering weight on the stepladder, almost breaking it. Giving a quick shake of the head to his colleague, he muttered,

'Gar nichts.'

Downstairs again, they made straight for the front door.

'Danke schön. Guten Tag,' said the first soldier who passed by them smartly and stepped out of the front door. But the second soldier stopped in front of Ellen, his blue eyes exploring her face, and lowering his gaze to rest on her blouse and her blouse buttons, causing her involuntarily to quickly check if they were done up. Slowly his eyes lingered. Suddenly he saluted her with that violent Nazi salute, clicked his heels and in seconds both of them were gone.

For several moments both women dare not move. Then Ellen wrapped her arms around her mother. Neither of them could speak. They waited, hugging each other, listening. After a few minutes Ellen went to the window to check the soldiers were out of sight.

'They've gone, Mum.'

'Thank God. I must go up and see if he's alright.'

'I'll go. You stay here and get your breath back.'

Climbing the stairs, Ellen fetched the stepladder and in spite of the fear of what she might find, she unlatched the attic door and peered in. It took a while for her eyes to adjust to the dark. 'Lukasz! Are you alright?' No response. Dread consumed her. Before going any further, she listened for his breathing or any movement but there wasn't a single sound. She panicked.

'Lukasz? Lukasz! Where are you? It's okay, they've gone.'

There was a shuffle and a shadow appeared in the darkness. Meg had followed her up and she was close behind her, flicking on a torch. The beam found Lukasz soaked to the skin and shivering, his eyes wild with fear. He had obviously done as he had been told.

Ellen peered into his face and smiled. 'I'll fetch a towel. You did well, Lukasz. I think we're going to be okay.' In one swift movement he reached out and grabbed hold of her hand, saying something in Polish and whimpering.

A Sea of Barbed Wire

'It's okay, it's okay, Lukasz. Get these wet clothes off and you'll soon feel better. Turning to her mother, she said, 'Can we raid Dad's wardrobe again for some more dry clothes?'

'Don't blame me if he complains when he gets home then. While I'm doing that, why don't you boil a kettle to make us all a nice hot cup of tea, we all need one; we can spare a little sugar too perhaps. I think we need it.'

Returning with a towel and carrying the hot drink, Ellen climbed up through the hatch door and blinked. It was hard to focus in the dark. 'Lukasz? I've brought you some tea.' Just a very thin slit of light shone down through a few loose tiles in the roof. A sheet of newspaper rustling revealed him still hunkered down in the corner by the chimney breast. It smelt damp in the attic but also of his sweat, of his wet clothes and urine. She wondered how the smell alone hadn't given him away.

He stood up, as far as he could because of the low beams, and he was tall. He took the cup of tea from her and put it down on the floor. Her eyes had grown accustomed to the dark, and she saw his face more clearly now, how his deep brown eyes gazed at her. He said something, which must have meant 'thank you' and then something else happened which she couldn't understand. He reached out and held her gently by her shoulders. 'You like my sister, Irena, very much.' He chuckled and released her, and the warmth of his sudden relaxed laugh delighted her. In the face of such danger, Ellen wondered how he could laugh. Then he pointed to his shirt, pinched the soaking fabric away from his chest, and tugged at it, pulling a face. 'It horrible. Very cold!'

She giggled. 'Don't worry, my mother's coming with some clean clothes in a minute.' He nodded, still smiling, but she didn't know if he understood. All she knew was there seemed to be a new bond between them which wasn't there before. So she climbed back down the stepladder, hoping her mother didn't see her cheeks were flushed with excitement. Meg was there at the foot of the ladder when she got to the last step. Not much passed her mother's scrutiny and she looked at her twice before ascending the ladder with the clothes slung over her arm. 'Don't you go getting soft over that young man, Ellie. We've got enough to worry about without you losing your heart to a runaway.'

'I'm not, Mum, why do you say that?' But her mother's stare was enough to betray her, and it brought the colour to her cheeks once more.

'Helping another human being who's running for his life is one thing. Getting involved with him romantically is quite another. Keep your distance, Ellie, and don't go showing him your pretty face too often or I'll have to turn him out on the street. Do you hear me?'

She couldn't speak. How could her mother tell what she had just experienced in those few seconds, in one simple glance?

'I repeat, do you understand?'

'Yes, Mum, but nothing's going on. I'm dating Robert anyway, you know I am.'

'Just you remember that then. We're in this together. No flighty ideas, girl, keep your head or you could get us all deported. Romance can loosen your tongue. Can't I leave you alone with him for five minutes?' With a sigh, Meg mounted the ladder. 'Nothing, mmm …' she repeated to herself thoughtfully. When she had gone, Ellen walked over to the window and looked out. Something had happened just then, and it had given her the most wonderful feeling, such excitement she had never ever experienced before.

Chapter 6

Although cold, it was daylight, and the birds were singing when Lucy got up. Her little boy Charlie was still sleeping peacefully and when she lifted him from his cot he barely stirred. She wrapped him up in a blanket, carried him to his pram and tucked him in. Cosy in his pyjamas, he was warm and smelt clean and babyish and he just stretched and whimpered a bit in protest at being disturbed. Lucy kissed his rosy cheeks and reassured him with a few words, and with a pang of regret, she set off pushing the pushchair with determination. It was soon after six o'clock in the morning, just after the night-time curfew had finished. Ever since Peter had gone off to fight, Lucy had lived like a single mother, alone and lonely. Daisy, her mother-in-law, although helpful in having Charlie for her every day, wasn't exactly supportive. In fact, at times she was barely even friendly. Efficiency was her strong point, friendliness and companionship were not.

The sky was beautiful in shades of pink and lilac when she set off at that time in the morning pushing the pram. Autumn was in the air, leaves were turning russet brown, blackberries were ripening on the hedges and drifts of dew laden cobwebs decorated the hedgerows. A chorus of birds celebrated the arrival of a new day. Lucy could have felt vulnerable, being out so early on her own, but she didn't. There were always German

A Sea of Barbed Wire

soldiers patrolling around, but far from being afraid of them she rather liked them, and anyway, Franz wouldn't let any harm come to her. She wasn't the kind of girl to let things like rumours worry her, and although they were technically the enemy, since she had been going with Franz and got to know a few of his friends, she thought they were rather nice. A flick of her curly blonde hair and the sway of her plump body often turned the soldiers' heads, and she would smile to herself if one or two soldiers watched her pass. If they called out to her, she would give them one of her looks, a cheeky smile tossed over her shoulder and a wiggle of her hips.

When she reached her mother-in-law's house, the door would already be ajar as Daisy would be expecting her. No more than a few words were exchanged usually, as the toddler was carried inside. Within minutes Lucy was on her way back home to pick up her sandwiches, climb on her bicycle, and set off for work. Over the rooftops, the calm sea spun a landscape of paradise in the dawn light like a giant saucer of azure blue. Beyond, in the far distance, the islands of Herm and Sark floated below a bank of pink and lilac clouds, sometimes giving the illusion of mountains, while other days they were barely visible at all, lost in a vapour of sea-mist.

As she cycled to the bakery, Lucy sometimes met other locals out and about, either going to work or walking their dogs. Most walked or rode bicycles because cars for civilians were no longer permitted. The Germans had requisitioned the best motor cars, the Mercedes and Rovers, for themselves. They drove these vehicles recklessly and at speeds dangerous for

Guernsey's narrow lanes and blind corners. Also, within a year of their arrival, they had ordered that all traffic should drive on the right-hand side of the road rather than the left. So many road signs went up, the street corners were bizarrely littered with them, tacked up with arrows here, there, and everywhere – and written in German. But Lucy was wary, she knew they didn't obey their own rules of the road and took little notice of others. People had been run over or knocked off their bikes callously. Accidents often happened if German soldiers were drunk, careering round blind corners in Guernsey with no thought as to who might be coming.

Petrol was rationed and in short supply, but some workers were allowed to keep cars or vans: doctors, priests, and agricultural workers. Buses had disappeared from the roads and were replaced with cranky horse-drawn carts; not an easy ride especially since the roads had been carved up and damaged by tanks and lorries carrying weapons and building materials. When heavy army vehicles passed Lucy, she could easily have been knocked off her bicycle but with her blonde hair flying and her skirt tucked up they paid her more attention than some might receive. But when a rumour went round that someone had been deliberately knocked down and killed by a German Officer who was intoxicated, she took the story back to her boyfriend Franz who condemned the cruel act as vehemently as she did. Stories often travelled round the island, not all of them true and some were embellished to add to their entertainment value. Most wrong doings on the part of the army were denied, but the German judiciary did act occasionally to bring the perpetrators to justice. Such tales that couldn't be excused by being

A Sea of Barbed Wire

called an 'act of war' were treated seriously. But over two years into the Occupation, the new laws islanders had to abide by multiplied.

Lorries that used to carry supplies like sacks of potatoes and tomatoes, passed Lucy now carrying troops of soldiers, wretched looking prisoners, or ammunition. They also carried tons of cement that they were using to build their fortified bunkers. The ill-fated foreign workers were brought over on ships, transported in disgusting conditions, and herded onto open-top vehicles for transport to their workplace like cattle. The camps where they were being held were filthy, damp and vermin infested. They had such poor sanitation, diseases such as dysentery and tuberculosis began to spread rapidly. When such vehicles passed her along the road, she would keep her eyes averted; the hungry stare of the dirt covered men, sitting or standing in the lorries in their pitiful clothes, confused and upset her and again she related such incidents to Franz in the evenings – and he too condemned such treatment.

She enjoyed describing to him how the island used to be: when shops were fully stocked with good fresh food and lovely new clothes and how she was able to go out and enjoy herself and buy nice things. Now she would complain she didn't have much money and there was nothing pretty to buy. Then he would tuck some notes into her blouse and tell her to treat herself.

When Lucy arrived at work, Ellen called to her as she was putting her bicycle away out of sight in the shed:

'Have you heard? Dora's husband's been arrested because they found out he's been keeping racing pigeons! They must think he's been sending secret messages to London. Anyway, he's been taken away and he'll probably be charged.'

Lucy chuckled. 'You've got to laugh haven't you – I mean seriously? Pigeons?'

Ellen stood watching Lucy take her sandwiches out of the saddlebag, imagining what awful interrogation the harmless man must be going through. 'Poor Dora! She must be out of her mind with worry. Honestly, they suspect everyone. Do they think we're all criminals? I wish I'd been there.'

'You'll be up there, being interrogated too, if you're not careful!'

'But it's not right, is it! We just allow them to trample all over us. They're ruining our island, picking on innocent people, building those hideous concrete bunkers and throwing their weight around.'

'And eatin' all our food!' said Lucy with a sparkle in her eye. 'Still, there is a war on. We have to live with it. They're good fun anyway, I think! At least it's not borin' having them around.' She studied her friend's face. 'You take life too seriously, Ellie. The war won't last forever, although I wouldn't mind it lastin' for a little while longer,' she added with a giggle.

Ellen looked at her curiously. 'You can't actually be enjoying the occupation, surely!'

'Why not? It beats the usual washin' and ironin', going to bed, getting' up, more washin', ugh! It was so borin' before! Now I never know what's goin' to happen next. I think it's quite excitin'.'

'You are a nutcase, you really are!'

That night Ellen told her father about Dora's husband and his racing pigeons.

A Sea of Barbed Wire

'They're just bullies,' he replied. 'So, they're accusing him of sending a message out to the Allies on the leg of a pigeon?' He chuckled. 'Well, it beats the usual I suppose. Selfish lot, they are. I've just about had enough of their arrogance.'

'But you wouldn't cross them, would you, Dad? It's so dangerous to challenge them, that's the trouble.' She remembered then what she had said to Lucy. How courageous was she really? Not very. Her friends were getting themselves in trouble for doing simple acts of kindness or going about their lives and trying to make the best of the situation. She gave a deep sigh of frustration. 'Dad, how I would love to have the courage to stand up to them, they're so cruel!'

'Then let's hope you never get the opportunity to then, love.' He looked up at her over his reading glasses. 'I mean it, keep your head down or we'll all be in the soup.'

Chapter 7

As a penalty inflicted on the population of the whole island for some misdemeanour, a night-time curfew had been temporarily brought forward from 10pm to 9pm. The locals soon learned the reason. A few adventurous young men had attempted an escape to England. So, however friendly the occupiers liked to appear, some things reminded the islanders that they were being held hostage. The risk of attempting to escape carried the penalty of death and had repercussions for all the people of Guernsey. Their island had become their prison.

Having to be back home so early, it wasn't easy for Ellen and Robert to meet and get to know each other. After the curfew deadline it was prohibited to be outside, the evenings were drawing in fast. It was also a fair distance to walk between their houses. Not many people dared to break the curfew time, the penalty was too great. It wasn't just the soldiers they had to avoid; some locals had been encouraged to keep an eye out and give their neighbours away if they noticed anything untoward. They were enticed by the offer of a financial reward, extra rations and cigarettes which was sheer betrayal when anyone took it up and reported people. As it was, the streets were patrolled by German soldiers, and the coastline, the beaches and the skies overhead were monitored continually. Islanders were careful to get home in time; even farmers weren't permitted to be out tending their animals during curfew.

Ways of how to explain their decision to hide Lukasz were teeming through her head but making no sense. She couldn't think how to phrase it in a way that wouldn't sound irresponsible. What they had done had endangered all of their lives, and now even Robert could be involved. She sipped her tea and grimaced. This wasn't real tea, from India or Ceylon; that was unobtainable unless one could afford to buy it on the blackmarket. Their substitute was made of dried crushed bramble leaves and it tasted bitter, but at least it was hot. After two years of shortages, Ellen had forgotten what proper tea tasted like anyway. Sometimes she sneaked a bit of sugar from their rations to make it a bit sweeter. Those people who had the money, and took the risk, were able to buy good tea on the black market, but it was ridiculously expensive. To deal in any blackmarket goods was illegal, but the Germans' idea of what was lawful wasn't hers.

'I think that's Rob coming now, Dad,' she said as she spotted him cycling up the road. 'We shouldn't say anything about *you know who*, should we?' She bit her lip. It was awkward keeping it from Robert, but she didn't feel able to tell him without it sounding as if they had all gone mad. Actually, she supposed they had, but she didn't regret it. They could never have turned Lukasz away.

'No, we won't mention it, love. No point in mixing him up in all this. The less people know the better.'

Within minutes he arrived, leant his bicycle inside the front gate and approached the house. He was looking handsome in his dark, grey-striped business suit and white shirt. It wasn't until he came closer that you could see it hung loose on him when he removed his bicycle clips. She could see the bottom of his trousers were frayed and spattered in mud. Bringing the formality of the bank with him, he looked older than his twenty-five years. Studious and intelligent, he had a mop of dark hair, and he wore thick black rimmed glasses which made his eyes appear bigger than they actually were. Behind these, he had an honest expression and a fresh-faced complexion. Born in the West Country, Robert had come to Guernsey when he was nine years old with his parents, but they had moved back there before the war. Pleased with his position at the bank in town, when they left the island Robert had stayed and taken lodgings in St. Peter Port. He was still living there in furnished rooms and the arrangement suited him well.

'Hello, love. Give us a kiss then,' he whispered as he came in the door.

She could smell the office on him, ink or papers or money perhaps and that always made her feel a bit queasy. His lips, as he brushed them with hers, were dry and cool.

'Mum's upstairs. Shall I make you a cuppa?'

He thanked her, flinging his briefcase down on the armchair and greeting her father with a handshake. Going into the kitchen to fill the kettle, Ellen heard the men speaking together in a low tone. She returned bearing cups and saucers on a tray.

'They'd better not deport any more local people or …'

'Or what Rob? I hate missing out on any news. Tell me!'

A Sea of Barbed Wire

'There's a new deportation order going out. All non-Guernsey born men between the ages of sixteen and seventy are to be deported, along with their wives and children if they have any.'

'Robert! They won't deport you, will they?'

'I hope not. Since the Manager evacuated, they need me at the bank more than ever. I might be made Senior Clerk now because there'll only be me left to do the accounts when the two juniors go and neither of them are experienced enough. One thing the German Officers like is their money. No, they won't call me in. They'd better not do anyway.' He took off his glasses and polished the lenses nervously. 'Anyway,' he added. 'I'm glad I stayed in Guernsey. If they'd signed me up to the army when war was declared with the other lads, let's face it, I wouldn't have been much use with a gun.' Still without his glasses on, he peered about with pale unfocussed eyes and squinted at Ellen, blinking in an exaggerated fashion, making a joke of it.

'Where did they send those who were deported before?' she asked.

He replaced his glasses and focused on her, straight-faced. 'An internment camp at Biberach in Germany. Some of the others I was at school with are there. At least I'll know someone if they do send me there,' he added, perhaps to console himself, but a shadow passed across his face. The kettle boiled, the sound of the whistle rose higher and higher. Reluctantly Ellen went to make the tea, saying: 'Well, let's hope they don't send you away.'

He smiled at her, raising his eyebrows. They could never relax for long; there was always some new threat, some new rule or demand issued by the occupying forces, instigating reprisals for any misdemeanour by one of the islanders. It didn't take much for the Germans to be issuing more restrictions or cutting down rations even further. When she returned from the kitchen, Rob and her father were chuckling about something.

'It's not funny, Dad!'

'It's alright. I'm not really joking; it's just sometimes they do over-react about the most trivial of things. What they say, goes, love. You've heard all the stories … You know what they're like by now. You can't reason with them.'

'Well, I've got a feeling the war will be over soon,' she announced, pouring the tea. Passing a cup and saucer to her boyfriend, she placed another beside her father's chair.

Albert looked over the top of his newspaper. 'Be alright wouldn't it, Rob, if women could predict the future?'

'Perhaps they can,' he replied, winking at Ellen. 'Here's hoping!' Raising his cup of tea to Albert, he said, 'Cheers!

However, then he grew more serious, putting down his cup.

'There's something else too actually.' He was looking directly at Albert. 'We're all going crazy at the bank now. The German Reichsmark is falling, it's apparently useless to us now, but they insist we keep it as our common currency. Two years ago, when the island was ordered to use those instead of our own currency, we knew it wouldn't work. Outside of Germany they're worthless.' He blinked, watching Albert's face. 'I'm worried. The island's going bankrupt and rapidly.'

A Sea of Barbed Wire

'That's virtually what I've been trading in since the Occupation started. So my pharmacy is running on a currency that won't have any monetary value when the war's over?'

'I'm afraid that could be true. The bank put all the English notes and deposits in the vault and sent some for safekeeping to London when the evacuation began. They can't get their hands on that, but the day-to-day transactions must continue using the Reichsmark, whether we like it or not.' He chewed a fingernail. He had quite thick stubby fingers and the fingertips on his right hand were stained with ink. 'Businesses have to accept them as payment for goods and services even if they know they're not worth anything.'

Albert was looking increasingly annoyed. 'What do they say its value is now compared to Guernsey currency then?'

'At the moment it's just under ten Reichsmarks to the pound.'

'Are they trying to fiddle us out of our own hard-earned cash?'

'It's possible and it wouldn't surprise me. I don't know exactly. It could be the Reichsmark won't be worth anything to us at the end of the war. As yet, I don't know any more than what I've told you. I've no doubt they'll be giving us loads more orders to comply with in the future.'

'Well, you'll stand up to them, lad, won't you!'

'It's not much good trying to disobey them,' replied Robert, looking at Albert steadily. 'I'm only a clerk, it's out of my hands.'

'Leave him alone, Dad. He only works there, who knows what the Germans are going to demand next.'

At that moment Meg could be heard coming down the stairs and the floorboards creaked as she reached the bottom and entered the sitting room carrying an armful of sheets. 'Ellie, help me with folding these sheets, will you?'

'Okay, Mum.' She stood up and took two corners, stepping backwards and folding them once, twice and putting the edges together. They repeated this graceful movement several times. Meg had just picked up the last sheet when suddenly there was a loud thump that sounded above their heads. They all heard it.

'What on earth was that?' said Robert, gazing at the ceiling.

Thinking quickly, Ellen said, 'Did you let that cat upstairs again, Mum? He must have knocked something over.'

'Dratted cat!' said Albert, burying his head in the newspaper.

Meg picked up the pile of sheets. 'He must have sneaked in and followed me upstairs,' she said. 'I'll go up and see to him and put these sheets away while I'm up there.'

'Do you want me to take them, Mum?' Ellen was eyeing her keenly.

'No thanks, love, I can manage.' But her stare told Ellen that her mother was worried. No-one else must know, least of all someone like Robert who they hadn't known for long. When it came to defying the Germans, no-one outside the family could be trusted completely. Everyone was living on their nerves.

Chapter 8

That night Ellen lay in bed wondering about Lukasz who was sleeping in the attic above her head. How much longer could he stay there, how much longer could they keep their secret safe and where else could they hide him? Her pulse began to accelerate, and she tossed and turned. She wished she could speak Polish and get the chance to talk to him more because she longed to ask him about himself, his home, his background and where he worked before the war.

The next day when she climbed up to the attic to take him some breakfast – such as it was – and some fresh drinking water, she found him lying on the pile of blankets, which served as his bed, just staring at the ceiling. His chest was bare, and his arms were stretched up and clasped behind his head. He sat up and mimed the act of writing, pretending to scribble on the palm of his hand. 'You …have …pencil?' He motioned with his hand. 'Please?'

'Yes, I'll see what I can find.' Putting down the jug of water she went back down the stairs. Her mother probably wouldn't approve of giving Lukasz anything like that as she had said before – "If the place is being searched the soldiers might pick up anything like that and it would give us away." Under her bed, Ellen kept a box containing some things she was saving, and she retrieved an old notebook which only had the first few pages written on, which she tore out. Then she rummaged around for a pencil and went back up to him. Lukasz stared at the articles she offered him curiously. He took the notebook and leafed through the blank pages with an expression of rapture on his face.

'What are you going to write?' she asked, jumping at the chance to find out something about him. The candle flickered and spat in the draught. He was fingering the pencil and the notebook thoughtfully. As she stood there in the semi-darkness waiting, he looked up at her finally.

'I write letter. I write letter to my mother and my sister. I tell them not worry. I okay.'

The bakery was quieter than it had ever been. There wasn't so much of the friendly banter, people popping in, and deliveries coming and going. Work was intense and practical, and all the time George hovered around in the background, his anxiety about the business and the supplies permeating the atmosphere. It was the cheerful company and warmth of the ovens that used to make the girls' work pleasant, and usually the hours flew by. There wasn't much that would put a dampener on the girls' spirits, but pride in their work was spoilt by the shortage of ingredients, and the awful state of the flour. They could understand why it was necessary to make it go further. However, the thinning down of good flour with other odd cereals, and mixing in the chaff, the husks, with the good flour, resulted in bread that was coarse and dry. It played havoc with the older folks' digestion. The butter ration was meagre, in spite of having the island's own Guernsey dairy herd, it didn't make eating the bread much easier either. But people were glad to have anything to eat. None of them could forget the first few weeks of the Occupation, in 1940, when the German soldiers were strolling through the streets of St. Peter Port licking open packets of butter as if they were ice-creams.

George, their boss, was so quiet one morning it worried Ellen. 'I wonder how much longer our jobs are safe,' she whispered.

'You and me both. Still, we have to keep goin', eh? Are you out with Robert tonight?'

'I doubt it, the films they're showing are all dwarfed by that propaganda stuff, it's awful especially when they tell us we have to clap and applaud Hitler, but I'm scared not to. It's not like it used to be. I don't like all the German soldiers in there. They sit on one side, and we have to sit on the other. It's awkward, especially when they cheer every time that ugly mutt shows his face. They look across at us to make sure we're clapping too. It's weird.'

Lucy giggled. 'Huh! I wouldn't clap my hands for Hitler, even if they paid me!'

'Ssh, be careful! Someone might hear you.'

'I don't care if they do. I'd tell him where to stick his stupid war if he came in here.'

'Lucy!'

'Don't mind me. I'm not scared of him or his soldiers. They can't stand him either, half of them! I bet they'd take a pot shot at him if they had half the chance.' She looked across at Ellen since there had been no more reprimands and caught her staring into space. 'What's up? Don't let it get to you, it's not worth it.'

'You know, Lucy,' she replied. 'I never thought it would be like this.'

'What, the war you mean?'

'I mean the occupation. I thought they'd be here and gone again in a few weeks, out there conquering the world with their bombs and big ideas – not staying here on our little island building those ugly monstrosities and making it all so horrible. And where are all the men now who boarded the boats to sign up? I remember seeing them looking so pleased with themselves and excited and proud to be going to defend their country.'

'You're right. Wouldn't I like to know where my Pete is! I haven't heard so much as a word from him since I kissed him goodbye on the harbour over two years ago. He got it in his head to sign up and there wasn't much I could do to change his mind.'

'Of course, I remember that day. I'm sorry, and there's me feeling sorry for myself. It must be so hard for you.'

'Oh, he'll probably come sailin' back one of these days. As soon as the war's over he'll come rollin' in, battle scarred and weary an' expectin' me to call him a hero. I wonder if I'll even recognise him.'

'You must miss him terribly though.'

She took a while to answer. 'No, not really. To tell you the truth, I've got used to it now. And I've got Franz, he cheers me up. My little Charlie keeps me company, too much company sometimes when he won't sleep at night!'

'It's a shame Charlie keeps you awake. Do you think he's hungry?'

'We're all hungry, eh? I try my best. I give him a boiled egg nearly every day and my mother-in-law saves extra for him. I don't know what she gives him while I'm at work though. I've told her not to give him too much mashed swede, it gives him tummy ache, but she always says:' Here, Lucy fell into imitating her mother-in-law's sing-song voice: '"*It didn't do no harm to my Pete. We want him to grow up a strong healthy little man like his dad, don't we?*" Honestly, I can't tell her anything.' Her imitation of Daisy made Ellen laugh.

But Lucy continued: 'Franz said he thought the war would be over in a few months. And it's two years and counting … It'll get even harder if our jobs go. There's only my wage comin' in and my littlun is needin' new shoes now he's started walkin'. Not that there's any left in the shops anyway even if I could afford to buy them.'

'You could ask your mother-in-law to help.'

'Oh, she knows he needs shoes. I wouldn't be surprised if he turns up wearin' a new pair of shoes when I go and collect him after work one of these days.'

'It is alright, isn't it? Her looking after him for you every day?'

'I suppose so. What choice have I got anyway? Tryin' to cope with the bills on my own isn't fun I can tell you. I've given up payin' the rent. My landlord's good to me though, he knows how things stand. What with that lot,' she said, waving a hand in the direction of the road, 'and with Pete away fightin', he's not forcin' me to pay up. Well, I haven't got the money anyway, full stop. He could chuck me out on the street if he wanted to, but he wouldn't, he's too kind-hearted!' She winked. 'I know he wouldn't because he's got a soft spot for me. Anyway, where else would he get a nice pretty tenant like me?'

Ellen sighed. 'I'm lucky I still live at home, and don't have to pay the bills. I give my parents a bit towards my keep, but it's not like running a house.'

It was time for their mid-morning break, and when George gave them a sign, they left their work and went into the kitchen. There, they were alone and having boiled the kettle, sat down for a quick snack. It was only ten o' clock but they had started work at six-thirty.

'Talking of landlords,' said Ellen, continuing their line of thought. 'The Germans seem to have a liking for our houses, don't they.' She looked twice at her coffee and pulled a face. 'Oh, this is so awful! I don't remember what real coffee tastes like anymore. Yeh, so I noticed the German officers have moved into one of those big houses along The Queen's Road. They don't care who they chuck out, do they.'

'Huh! I bet they won't be payin' any rent for that!' Lucy replied and cuddled her coffee cup, warming her hands.

'Anyway, our jobs are safe for now I suppose. Everyone needs bread after all.'

'Let's hope so, but the way things are goin' we won't have any flour left to work with. What they try to pass off as flour these days is more like the stuff Pete used to mix in a bucket and plaster the walls with!' Lucy was chuckling. 'Oh dear, I remember those days of him comin' home from work covered from head to foot in plaster an' leavin' huge white footprints across the carpet like a big snowman!'

When Lucy opened her heart to Ellen like this, she longed to tell her about Lukasz. If only she could share her anxiety, talk about him, say how difficult it was to keep a secret – she knew Lucy would understand about keeping things quiet. But she couldn't say anything. It wouldn't be fair, and it would endanger her life and that of her little boy. To involve anyone else was too great a risk. So they went back to work, each with their own thoughts. Ellen knew why Lucy was quiet at times and she understood. As for her own secret, it had to remain a secret for everyone's sake.

Chapter 9

Rising from her bed while it was still dark, Ellen washed in cold water, dressed and went downstairs to make some tea. It was freezing in the house. The fire from the night before had gone out and what little warmth remained was of no use. The fact that Lucy trusted her enough to tell her about Franz, made keeping her own secret even more deceitful. But hiding Lukasz wasn't an innocent secret like that of falling in love with a handsome soldier when you're lonely. Sheltering an escaped prisoner was deliberate and the risk of betraying her whole family to the Germans was reckless. And yet, as the minutes passed and the time drew near for her to leave for work again, she was no nearer deciding what to do about it. Her mouth felt sour, and she felt shivery from lack of sleep.

She put the kettle on to make tea. Pouring boiling water, she stirred the pot, her thoughts miles away. It was Lucy's honesty that had touched her. That she had trusted her –putting her own future in her hands – the responsibility gnawed away at her conscience. What is a friendship, she asked herself, if you can't trust your own friend?

Since their house had been searched, they had allowed Lukasz to come down and use the bathroom when it was safe to do so. But usually, Ellen and her mother continued to routinely carry a bowl of hot water

A Sea of Barbed Wire

up to the attic for him to wash and shave, and to take him meals. As time went on, they began to relax, allowing him downstairs more and more, to sit with them when the coast was clear. Lukasz had been with them for several weeks when their relaxation came to an abrupt end. News came of an escaped prisoner being discovered in a woman's house. He had been hauled out of his hiding place in the garden shed and shot dead in front of her. The woman was taken away and charged. It caused a blanket of fear to descend on Ellen and her family but not a word was revealed to Lukasz. After work when the house was quiet, Ellen would sometimes go up to keep him company, hidden away as he was in the half dark. She would chat to him about anything that she could think of, realising that less than half of it he would understand. It was hardly a life for him, she thought, cramped up in there with nothing to do all day. So, his secret existence continued, his wounds healed, and he became stronger. But she knew his confinement couldn't go on much longer.

Arriving at work, Ellen found Lucy already busy working. Inside, she took off her coat and went to the kitchen to make herself a hot drink. George was in there, poring over some sheets of invoices and order papers.

'Good morning, Ellen. We'll be finishing early today unless the next lot of flour comes in. They've said it will be today, but I won't hold my breath.'

'Okay, George. I wouldn't mind actually. I hardly had a wink of sleep.'

'No sleep! You youngsters have nothing to worry about, eh? Take a bit of advice from me and don't ever get any big ideas about running a business. It's not worth it. It gives me nothing but trouble. You've got your whole life ahead of you, Ellen. Between you and me, if you want to spread your wings and see a bit of the world when this war's over then why don't you, eh? You're only young once. If I had a daughter, I'd say the same to her, don't go committing yourself to anything or getting married and signing your life away before you're ready. But that's just an old man talking. Perhaps I'm wishing I was young again myself. Don't mind me.'

'Thanks, I'll remember what you've said, and I haven't got any plans on marrying any time soon anyway! But let's hope all this won't go on much longer. Perhaps they're right and it'll be over by Christmas.'

'I can't see that happening myself, Ellen, but I hope you're right.' He folded up his papers and stood up.

'I'd better get on, I suppose,' she said, leaving him and going to join Lucy.

Lucy was already loading up the first batch of dough in the bread tins.

'You must have started early. Any reason?'

'Between you and me, I'm hoping to see Franz this afternoon, so I thought I'd get here early,'

'George just said we might be sent home early anyway. He doesn't think the flour order is going to arrive.'

'Oh, that's alright then.' She giggled, sounding very light-hearted.

'How's little Charlie?'

'He's fine. I dropped him off at my mother-in-law's before she was expectin' me. She's a miserable old bag, that woman, does nothin' but complain.'

'Perhaps she finds having him too hard work.'

A Sea of Barbed Wire

'Don't think so. She keeps sayin' he could always stay the night, save me havin' to bring him to and fro. Who does she think she is? As if I wouldn't want my little boy with me! I hardly have time with him as it is.'

Ellen couldn't stop herself. 'How do you manage then, with him to look after and going out with your man in the evening?'

'Charlie's asleep in his cot by seven. I'm always back before curfew so he's okay. He can't go anywhere exactly, can he, eh?'

'You leave him alone? Without a babysitter? But Lucy – think of the risks. And anyway, what if anyone finds out?' The colour drained from Lucy's cheeks. In an instant her mood had changed.

'You won't report me, will you? I wouldn't have told you but – Oh, Ellie! I think I'm fallin' in love with Franz! I just have to tell someone and well, you and me, we've known each other a long time. You know what it's been like for me, with Charlie just a new-born baby in my arms when Pete went waltzin' off to fight for his country. He didn't care! What about me? He could've carried on workin' here. He didn't even want to stay! As soon as the call went out, he was off. You couldn't see him for dust.'

Ellen nodded, knowing full well how some of the young men, boys even, had leapt at the chance of adventure, of leaving the island for the first time in their lives. And even George had boosted her confidence in being stronger, planning for the future and seeing the world. Since the occupation, freedom had never been so important.

'Don't worry, I won't breathe a word. But please be careful. I can't bear to think what would happen to you if anyone found out.'

Ellen got home from work mid-afternoon to find her mother was out, which wasn't unusual as she would either be stuck in a queue shopping or visiting her nan. So she boiled the kettle and carried some tea up to the attic for Lukasz to keep him company. Fetching the stepladder, she climbed up, tapped on the attic door but there was no response. Sometimes he would reach out his hand and help her up into the attic itself so they could talk but it was strangely, horribly quiet. She had an awful feeling something was wrong. She waited and tapped again, listening. Then she heard a scuffling and in a moment of panic she put the cup down, spilling some of its contents, and thrust her hand upwards, pushing the trap door up.

'Lukasz? Are you alright?' She heard a moan. Through the darkness she could see him at last. As her eyes became accustomed to the gloom, she saw Lukasz sitting on the floor huddled against the wall, muttering in his own language words that sounded to her like cursing.

'What's happened? Are you alright?'

'Sorry, so sorry …it my leg. I have – how you say? The cramp. It nothing.' Looking up at her he pulled a face. 'I scare you. I sorry.'

In the dim light she saw he was rubbing his calf-muscle. The air was dank with the man's sweat and the tang of urine from the bucket. With a sudden rush of pity for him, she wondered how such a strong man could cope, hiding away crouched in the dark. It was so degrading for him, as if after all he was still a prisoner. He was even unable to stand up to his full height as the roof was so low and the beams stretched above his head. But she knew he would argue that pride had been stolen from him long ago, when his family was attacked and he was captured.

'Has the pain gone yet?'

'Yes. It going. Thank you.' Looking up at her, she caught another grimace of pain flash across his face. Moving back towards the hatch, she saw she had spilled some of the tea. Moving stiffly, he stood up as straight as he was able to but stooping to avoid hitting his head on the beams. He took the tea from her and thanked her. She wanted to say something, some words of encouragement to cheer him up.

'Do you feel alright, Lukasz? I mean, apart from the cramp, how are you coping with all this?' She swept her hand across the attic space and frowned. 'It must be so hard.'

'I am okay. I have the pain in my legs. I hungry but...'

'I'll try to get you more food, but you know we don't have much either. There's hardly any food to buy in the shops.'

Lukasz was shaking his head. 'I know. I know. Don't worry. I not stay here long. Too dangerous for you. For your family. You ...your mother ...she very kind.'

Suddenly, outside the house, very close, they heard several gunshots. They both froze.

'Someone's coming!' she cried. 'Oh, Lukasz! What shall we do?'

Lukasz was muttering under his breath, but in Polish and she couldn't understand him. He started gathering his bedding together. 'They not find me here. I go. I must go! Help me please!' he cried. Suddenly he was holding her, listening, 'Ssh, ssh!' His breath was coming in gasps. 'They come! They come for me!'

'Wait!' she whispered. 'No, I don't think they're coming here. You can't leave now. They'll see you. Be quiet, Lukasz and keep still. Don't move!' She withdrew herself from his arms and closed the attic door, shutting them both in. Thrust into darkness, they stood together, hardly daring to breathe. 'They'll be gone past soon. Don't worry,' she whispered, remembering with dread that she had left the step-ladder there on the landing.

They both waited, while Ellen kept hoping what she said to Lukasz to quieten him was true. But gradually the noise receded. There were no more shots and Lukasz turned and gazed at her, rubbing the back of his neck as if it was stiff.

'I not stay here. I make danger for you. I not like that.'

'But if you run away, they'll capture you again! What would happen to you?'

He shrugged his shoulders, smiled, pointed to his temple, shut his eyes and said, 'Boom!'

She was caught out for a moment and stared at him, but he chuckled, 'Boom! Boom!'

She couldn't understand how he could joke about it. How could he say that, with such detachment, as if it was nothing!

'Don't, Lukasz! That's not funny.'

'I happy to be here, to see you, but I must go, to save you…' He just mumbled the rest of the sentence in his own language, becoming suddenly serious and looking distressed.

'No Lukasz, stay here, please, we want to help you.'

'You, your family, you already help me. If I stay, it very bad!'

She caught sight of his face then, as a shaft of light slanted through the roof space, probably from a missing tile. He looked gaunt, with his deep brown eyes reflecting his spirit which went beyond fear to somewhere else, a place haunted by death.

'You do understand, don't you, Lukasz? There's nowhere for you to go. The Germans are everywhere on the island. There are spies out too, people who would betray you if they saw you. Wait, lie down again and rest.'

Like an obedient dog his defiance wavered and casting his eyes back to the eaves where he had been, he shrank back and moved away from her. He began spreading out his bed again slowly and methodically. But then he turned, hesitating once more.

'Ellie?'

She put her finger to her lips and shook her head. 'No more. We'll be alright, trust me.' She left him then and opened the attic door. Light flooded in, causing her to blink and almost lose her balance. Then, as he stepped forward to help her, taking hold of her hand, she looked into his eyes. Perhaps needing comfort, reassurance, whatever it was, suddenly he put his arms around her and hugged her. They needed each other so badly. When he held her, it was like a bolt of lightning shooting through her and she felt as if she was dissolving into him. Suddenly everything, her whole perspective on life, changed. His hold on her was so vibrant, so exciting, so loving and strong. She felt his warm body against hers and a shudder of desire and reassurance passed through her.

It wasn't until she was in the kitchen that she came to realise what had happened. Whatever the gunshots were outside, they had stopped as quickly as they had started, and she found herself trembling. Perhaps it was because she was feeling so hungry that emotions were getting the better of her. She went to look at what pitiful reserves of food there were in the pantry from the meagre rations allowed them, but she couldn't find anything that was spare.

Chapter 10

Managing to put some distance between himself and the experience, Lukasz lit the candle beside him, drew out the notebook and began to write, continuing the story of his capture and imprisonment. His letters had taken on the form of a diary. Finally, having written as much as he could, he lay back on the mattress, stretching his arms up behind his head. His breathing had steadied now and he felt hungry. He knew he must try to forget it, but he was always so hungry. When again he began drifting between sleep and wakefulness, the images of Ellen became confused with memories of girls he had lain with in the past and it was all unreal. He dreamt of warmth, of laying in a woman's arms and feeling her soft hair on his neck.

Suddenly he awoke with a start. The candle had burnt down to its base and was fizzing and spluttering as the wick drowned in its own liquid wax. Ashamed of having forgotten it, he realised the danger of setting fire to his clothes, the mattress, and the house itself. He blew out the remains of it and lay seething with anger and frustration at himself. How much longer must he be cooped up in here anyway, fed and watered and kept restrained like an animal in a cage? Adrenalin flowed like an electric shock through his limbs, his muscles tensed up and he felt as if he could burst out of the attic and run, just run free and fling his arms in the air regardless of his captors. Reality soon came over him however. If he did such a thing, gun fire would bring him down as surely as the crows he shot across the fields with his father. Reminded again and again of the horrors he had escaped, his urge to escape the sanctuary the family had offered him evaporated as quickly as it had begun. But even so, his heart pounded within him as he lay back breathing deeply, panting and longing for freedom.

Ellen's hands were becoming rough and sore. Due to the shortage of fat in their diet, everyone's skin was dry and prone to splitting. She always tried to keep her hands clean as she was mixing flour and kneading bread all day. The precious bar of soap that Dora had given her would soon be gone. One suggestion for an alternative to soap she had heard was to wash with mud, but that idea had been received with jollity and had caused a ripple of laughter through the bakery.

'Might improve the taste of the bread though!' quipped Lucy. She was always the one to lighten the mood and cheer people up. To have enough hot water to take a bath anyway wasn't easy either as they had been told to conserve water whenever possible. They weren't allowed to use the gas during curfew hours. Two years into the occupation and the lack of provisions was making its mark. How the women would have loved to put on some lipstick, try a different hairstyle, and go out without the restrictions imposed on them. German soldiers sometimes attended the social events that were held in the parish hall, their unexpected presence causing a flurry of giggles and nervous sideways glances from the girls present. But it hadn't escaped Ellen's notice either that the once fit and muscular German soldiers who used to come and make eyes at them were looking thin and their faces were pale and gaunt. Some never dropped their severe expression even while dancing, but sometimes Ellen felt sorry for them. They looked so young, and she wondered what their backgrounds were, whether they had girlfriends back home and what their families were like. What was the war all about, she wondered, if both sides suffered like this. There were no winners. There was just destruction, the ruin of many lives and the death of thousands.

One Saturday morning, Ellen set out to do some shopping, more in hope than anything. She had a list from her mother, who had asked her to purchase any basic ingredients that were available and any fresh vegetables or fruit. She passed some German soldiers who were standing around smoking and tried to keep her eyes cast down. But curiosity got the better of her sometimes and she glanced up, only to accidentally catch the eye of one of the soldiers. It set her off blushing and she had to look away again quickly. She daren't admit it to herself but it didn't surprise her that Lucy had fallen for one of those boys, with their blonde hair and blue eyes. It was then she began to wonder what Lucy's boyfriend looked like. He could easily have been among those she just passed.

The High Street was packed with queues of people outside shops. They stood patiently, their empty shopping bags swinging, some babies crying, and some conversations that Ellen could only catch snippets of all gave the same message – times were hard. The queues clung to the pavements, prams and pushchairs, whimpering dogs on leads, pleading children tugging at their mothers' skirts. Down the middle of the road three German Officers were walking side by side talking loudly in their sharp staccato language which neither Ellen nor any of those they passed, could understand.

She joined the queue outside the grocery store, hoping to buy potatoes, cabbage, and swedes. She stood for an hour, shuffling forward occasionally, and the women who came away from the shop carrying their purchases were invariably disappointed. They came shaking their heads, complaining that they couldn't get what they wanted and that they had been forced to leave with next to nothing to feed their families for the weekend.

At last, it was her turn to step into the shop. There were four women in front of her and some friendly banter was going on. Even in the direst of circumstances, the locals managed to keep their sense of humour. It cheered her up to hear them pulling the shopkeeper's leg. Finally, she had reached the counter. Asking for what she wanted, she knew was pointless because she could already see the shelves were virtually empty. The shopkeeper apologised.

'Tell your mother, dear, that I'd give her half of mine if I could, but there isn't a single cabbage left.' Saying this he nodded towards the road where, at that moment, a group of off-duty soldiers were passing, larking about and full of jollity, and weighed down with parcels of shopping. She came away with a few parsnips and two carrots. At another shop she managed to buy a tin of plums and a small portion of cheese. A group of soldiers, shepherding a straggly line of prisoners passed her. Some of the prisoners had bare feet. She felt herself blushing, this time out of shame. As she walked on carrying her shopping, one of them looked her in the eye. When she got home, she told her mother about what she had seen.

'Those poor men, they looked half-alive and so weak. Can't we help them?'

'Listen Ellie, it could be your father there among them one of these days. We've got one of their prisoners here remember and the punishment for such a crime could be worse than that. Lukasz grows in strength every day because we feed him and give him shelter. He's a fine young man but how much longer can we hide him from them? One slip of the tongue and they would come for him, and for us too. I hate to think what would happen to us. I've heard my friends talk about a local woman who helped an escaped prisoner. She didn't manage to hide him for long before they were tipped off by a so-called neighbour. The soldiers came and turned her house upside down. He was found and dragged out of the house, and I don't know what happened to him, shot dead most likely. We don't know what's happened to her, but if she's lucky, she will have been put on a boat to Germany and held in their prison camp. The women I know, they all speak behind their hands and whisper and tell me she must have been crazy, that they wouldn't take a chance like that if they were paid a thousand pounds. And do you know what I say? I tell them I wouldn't dream of doing such a thing either! I've lied to save Lukasz. But now I lie to save us all,' she added. 'God help me, Ellie, I don't know what I'm doing these days. I think we've all taken leave of our senses.'

The colour had drained from her face and as she turned away, Ellen realised it was just as hard if not harder for her mother than it was for her. They were trapped as a family by their secret, and therefore isolated from their friends. They were stuck, unable to go forward safely, but also unable to turn back. The price they would pay, if they surrendered him now, would be too high. The Germans would give them no credit for their honesty. There was no way back for them.

Chapter 11

Lukasz was becoming more restless and the cramps in his legs more frequent. When it was quiet and there were no soldiers about, they let him come down into the main part of the house, use the bathroom and wash. Items like soap, shampoo, toothpaste were virtually impossible to come by, but the states issued hard blocks of household soap which were a better alternative to no soap at all. Getting hold of a whole bar of fragrant soap from France was a delight, but it didn't happen very often. They cut it up and savoured each piece, but it was a luxury they rarely enjoyed.

Ellen had begun to notice a certain restlessness in his behaviour. He no longer smiled much in gratitude but looked increasingly anxious when she brought him a bowl of food or a piece of fruit. He never saw the daylight and the sun hadn't shone on his face for weeks. One day when she took him an apple, he was about to take it and then held up his hand in denial and refused it. She was taken aback.

'What's the matter? Are you ill?'

He shook his head and pushed the hand which held the apple away. Helplessly she offered it to him again. 'But you must eat!' she insisted. But he wouldn't take it. Eventually she climbed back down the ladder, puzzled, and upset. She didn't tell her mother he had refused the apple. After that, she didn't want to eat it herself either and she replaced it in the kitchen cupboard, wondering about him and why he wouldn't eat.

That evening however, Ellen was curious to know if Lukasz had accepted his share of the hot dinner her mother had taken up to him. But her hands were empty when she came down and she showed no sign that anything had changed. There was a lot more tension in the house now. Albert, against his wife's wishes, had obtained a crystal radio set. He was delighted with it, and that evening he brought it out and switched it on to tune in to the BBC News. The deep voice of the newsreader emitted a low rumble late into the night. The sound of it terrified Ellen and her mother, in case there was anyone going past who might hear it. It wasn't helping their nerves, having another illegal item hidden away in their home that was threatening their lives by its very existence. If any soldier walking past heard the low mellow voice of the newsreader coming directly from London, he wouldn't have hesitated to knock or even break the door down to arrest all of them.

One evening, when they were eating their evening meal which consisted of boiled potatoes, carrots and a few sprigs of cauliflower, Ellen was feeling particularly worried about Lukasz. 'Mum, do you think Lukasz is eating enough?'

Meg looked up from her plate in amazement. 'What a question to ask! Of course, he's not. None of us are!'

Albert, on the other hand, gazed at her quite kindly. 'We all get by as best we can, love, don't we, till something happens to change it, eh?'

'He's so confined up there. I was wondering if we could move him, give him a bit more space. He's getting awful cramps in his legs and he can't get any exercise.'

Her parents looked at each other; her father raised his eyebrows. 'You want to give him more room, is it?'

'I don't know where else we can hide him, unless –' Ellen had had an idea. 'Supposing we clear out the cellar?'

'And where do you propose we put everything? This isn't a big house you know, love.'

*

It had been raining all day and the wind was howling round the house. Ellen had arranged to meet her boyfriend in town after he finished work, but she wasn't sure about going now. If her coat got soaked through it would take days to dry it out without the heat from a fire and she didn't have another one. In such a wind the umbrella was useless. Coal was in such short supply they struggled to heat water for baths and dry the washing. Joan usually managed to get them some logs to make a fire in the evenings, but the heat from them was short-lived. However, by four o'clock the wind had dropped considerably. The rain continued to fall but it wasn't so heavy and not having seen Robert for a whole week, in spite of the effort it would take she decided she should go. He had telephoned twice to tell her he was too busy, with accounts to do in the bank keeping him back sometimes until near on the curfew hour. So buttoning herself up against the cold, she set off. It was already getting dark.

Walking into town from the Rohais, even when it was warm and sunny, was quite a distance and with her stomach crying out for something to eat she soon began to feel weak. It was perhaps a walk of only a mile and a half, but after only a short while she needed to rest. Seeing an empty bench ahead sheltered by trees, she decided to stop for a while. It was quiet on St. Julian's Avenue, with barely a vehicle on the road.

Out of the dim light and misty rain she could see some people coming up the hill. It was a couple, walking arm in arm, a man and his girl by the sounds of the giggles that came on the breeze. The pavement being so narrow at that point, she noticed the man was protecting his girl from the wet road and the splashes from puddles as German army vehicles tore past. He was holding his raincoat over both of them and had his arm around her shoulders. Ellen continued to sit there, getting her strength back.

Just as she was beginning to feel better and had decided to walk on, the girl gave a shriek of laughter. The young couple were upon her now, passing the bench within a few feet of her. Ellen stayed where she was, keeping as still as she could. Her heart began pounding. It wasn't that she was afraid, but just wished the ground would open up and swallow her because it wasn't any young couple. Having recognised the laughter, she knew immediately it was Lucy. A glimpse of the man's boots told her more; they were jackboots, German army boots. Ellen felt as if she couldn't speak to her, even though she was only feet away. It was as if a barrier was between them. Lucy's face was concealed beneath her boyfriend's outstretched jacket. They passed on by without seeing her.

The moment passed and it was as if it had never happened. The young couple had gone by and were walking on up the hill. Ellen sighed; she thought she could always tell Lucy that she thought she had seen her with her boyfriend but wasn't sure. Otherwise, how could she explain that she hadn't said hello? Hurrying now, she continued to fret over what she should do. It was five-thirty when she got to Church Square and to her relief Robert was waiting for her. She managed to stop herself telling him about seeing Lucy, much as she was tempted to let the whole story pour out. At once she found herself having to keep another secret from him. But withholding information on something that had just happened was so hard that, without her meaning to, it caused Robert to look at her anxiously. 'Are you alright? You're very quiet tonight.'

It was true. A chasm had opened up between them and Ellen felt tense and awkward. 'I'm sorry. I'm just tired I suppose, and hungry of course! You must be too.'

'Yes, another exhausting day. I don't have the answers to my customers' questions these days. I assure them their money is safe, but when I tell them they can't withdraw much money at a time, they get the impression it's in danger.'

'Is it though? Their money is safe, isn't it?'

'Safe as it'll ever be, but none of us know what they are going to demand next.'

She snatched a quick glance at his face and noticed how pale and strained he looked. They hadn't known each other that long but he had never appeared so burdened; he looked almost middle-aged. She held his arm as they walked along the street together towards his place. Ellen had brought with her two small potatoes she had saved and baked in their jackets overnight in the hot ashes of the fire. Also, she had some cheese and two boiled eggs carefully wrapped in newspaper. She felt almost faint with hunger.

As they walked, Robert told her a bit about his work, and she had previously thought of several things to tell him that had happened during the week. But she couldn't tell him the things which were dominating her thoughts, causing her pulse to run at an alarming rate. The more she tried to act naturally, the less she could think of to talk about. Having to censor her own conversation made her appear tense and awkward, as if she was hiding something, which of course she was. Where the usual topics they used to chatter about had disappeared to, she had no idea. No sooner had she thought of something to tell him, then she remembered that if she told him *that* she might accidentally tell him about *the other thing*. To even confide in Robert hypothetically about the terrible risk she and her parents were running in concealing an escaped prisoner was impossible. And she couldn't tell him about Lucy's new boyfriend, since she had promised not to tell a soul.

They came to the house; Robert's apartment was upstairs. Ellen set off climbing the stairs before him, carrying their supper in a shopping bag. His keys rattled in his hand and his breath was coming in short gasps behind her. He unlocked the door to his room and switched on the light before he stood back to let her in. It was a poor little room. It occurred to her every time she went there that for a young man holding a responsible position at the bank it should have been better. But the war had limited his choice of accommodation and for once she was glad of its obscurity. His apartment was tucked away at the top of Mill Street in St. Peter Port, in a terrace of shops and houses on a narrow street that climbed up the hill above the town. His room was at the back of the house, receiving barely any sunlight and had no views of the sea. Any grander and he, as many others, could be in danger of being thrown out in favour of soldiers being billeted there. He took her coat and hung it up although she could have done with keeping it on. She felt so cold in there she had started to shiver but she sat down, missing the warmth of her coat and unconsciously clutching her handbag on her lap as if it was in danger of being torn from her arms. He stood before her, rather vacantly. 'I'll just go and fill the kettle; I'll be in the kitchen out the back.' When he came in again, she said, 'I'm quite chilled at the moment, Rob, I think I'd better put my coat back on.' She tried to smile but it didn't quite work.

Fetching her coat, he apologised and helped her put it on, scrutinising her face as he did so. 'Are you sure you're not worried about something, Ellie? You don't seem yourself.'

She shrugged. 'I am worried, of course I am, but only about the usual, you know …' She struggled to remember what she could be worried about that was safe to tell him. The secrecy was disorientating. Her eyes desperately travelled round the room, taking in the single bed, the lamp on a rickety table beside it with the cracked lampshade, the table where Robert usually spread his papers to do his figures and accounting in the evenings. It was all so sad; it was all so terribly dull she felt she was going to cry.

'It's no good any of us worrying about that lot.' He was gesturing with his head as if the whole German army were just outside the door. 'We're all in the same boat, Ellie, and we've just got to stick it out together, haven't we?' He came and sat down beside her, taking hold of both her hands and peering up into her face as if she was a child. 'Don't worry, my love, we'll take each day as it comes, eh? We've still got each other.' He kissed her fleetingly on the cheek. His lips felt cold against her face. Suddenly she was weeping.

'Oh, I'm sorry, I think I'd better go!' The sobs came heaving in her chest, hurting her throat like pebbles.

'Sweetheart, don't! You're overtired, that's what it is. I should never have expected you to walk into town to meet me tonight, what a foolish idea! And your coat, it feels wet through! Oh, what was I thinking of!'

'I'm sorry, I'm alright now, really.' She sniffed and felt for her handkerchief, but it was wet in her pocket. 'Look, let's have our supper and then you can walk me back.' She managed a smile. 'Do you have any tea? I could really do with a hot cuppa, and a spoonful of sugar if you have any.'

To her relief, Robert agreed he had a little and left her to go back to the kitchen and make it. She sighed and tried to pull herself together. Inwardly, she gave herself a good talking to. Go under now, she murmured under her breath, and you'll take everyone else with you.

Chapter 12

By the afternoon the weather had worsened and when Ellen arrived, she found her father was already home. In spite of the cold wind, the brisk walk home had revived her and put some colour in her cheeks. Realising how much Lukasz was missing, that he had been shut in the attic all the time she had been out at work, and had been up there for days on end, she said, 'Dad, what can we do about him getting no fresh air?'

Albert took a deep breath and sighed. 'Can't be helped. Leave him be, love. The war could be over in a couple of months, we'll keep hoping, eh?'

'But what if …'

'Never mind what if …I'm going out in the yard to fix up some firewood. There, sounds like your mother's home now.'

Sure enough, Meg had just come in the door, stamping her feet to get the circulation going. 'My feet got so cold standing in the queue for so long and all I managed to buy was a pathetic tin of spam and a cauliflower!'

'Better than nothing, Mum!' She took her mother's basket from her. Having heard her parents talking the previous night, she was beginning to realise that the whole idea of hiding someone for year after year, waiting for the war to end, was futile. None of them knew how long the occupation was going to last.

Every day Lukasz grew stronger. He was eating more than when he was a prisoner, even if it wasn't much, and his wounds had healed. But as each day passed, she knew he couldn't remain cramped in that small space indefinitely. The freedom they had offered him by concealing him, was temporary and risky. Being free wasn't about being locked away, hiding and in fear of being discovered. It was a very poor kind of freedom if that was the case.

While food was the main topic of conversation at work and in the street, the novelty of women striving to lose a few pounds had long ago lost its charm. There was nothing else on people's minds except where the next mouthful was coming from. Ellen often wondered what the poor diet was doing to their bodies. Now, as she looked at her mother standing at the kitchen sink, she saw how slim her hips had become and how bony her arms were; they used to be pink and plump. With a shock she noticed too, how thin her face was when she turned to speak to her:

'Well, don't just sit there, love. Aren't you going to come and dry up for me?'

Ellen went quickly and picked up a tea towel.

'When you're done would you make us a cuppa love, and take one up for …?' She raised her eyes. His name was rarely mentioned. It was a kind of unspoken precaution.

'Mum, I wish we could find somewhere else for him, somewhere with more room and brighter,' she whispered. Having to talk in phrases that were open to interpretation was now a habit of theirs.

'We've been thinking about what you suggested, actually. Your father and I might make a few changes

A Sea of Barbed Wire

soon, move a few bits around, give him a bit more space.' She finished washing up, dried her hands on her apron and went to sit in her armchair.

'Half fill the kettle will you, love, we're having to save the water now. When I've had a rest, I'll go and fetch in some of that firewood. I can hear your father outside sawing again.'

'I'll get it in, Mum, you stay here and rest.'

When Ellen carried the tea up to Lukasz, she found him writing in the notebook she had given him. 'Here's your tea, Lukasz!'

His hand came through the gap and as he lifted the door wider, the light fell across his face, and open shirt. He reached through and took it from her, thanking her.

'You come up. We talk?'

She agreed, climbed up further and crawled into the attic. 'How are you? You must be so bored! Are you alright?'

He nodded with a brief smile. 'Yes, yes. I okay.' Returning to his corner, he sank back into the gloom on his heels and drank a little from his cup.

'The tea,' said Ellen, wrinkling her nose. 'I'm sorry, it's horrible!'

A deep laugh rumbled up from his chest and he said, 'It horrible, yes!'

She laughed too, delighted to be sharing a joke with him. Serious again. 'I wish ...' she began. 'I wish we could do more for you.'

'More?' he replied, echoing the word, looking puzzled.

'More to help you.' She looked around, gesturing to the limited roof space, and waving a hand at the rough floor and the old boxes stored there. It was such a dingy place to spend any time in; already to her it was feeling claustrophobic. Lukasz pushed back his dark hair to reveal an ugly dry scab on his forehead. 'It better. Me feel better.' He lowered his voice to a hoarse whisper. 'My life, Ellie …My life, it is yours.' The genuine affection in his eyes held her gaze for a moment.

'Don't be silly! It's not just me. It's my mother and father. We all had to help you.'

'Please, Ellie. It is you who think of Lukasz. You, my friend.'

'We're all your friend Lukasz.'

'But you are for me,' he said and taking hold of her hand he kissed it and turned her hand over to let his lips linger on the inside of her wrist.

Reluctantly she snatched it back. 'No, no Lukasz, you mustn't!'

'I sorry. I not mean to …'

'It's okay, but please …don't do that!'

She left him quickly and climbed back down, her head reeling. His touch, the intensity of his look, the warmth of his lips thrilled her but she hardly dared admit it to herself. Never had she experienced what she had just then. It had felt like an electric current shooting through her body.

Chapter 13

The following afternoon Ellen returned from work feeling very despondent.

'George said there's no more work for me now. My job's finished, Mum.'

'What! He's dismissed you? What do you mean?'

'No, not dismissed me exactly, but...' Her breath was coming in short gasps from the effort of hurrying home. Without much to eat, the physical exertion of walking home had drained what little strength she had.

'Here, love, come and sit down.'

'It could be just for a week or two, but it could be much longer. There's no flour left to work with. The Germans have requisitioned the latest delivery of flour and there's no sign of any more coming. George said until he can get more supplies, and providing the Germans don't commandeer it again, there'll be no work for any of us.'

Meg sighed. 'So that means no bread for us either. I could've guessed as much.' She sat down beside her. 'I suppose we have to make do with whatever we can get now.' Tears flooded her eyes. It was a bitter blow. 'I don't know how we're going to manage love, I don't really.'

'Everyone needs bread, but George can't afford to pay us without work.'

'Oh love, how can we feed him upstairs if we can't even feed ourselves? I'll go and see your nan tomorrow, see if she can spare any flour. We can make some soda bread if we can get enough. If not, we still have plenty of potatoes for now. We'll get by somehow.'

'I've been thinking, Mum. Wouldn't it be better for him in the cellar?'

This question was met with astonishment. 'Is that all you think about? I've said this before, Ellie. There's no room down there for him, love. It's full of your father's tools, fishing rods, coal sacks – not that we're able to get much coal these days – but lots of old stuff and -'

'But couldn't we clear it out? We could get rid of some stuff, sell some to make room for him. We could if we tried, Mum. You know how the shops are selling second-hand goods, you said so yourself with your wedding-dress. If the Germans come to search the house again, last time they didn't notice we had a cellar. We could cover the trapdoor that leads to it, put a carpet over it or something and it won't show at all. At least it's got a small window to give him a bit of air and he'd have more room.'

Meg appeared to be warming to the idea. 'I must admit, it would be easier than having to climb up into the attic every time we take him a meal. I'll speak to your father. It's about time we cleared out the place anyway, we might even find something in there we can make use of ourselves.'

On Sunday morning Ellen was woken by something going on downstairs. Dressing hastily, she crept down fearing the worst. The German soldiers had been known to arrive early and without warning. But to her amazement she saw Lukasz there with her father. Her mother was in the kitchen. They had the cellar trap door open and there was stuff all over the place. She had never seen Lukasz in daylight before. He looked well, his height and physical strength seemed to dominate the room. He was, she had to admit, very striking.

'What's going on? You're busy!' She was smiling, knowing very well what was happening.

'I talked to your father last night and he thought your idea could work.' Lukasz glanced at Ellen; he nodded and smiled a little, but his eyes didn't linger on her. His unfamiliar voice and language gave the scene alarming vividness. For a few minutes she stood and watched, hardly able to believe her eyes that Lukasz was there helping her father heave and lift the boxes out of the cellar. Albert easily became breathless. 'I'm not up to this kind of work, not like I used to be.'

'I help you,' said Lukasz. 'At home I work with my father. He has land, I plough with horses, it very hard work. I get strong.'

They were interested to hear about his past. He described the farm as they shifted the stuff together and seemed more and more relaxed. Wearing an old white shirt of her father's and his trousers too, which were far too wide on the waist but tied round with string, his dark hair hung in greasy locks to his shoulders. In the heavy task of moving the stuff, inhibitions had been forgotten, especially when suddenly Lukasz caught his hand on the sharp edge of a tea chest and yelled some expletive in Polish.

'Ssh!' they all chorused. A hush descended on them in their fear of being heard. The task and the danger involved, had brought them all together as they heaved and shifted boxes, and discovered things they had long forgotten. The task, and the camaraderie had lifted all their spirits.

Ellen went outside to make some space in the outside toilet, hoping it would be possible, by packing things floor to ceiling, to still leave room for the privy to still be used. A fresh breeze was blowing. Opening the wooden door, she didn't see much potential in there to store much. It was such a small space. She pulled the sack of coal out – the last of the coal they had. There were wellingtons, which could go indoors, and some old coats they used for gardening, hanging on the door. Several boxes were already stacked up in there; things which they had brought down from the attic before. After ten minutes or so, she had shifted quite a bit, lodged some behind the toilet seat and some she took indoors to put back in the attic.

Back indoors, she stooped to pick up a box of tools. Next, up came a box of books from the cellar and Ellen looked through them eagerly – they were so short of anything to read.

'We could let the library have some of these books.' Ellen was eagerly leafing through one. 'People are saying they've read all the books they've got twice over and the library hasn't got many left. The Germans have taken half of them. I don't know if they read them or burn them to keep warm.'

'Well, I'm not giving them any of my books,' declared Albert, suddenly banging down one book on top of another in temper. 'God knows I've got nothing else to spend my time on. No fun in going out, nothing in the newspapers you can believe. It's a poor state of affairs, it really is.' He straightened up. 'Here, lad, let's get this stuff sorted. I'm all done in.'

Lukasz looked at him anxiously in response to this sudden change of tone. 'I give you much trouble, Sir. I sorry. It too much ...I go!'

'No, no Lukasz. It's alright,' said Meg in a soothing tone. 'It's okay, my husband is tired, that's all. He's a little fed-up too, don't worry. We'll get you downstairs and you'll be fine.'

But Lukasz continued to speak rapidly. None of them could understand until he finished with the words: 'I give you much trouble! I must go!'

Meg stepped in to reassure him, putting a firm hand on his arm. 'Listen, Lukasz. Be quiet. When the war is finished, we'll all be okay, understand? All will be well, Lukasz. Trust me.' Saying this, she nodded to her husband. 'Alright, Bert? We're nearly finished.'

Ellen couldn't help admiring her mother at that moment. In the face of all that had happened, she remained calm and positive.

They finished storing things around the house, and finally Albert emerged from the cellar wiping his hands on a rag. 'That's about it then,' he said, and turning to Lukasz, added, 'It ain't no palace, lad, but it might do you for a bit.'

'Let me have a look,' cried Ellen, slipping past them, and stepping down through the trap door. The cellar was easily concealed as it was accessed by a trapdoor that blended into the floor itself when it was closed. She descended the rough brick steps, and it grew darker. The small window cast a little light, illuminating a cavern about ten-foot square. Its walls were half-plaster and half brickwork; between the wall and the ceiling on the far side was the tiny square of a window through which a gentle breeze blew. This was probably visible from the garden, especially at night if there was a candle alight. They would have to conceal this from outside, but at least that gap would give Lukasz some fresh air even if it was rather draughty. The cellar ceiling was higher than the attic, high enough for a tall man like Lukasz to stand up straight and it would give him some space to move around. For too long he had been stooping down under the eaves unable to stand up straight or walk about.

'Right, can you get this lot up in the attic,' said Albert, breathing heavily, 'I need to sit-down.'
Lukasz picked up the large box and carried it up the stairs. They heard his heavy footsteps tramping across the landing and the rattle of the stepladder.

When he was out of earshot, Meg said, 'I hope to God they don't come looking for him again. We need to hide this trapdoor. I'll get the rug down from our bedroom straight away.'

When he returned, he was carrying his roll of bedding and he descended with it into the cellar in silence.

That night Ellen lay in bed thinking about him stretched out on his bed in the dark. At least now he had a thin slice of a window, a little fresh air, and he could walk about and look up at the stars.

The family relaxed a little over the next few days. Often, once the curfew was in force and they knew no-one would call, they left the trapdoor open and Lukasz came up to stretch his legs. They invited him to sit and

A Sea of Barbed Wire

talk with them in the evening. They could even listen to the radio as long as they kept it on very low.

Ellen was alone in the house when she heard the trap door open. Lukasz appeared, pushing back the rug and climbing out, his hair flopping over his eyes.

'Hello, Lukasz!' She was a little surprised and concerned but smiled warmly. 'You're taking a chance, aren't you, wandering about in the middle of the day?' She returned to the kitchen, her hands covered in flour.

'What you do there?' he asked, regarding the mixing bowl, the scales and their precious ration of flour. He was blinking against the light.

'Making soda bread,' she replied. He didn't understand but Ellen started talking to him in a business-like way, thumping and kneading the bread dough as she worked. He was probably lonely and bored, she thought, being confined to the cellar for hours at a time. 'I can't go to work at the moment, in the bakery,' she explained, 'so I thought I would make some here. We can't manage without bread, even if it is made with horrible flour.'

'Horrible?' He echoed her and chuckled. He seemed to like that word.

'Yes, look at this.' And she ran her fingers through it revealing the lumpy texture that made the flour so coarse and grey in colour. Her nan had given them some but it was very rough, with the usual bits of wheat and oat husk in it.

Lukasz stood watching her. 'My mother – she do this too. She make the bread. My mother - if she be dead, I not know. Ellie! They kill my father. They kill me too.' He thumped himself in the chest, his dark eyes flashing and his face contorting in anguish, so rapidly did his moods change. She stopped what she was doing. 'I understand, but we hope and pray the war will be over soon.'

He nodded. 'I pray too. I pray for my family, for my poor sister.'

Returning her attention to the bread making, she patted the dough into a loaf shape, covered it with a cloth and wiped her hands. 'I'll leave it to prove now. Later, when it's out of the oven, you can have some if you like.'

'You go to work?'

'Yes, I work at the bakery, making bread, like this. There's no work for me there at the moment.' She continued chatting to him even though she guessed half of what she said he didn't comprehend. But talking was a way of helping him feel more secure. More than anything she wanted him to trust her, to trust her parents and not try to run away.

'What is it, the bakery?' He pronounced it carefully.

She explained, pointing to her own dough and making various signs and hand-movements, describing what her job entailed. They were having quite an animated conversation when they heard voices outside. She peeped out of the window and saw her father talking to someone standing at the gate. It was a German soldier.

'Lukasz! Quickly, hide!' She pointed to the cellar. In a flash Lukasz disappeared. With trembling fingers, she folded the trapdoor down, and shifted the rug back over it. The manoeuvre took no more than a couple of minutes, but when her father came in, she felt her heart pounding.

'Cold out there,' he said, breathing quite heavily as he sat down and removed his boots. 'Too cold to stand around talking to that lot! I told him, I'm not freezing to death for you or anyone.' He tossed his head in the direction of the road.

'I thought he was about to come in, Dad. You didn't offend him, did you?'

'I don't care if I did.'

Ellen began removing the teacloth covering the dough she had left to rise only a few minutes before. It was too soon but it was a welcome distraction. For something to do, to occupy her while she recovered her nerves, she began to knead the dough again, slowly and methodically. It was a task she found relaxing even when she was at work, and it helped her to get back on an even keel.

'That German stopped when I was talking to old Ron out there. Ron's wife hasn't been too good.'

'Sorry to hear that, Dad. Has she seen the doctor then?'

'The doctor says it's not medicine she needs, it's some good food, vitamins and protein. I wish I could give her a prescription for things like that! He told Ron to give her plenty of eggs and some decent fruit. Of course, Ron can't do that, none of us can. I was tempted to tell that German what the doctor had said.'

'He probably would have agreed with you though, Dad. They're all hungry now, even the soldiers don't get enough by the look of them. You can still give out some prescriptions though, can't you?'

'Some, but what I do isn't half enough, love. I can't give them food and that's what my patients need above everything else. The supplies of drugs aren't reliable, we haven't got a couple of aspirins to rub together at the moment, let alone penicillin or cough mixture. I dread to see their faces sometimes when I have to turn them away empty handed. It'd be nice to give them something like a nice bottle of fresh orange juice. It would do those folks a world of good, better than any medicine.'

'Oh, if only!' Ellen sighed. She saw how worn out he was, the unreliability of deliveries had almost beaten him. How this war was wearing everyone down. She wondered how much longer they could hold out; how much more anxiety and shortage of food they could bear. Albert raised his head suddenly as if listening, 'How's he been?' he asked quietly, nodding in the direction of the trapdoor.

'Oh, fine, I made him some tea and he came up to stretch his legs for a few minutes.'

Her reply seemed normal enough, but it seemed to hang in the air awkwardly and she found herself wondering why he hadn't responded. Perhaps it was her imagination, but there was just a little too much delay.

'You know he can't stay here, love.'

Ellen shot him a look that betrayed more than she meant it to.

'But Dad!'

'I'm going to see about him.'

That statement alone sent waves of fear shuddering down her body.

'See about him? What do you mean? Mum said he could stay here for -'

'Never mind what your mother said. Your mother's not heard half of what I have, an' she's got a soft heart in her that doesn't do her, or any of us, any good.'

Ellen slapped the dough down on the table impatiently, flung it back into the loaf tin and threw the cloth over it. 'Dad! For heaven's sake! Why don't people stand up to the Germans more? They've got no right to keep us all in a state of fear, creeping around on eggshells and trying to please them all the time. As it is we're obeying every little rule they feel like imposing on us. Why should they persecute us, we haven't done anything wrong?!'

Her father stood up, raising himself up taller than his usual stance and he faced her sternly. 'Ellen. Any more of that language, my girl, and you'll have us all thrown into prison. *We haven't done anything wrong!* Who do you think that man is down there who we've been sheltering for I don't know how long? Father bloody Christmas?'

'Ssh! Don't! Someone will hear you.'

'Well, maybe it would be better if they did. Bring an end to this infernal vacuum that we've got ourselves into.' He took off his coat, and sighing in resignation hung it on the back of the kitchen door and stormed off saying he was going to have a lie down. She heard his heavy steps climbing the stairs. Never in her life had she seen her father in a temper or depressed and unable to cope. Then, she realised, Lukasz might have heard every word of what he had just said.

Chapter 14

It was fortunate in a way, that Ellen didn't have to go to work the rest of the week. Seeing Lucy out with her soldier had brought home the reality of the situation she found herself in. Lucy appeared to give little thought to the future, she was living for the moment and dealing with her life as best she could, and who could blame her? Well, lots of people actually but where did that leave Ellen? Gradually she was becoming isolated by her burden of secrecy and unable to relax. In the end, she thought, wouldn't it be better to be honest and open about things? But there was too much risk involved.

It wasn't often Robert came to their house. With the curfew being imposed it was difficult for him to get back in time anyway. Even if she had told him about Lukasz, which she still hadn't, it would immediately involve him and risk his life as well as their own. Actually, she wasn't sure how he would react to them having done such a thing. Ellen took a peep at the dough she had left to rise under the teacloth and groaned. It needed warmth. Part of the problem was that the house was so cold. They couldn't light the fire until the evening as fuel was short and being able to purchase paraffin was a thing of the past, so the paraffin heater was useless. They needed the bread for breakfast so resigning herself to the fact that it would have to do

A Sea of Barbed Wire

as it is, she lit the oven and placed the bowl with the dough on top of the cooker to encourage it to rise a little more while the oven was heating up. Then she made some tea and took it up to her father who was having a lie-down. She found him fast asleep on the bed and placing the cup beside him, she crept out. However, when he came downstairs half an hour later, he seemed in a better mood. The loaf was in the oven, and the fragrance of bread baking permeated the house. He sat down and took up his paper.

'Smells good, love. Where's your mother?'

'She's gone shopping and then to see Nan. She said she'll be back by five.'

'Folks are saying the curfew's been extended again. Got to be indoors even earlier now. If Robert's coming here after work, he'll have to get a move on. Takes him how long to walk home?'

'Half an hour at least, Dad…actually, I was thinking …I don't know what we should do about Rob. I mean, whether to tell him or not.'

'There's no need for the man to know, surely. No use worrying the poor chap. He's got enough on his plate with the bank I should think.'

'But I find it so hard keeping secrets.'

'Then you'd better start getting used to it, Ellie. We've got one hell of a big secret that plenty of people would love to know about. There are some folks who'd give their right eye for a big fat secret like that – a nice little earner for them if they wanted to make a bit of cash and keep the Germans happy, eh?'

Her heart was feeling fit to burst. 'But Dad, what if Rob suspects something, or finds out somehow?'

'Ask your mother. It was her fault, and yours, for inviting the lad in and making a fuss of him. You women are too soft hearted, that's your trouble. Anyway, it isn't Robert you want to worry about – it's them.' Another toss of the head. 'We can only do what we can do, love. Same as we'd hope anyone else would do for us, if we were as hurt as he was when he turned up.'

Thankful that he was showing a little sympathy for Lukasz, Ellen went over and gave him a hug. He was surprised – it wasn't a thing she did very often. Getting on with some useful work was the best solution to dealing with a lot of problems. Somehow or other she knew she had to harden up to be able to cope with all this.

They say people can get used to anything over time. But ever since the German soldiers landed on Guernsey's small airport runway and came marching through the streets, the sight of them was alien and bizarre to all the islanders. They had never seen anything like it, apart from on film at the cinema. Ellen wondered what those soldiers were thinking as they stepped smartly past glasshouses filled with the colour and fragrance of freesias and vineries loaded with ripening tomatoes. Their heads must surely have turned briefly to catch a glimpse of the beautiful landscape on the island while they congratulated themselves on having claimed a tiny portion of British soil.

What did they think of the way Guernsey people lived their lives? Was it so different to their own? The memory of that first glimpse would be tucked away in their minds surely, with reminders of the family life they had left behind. Would they think of their own

A Sea of Barbed Wire

childhoods and how war had interrupted and destroyed it all? They would have memories of innocent times, distant from the strict German army discipline under which they were now held. Individual soldiers did show their compassionate side sometimes, giving sweets to the children who hung around watching them doing their drills and sometimes imitating them, marching along behind them, their little legs moving in unison and their little arms swinging. Once, Ellen saw a soldier stop a Guernsey mother and ask her if he could hold her new-born baby, just for a few minutes. He told her that back home, the night before he had left, his wife had given birth to a baby boy and he had never had the chance to cradle it. A person's need for care and affection can never be suppressed completely; it was understandable that miles away from home their affections might wander as they looked towards local girls and began new relationships, however much these affairs were frowned on by the community.

There was a thump heard on the doorstep. It was Meg, who had put her shopping bag down on the doorstep. Ellen opened the door and carried her bag in for her. 'This feels light, Mum. There's not much left in the shops is there.' The bag, she noticed, contained just a few root vegetables. Meg made straight for the armchair before even taking off her coat and flung herself down. She looked exhausted.

'I've just made a cuppa Mum; shall I pour you one?'

'Please, love, and is there any sugar? Just a little would help. Oh dear, I feel quite weak and light-headed.' She kicked off her shoes.

'Didn't Nan have anything to give you for lunch?'

'Of course, a little bread and dripping, but I'm afraid it wasn't enough.' Here she abandoned any further explanation and continued to get her breath back, waving away any further questions as if they were flies. 'Thank goodness though, I think your nan's doing alright. I didn't expect her to be as capable as she is, with losing Gran'pa like that. Well – you never know what's round the corner.'

Ellen passed her a cup of tea. 'There's a little sugar in there, Mum.'

'Thank you dear, I've only been out since eleven o' clock but I feel as if I've been away a month. When I've got myself together, perhaps you'll help me get some dinner on. Nan gave us a tin of corned beef to go with the vegetables. It will be nice to have something different to taste.'

Her mother's once comfortably plump figure had been transformed by the inadequate provisions. The thought of them all sharing one small tin of corned beef made Ellen shudder. But there was no point in saying anything. The food available was so pitifully meagre. As for herself, she had lost a lot of weight too, and the novelty of finding her waist becoming nice and slim had long worn off.

There was a light tap on the door. A boy Ellen didn't recognise, skinny and half-scared, stood there. He handed her a note.

'Thank you! Wait there and I'll see if I can find something for you.' She returned with an oatmeal biscuit. He held out both hands and took it gratefully before cramming it into his mouth all in one go and racing off down the road on his thin little legs. The message was written crudely in pencil on brown paper which Ellen recognised was a piece of packaging paper from the bakery.

"Dear Ellen. Delivery arrived. Please return to work tomorrow at 6.30 am. George." She read it out loud and sighed.

'Don't you want to go back to work? I thought you were getting bored.'

'Yes, of course I do, Mum, it's just …'

'You've got used to having a lie-in, in the mornings, is that it?'

'Yes, no, well, something like that.'

'He must consider you a good worker. I'm sure he can't afford to pay anyone who doesn't pull their weight. And that means there'll be bread in the shops again. Thank goodness!'

Chapter 15

Their efforts, George said, had to be doubled up to supply the customers who were crying out for bread. All morning Ellen and Lucy were working hard. They were able to catch up with gossip, and it was a welcome distraction to be busy and talk about things they had heard on the grapevine. No mention, however, was made of anything personal; it was as if they were both avoiding the inevitable subject that was on both their minds. The situation was made more tense by their boss continually coming in and out of the work area bringing trolleys to take the dough to the ovens or bringing new sacks of flour in. Whenever Ellen felt tempted to start the inevitable confidential conversation, he suddenly reappeared again, his trolley squeaking as he came down the corridor. She looked at Lucy and raised her eyebrows and just like the old times, they both dissolved in laughter.

At work was the only time Ellen was able to actually feel warmed through. Being warm, and with the delicious smell of the freshly baked loaves, she soon relaxed, even if her stomach was pinched with hunger. She had decided that if Lucy was in love, she could only be happy for her. Love was such a special thing she almost envied her. How could she envy her friend for being in love with a soldier on the enemy's side? Perhaps that was part of the attraction: forbidden love, but whatever it was had transformed Lucy's face, she was buzzing with excitement and humming a tune as she worked. "There'll be bluebirds over …"

George came in. 'Right, girls. I'm just off for my tea break. Keep an eye on the time for me, eh? The next batch will have to come out in ten minutes. Oh, and don't let anyone hear you singing that song – or they'll have you, and I'm not joking.'

'Okay, George,' they replied in unison as he took off his overall and made his way back down the corridor. As soon as he was out of sight, their eyes met.

'Thank goodness he's gone,' said Lucy. 'I've got so much to tell you!'

'Right, fire away, I'm all ears!' replied Ellen, smiling. Cutting a new lump of dough, she began kneading it with the energy she needed to dispel her anxiety.

'Look! He gave me this!' whispered Lucy, her cheeks flushing as she unbuttoned her blouse and showed Ellen an exquisite gold heart on a chain that swung low between her breasts.

Ellen was more than a little surprised. 'It's beautiful! Where did he get such a thing?'

'I dunno! It would be rude to ask wouldn't it! But it's gorgeous, eh? Don't you think it's the sweetest little thing? I'll treasure it always.'

'He sounds very romantic, Lucy. It's lovely, you're very lucky, but aren't you getting yourself in too deep here? I mean, it can't last can it, and you'll be so upset when he -'

'When he what?' she demanded, raising her eyebrows. 'You're such a spoilsport, Ellie, you really are.'

'I'm just trying to be realistic.' She laid the dough aside and took another piece, sprinkling flour and rolling it thoughtfully on the wooden work surface. Perhaps Lucy was right. So, she tried to backtrack a bit. 'I was just thinking, hoping really, that the war will be over soon, and your boyfriend will be called back to Germany. You have to realise that. So much will change when the war is over.'

'But you're wrong there. Franz told me it'll go on at least another year or two. He hates it too, you know. Not all Germans are in favour of the war or support Hitler. Some of them hate him, Franz certainly does. He told me he longs for it all to end so we can all live normally again. He's longing to see his parents and friends back home, and his mother's not well at all. She's got a bad heart. And do you know what he said to me the other night? You'll never guess!'

'Ssh! Keep your voice down or you'll have us all in trouble. Oh no, look at the time. The bread!'

They both dropped what they were doing and rushed to the ovens, pulling open the doors and standing back as a blanket of heat and smoke hit them and billowed up towards the ceiling. Donning gloves, they retrieved a dozen loaves from the ovens. Several were scorched on top but fortunately they were fine, crusty and sweet smelling. Their fragrance filled the workroom.

'Phew!' they both cried in relief, doubling up in giggles again.

'Oh, it's good to have a laugh! You shouldn't take everything so seriously, Ellie, honestly! You're a real wet blanket sometimes!'

'I suppose I am,' she admitted. 'But it's hard not to be, in the times we're going through. I long for the war to end and for us to be free again, don't you?'

Lucy hung her head. 'When the war's over I won't be free. Pete will come back, and that's if *"I'm lucky"* as they say. He'll most likely expect to be greeted with open arms by his pretty little wife and expect me to call him a hero. And the trouble is, I don't even want to have him back.'

Ellen turned to her. 'Franz?'

Lucy nodded.

'I envy you. I know I shouldn't, but to be truly in love! It must feel wonderful!'

'It wasn't like this with Pete. I've changed, I know I have but I can't help it. I'm not the same girl I used to be, Ellie. I can't help bein' affected. It's not all my fault, is it?'

'What, that you love Franz? No, Lucy, don't worry.'

'But I am worried, Ellie! What can I do if he's sent away, sent to the Russian Front or somethin'? That's what they're all scared of.'

However, squeaking was heard coming down the corridor and their boss appeared. He gave a quick survey of the kitchen, saw the loaves cooling on the racks, admittedly looking a little more toasted than usual, but he said nothing about them, just nodded. 'You can take your break now, Ellen,' he said, 'Lucy, you go when she comes back. We've got to keep it up or we'll never be finished.'

With some relief, Ellen untied her apron and giving Lucy a smile, made her way down the corridor. All that waited for her was fifteen minutes sit-down and a hot cup of tea made from dried hawthorn leaves or something similar. She had brought with her a crust of bread and a small piece of cheese wrapped up in a piece of paper. Tonight, she would be able to take a fresh loaf home. As she sat down, she sighed with relief that she hadn't given her secret away. As for her feelings for Lukasz, she kept a special place in her heart for him. But she longed to be able to tell Lucy, talk about him, share her curiosity and excitement about him. But she mustn't reveal her true feelings, not to a single soul. Her heart felt fit to burst.

That afternoon when she got home, she placed a freshly baked loaf of bread on the table for her mother to find when she got back. The house was quiet. Keen to speak to Lukasz while they were alone, she pulled the rug back. She had made him some coffee from the ground acorns which was the substitute for coffee beans they were using. It tasted bitter if they had no sugar, but it was the best they could do. Before she went down, she checked out of the window to make sure no-one was around. It was generally quiet at that time of day, and feeling satisfied it was safe she pulled the rug across and tapped on the trapdoor. There wasn't a sound from below. She waited and presently a scuffling sound was heard. The door lifted up a few inches and His brown eyes appeared out of the gloom below.

'I've brought you some coffee, Lukasz. Do you want to come up and stretch your legs?'

He didn't reply but appeared to understand because he pushed the trapdoor up further and clambered out. The first thing she noticed, apart from the fact that his eyes were bloodshot, was the smell of his sweat. She was sorry, but it was impossible to allow him to use the bath very often. Also, they were so short of fuel to heat the water they hardly had enough for a bath themselves. The electricity and gas were rationed to the times they were allowed to use it. Lukasz came up and stood very tall beside her. She turned away, her heart pounding. 'Walk around a bit if you like. I'd say you could walk in the garden but I daren't let you go outside, it's too risky.'

'Risky? Riskee …riskeee' he echoed, trying out the new word for himself.

'You could be seen.'

He nodded, sipping the coffee.

'I'm sorry, she said, as she noticed him pulling a face. 'It's even more horrible than the tea.'

'You go work. I not help. Your father. Your mother. I stay here, I do no work … I do nothing. I wish …' He continued finishing what he wanted to say in Polish.

'I can't understand you but it's okay, Lukasz, you have to stay out of sight.'

'I feel it not right. I not chop the wood. I not work, nothing. I worry.'

'It's the war, Lukasz. It's not your fault.' How she longed to comfort him, to hug him, to show him it didn't matter, tell him that everything would be alright. Then she thought of Lucy. It was strange. Lucy had got herself into such a dangerous position and yet she didn't seem worried at all. But Ellen felt tied to her responsibilities, to her parents, to her secret. The war was something they shared, something they were all involved with. And sooner or later it would end, for better or for worse.

Lukasz was trapped. If he left them; if he attempted to escape from the island, his chances of survival were minimal. Young men had already tried already and failed. Several had drowned or been discovered, had to turn back and land right in the face of the enemy. The beaches were mined, the coasts were guarded all the way round. Going out in a boat was banned except for fishermen, and they had to be accompanied by a German soldier. Fishermen were allowed to fish only up to a perimeter of three miles from the coast. The seas around Guernsey were treacherous and the coast was watched day and night. There were lookouts and sentries on duty with searchlights everywhere. The islanders were actually being held captive, all of them.

Lukasz walked towards the window and looked out. His eyes were half closed and he blinked and squinted against the light even though the sun wasn't shining.

Ellen was afraid. 'Stand away from the window, Lukasz!'

He turned round quickly and faced her, not understanding. She tugged at his arm and pulled him away from the window. 'You could be seen! People might betray you.'

He mumbled a few words, but within seconds the tension lifted from his face and he smiled broadly at her.

'They see me, yeh?' He chuckled.

'I hope not, but -!'

He took her by the shoulders. 'We be okay.' His eyes searched hers for recognition. She nodded, swallowing hard as a tingle shot through her at his touch. For a moment she thought he was going to kiss her.

A Sea of Barbed Wire

'What you do, the sewing? The reading?' His focus on her intensified, but he let her go and picked up a book that was lying on the arm of the chair. He flicked through it and put it down again. Alone together, not shut away in the dark this time but in the sitting-room, his presence seemed more real, and closer. He had come alive in the daylight and was relaxed. Hearing him often breaking into his own language, although incomprehensible to her, was music to her ears. She liked to hear his accent and the tone of his voice, low and strong.

'I like to read, when I can see, before it gets too dark.' She picked up another book from the sideboard to show him. 'Come and sit down.' She indicated the seat beside her. Leafing through it, she began showing him pictures of England, streets of London, taxi cabs and buses. There were photographs of people boarding trains, and then others: rural scenes of farmworkers, cows, fields and shepherds driving herds of sheep.

'Ah, this, my father...' Suddenly Lukasz began speaking rapidly as if he was on home ground, evidently explaining the things he knew about, the life he understood.

'I work here...my home.' He pointed to a large photograph of a country scene where shire horses were pulling a plough.

'Your home, Lukasz?'

'My home. My father ...yes.' His face contorted in pain at some memory. 'My father dead. He shot.'

'I'm so sorry. The Nazis?'

He nodded. How she wished she could converse with him fluently. There was so much she wanted to know and share with him. His passion excited her; his was a new world which she longed to explore. Longing to continue the conversation, and ease his sadness, she noticed it was growing late and closing the book she said, 'Come on, Lukasz, you'd better go back down. My parents will be home any minute.'

With a hopeless kind of gesture, he stood up and went towards the trapdoor. For a brief moment he stopped and looked her straight in the eye, holding her gaze for more than a few seconds. It was a look filled with loneliness; that was the only way she could interpret it.

'My home,' he said, glancing again at the book in her hand.

'Here, take it.' She gave it to him. He took it, turned away and left her, descending the steps and pulling the trapdoor down over his head. Putting the rug back in place, she walked to the window and peered out as dusk fell. Sometimes she felt as trapped as he was.

Chapter 16

That night after eating their meagre dinner consisting entirely of boiled vegetables, Albert put down his knife and fork. Meg stood up and began clearing the plates away, glancing up at her husband as if she knew what was coming.

'We have to talk, all of us. 'Put those away, dear, and come and sit down. I've got something to say to you and Ellen.' It was unlike Albert to be so awake after a meal for one thing. He invariably fell asleep even if his hunger hadn't been satisfied.

'I've heard tell of some locals over Castel way who have been found sheltering an escaped prisoner. Don't know what's happened to them yet but I can guess. We can't afford that to happen here, it's one thing being a good Samaritan but it's quite another if my family's lives are put at risk. I probably shouldn't have allowed it in the first place.'

Ellen became scared. Her eyes instinctively went to the trapdoor. 'But Dad, he's -'

'Ssh, Ellie. Be quiet. Hear me out.'

Meg left the table, sat down in her armchair and picked up her knitting. 'Bert, I heard about that too, but we had no choice but to take the poor man in.'

'This is my house and I'm saying we can't go on, not any longer. I won't allow it. Look, dear, the risk is too great. Think of Ellen here. We can't keep hiding him.'

'And what do you expect us to do?' Meg demanded. 'Throw him out on the street tonight? He won't last five minutes.' Her needles clicked irritably. In the tension that followed, Ellen couldn't speak. Her thoughts were in turmoil. She was wrestling with her feelings, her care for Lukasz was up against the safety of her own parents. Her father began to tell them what he had heard. These 'quislings' as they were called, were despised by the islanders except no-one knew who they were. There were only suspicions, and this was worse in a way. Letters had been written, anonymously, to the Commandant and addressed to The Grange Hotel where the German army had their headquarters. If anyone was betrayed for hiding something, even a radio, the soldiers would go to their house, they would be arrested and interrogated, and if found guilty, deported to a German prisoner-of-war camp. That's if they were lucky to escape with their lives. People had been shot for defying them. Was it justifiable to protect one man while putting the lives of several others at risk?

Robert had a couple of days off and was able to go and see Ellen at home. She hadn't seen him for several days, but she was apprehensive now, particularly as he was coming to their house for tea. It was going to be a family gathering because it was Joan's birthday. Meg had managed to bake a birthday cake which had more grated carrot and potato in it than anything else.

'Come in, Mother, and sit down here by the fire. Not often we have a fire in the afternoon. It's a real treat.'

Ellen greeted her nan with a hug.

'You're looking pretty, dear. Are you expecting your young man tonight?'

'Yes, Nan, he's coming along soon.'

Joan looked around, inspecting the room. She hadn't been inside their house in a while. 'How have you been managing?'

'We get by as best we can, Mother.'

Grief hadn't changed her, in fact it seemed to have made her more resilient, more capable. 'I'll see what else I can get you. This time of year, there's not much left in the ground I'm afraid. I'll be sowing cabbage and cauliflower soon, but the land isn't producing much; you know how things are ... what with thieves plundering and Germans requisitioning whatever takes their fancy. Last week when the cabbage plants were just coming through, they drove one of their tanks straight over them and started doing manoeuvres, for heaven's sake! They churned up the whole field and laid half the crop to waste. They don't care.'

There wasn't a moment when Ellen wasn't acutely aware of Lukasz being only feet away from them under the floor in the cellar. Probably he could hear what was being discussed but he wouldn't understand. But her heart pounded within her when Joan began talking about the cruel treatment meted out to the prisoners and the Organisation Todt workers that she had witnessed recently. 'How wretched and poorly they look,' Joan complained. When Joan began talking about the local girls courting German soldiers it was as much as Ellen could do to stop herself blushing. The trouble was Joan wasn't slow to pick up on signs of discomfort. Within seconds she appeared to be scrutinising her granddaughter's face. It was as if Lucy's secret was already written there – the whole story.

Suddenly they both heard a man cough.

'Oh, so your father is home!' said Joan. 'I assumed he was still at work. The pharmacy was very busy when I called in there this morning.'

Ellen shot off her seat. 'I'll just give Mum a hand,' she mumbled, retreating into the kitchen. Meg was working at the sink. Inclining her head in the direction of the sitting-room Ellen said, 'Do you want me to do anything, Mum?' she asked, fixing her with a meaningful stare.

'No, thanks, keep your Nan happy and I'll be there in a minute.'

But Ellen whispered in her ear, 'We heard him cough,' she said, rolling her eyes in desperation.

Meg nodded and frowned. Then she spoke up with a cheerful tone: 'Would you just bring the milk jug, love? I'll bring these.' Picking up a pile of tea plates, she carried them through to the sitting room and Ellen followed her. Just as she placed them on the table a cough sounded again.

'He sounds bad, your Bert. What's he doing down there in the cellar?'

'It's not Bert, Mother.' Meg sat down. 'We hoped we wouldn't have to tell you. We didn't want to get anyone else involved, least of all you.'

'What on earth are you trying to say? Come on, out with it!'

'Any decent person with a conscience would have done the same, Mother. What do you do if someone comes to your door begging for help?' Meg took a deep breath. 'I'm afraid we're sheltering a young

A Sea of Barbed Wire

man. He escaped from the guards and came to the backdoor in a terrible state. We gave him some water but then he collapsed on the kitchen floor.'

The whole room seemed to absorb the silence that followed. Joan bowed her head as if thinking, then she looked up. 'Good for you!'

'So you're not angry? I thought you would be so against us doing anything like that.' Meg turned and included Ellen in the conversation. 'We just had to do something, didn't we!'

'No, of course I'm not angry, dear. If we can steal one life back from those evil Germans to make up for when they robbed us of Gran'pa, then it's only right. They don't deserve to have men slaving away for them, barely giving them a crust of bread to keep them going.' She hung her head and when she raised it again, they saw her face was wet with tears. If Max hadn't been late for the curfew that night, he would be with us now and I'm certain he would approve of what you're doing. If only this blessed war would end and allow those poor prisoners to go home.' Joan's composure had returned. 'So you're hiding him down there, in the cellar? Is he ill?'

'No, he's okay. He's much better than he was, but very confined of course. Bert's worried now and he's right, I suppose, we can't hide him forever.'

Joan looked furtively around the room. 'Who else knows?'

'Nan, we haven't told anyone yet.'

'Not even that boyfriend of yours?'

Ellen blushed. 'No, I don't know if I should.'

'But he's expected tonight you say? Then you must either put him off or tell him as soon as he gets here, Ellie. If he comes, he can either promise to keep his mouth shut or he'll have to stop seeing you.'

'But I don't know him well enough to trust him.'

Her nan looked at her. 'He might not want to be *in on it*, if you see what I mean. He has responsibility to the bank, and his career.' She smiled, amusement dancing in her eyes. 'You've certainly got yourselves into a corner. Well, this is one birthday present I wasn't expecting!' She looked at each of them, absorbing the fact of their dilemma with a philosophical shrug. 'They probably won't miss your poor prisoner. Just one more man presumed dead, another number dropping off their list. His absence will hardly be noticed, except they'll probably make a right song and dance about it if they do discover him gone. It's a wonder they haven't sent the troops out already to hunt him down.'

'Oh, but they have, Mother. It was nearly four weeks ago now. They even –.' Meg hesitated; she seemed to try to stop herself from pouring out the whole story but it wasn't working because Joan had her eyes on her.

'Even? What are you saying?'

Meg sighed. 'They've even been and searched the house already.'

Joan looked incredulous. 'Here? When? And what happened? Why didn't you tell me?'

'We were lucky, Mother, that's all I can say.' Perhaps she could hardly believe it herself.

'At first we had him hiding up in the attic, Nan.'

'There's no need to whisper now, dear. I know they say walls have ears, but I think these walls are thick enough. So you had him up in the roof?'

A Sea of Barbed Wire

'Yes, we moved him down to the cellar only the other day. He's more comfortable there, and he has a bit more room.'

Joan smiled. 'Well, I think you all deserve a medal. I'm proud of you. I'll do anything I can to help. Since those hooligan soldiers caused my dear Max to panic, I'll do anything to defy them. I can't bring Max back, but I can fight the suffering they're causing to everyone else.' Her curiosity continued. 'And Bert? He agreed to it? He's a braver man than I thought. Now,' she continued, 'tell me about your prisoner: where's he from? Does he speak English? Has he recovered?'

They were so surprised and relieved that she had taken it so well, Ellen had completely forgotten about Robert coming. Still in the mid flow of conversation, they heard footsteps approaching and a sharp knock on the back door. Ellen leapt up but her mother stopped her.

'Stay here and keep your nan company. I'll see to the door.'

Joan studied Ellen with a sympathetic smile. 'If he's the decent sort of man I think he is, he'll stand by us and our decision, don't you worry.'

'Oh, I hope so, Nan.'

Some whispering went on in the kitchen for more than a few minutes. Meg's tone was calm but suddenly they heard the back door slam.

'He hasn't gone again, has he?' cried Ellen.

Meg came into the room, visibly shaken.

'I told him straight out what we were doing. Probably not the best way to go about it but it's too late now.' Meg sat down with them again, but she wasn't relaxed.

'So he was very angry then, Mum?'

There was an awkward silence. 'Actually, I think he was completely shocked.'

Ellen stood up and grabbed her coat. 'I'm going after him.'

Not wanting to draw attention to herself, she didn't run but kept walking quickly until she saw him ahead. She caught him up and gasped, holding her side and breathless. 'Rob, please, we need to talk.' She glanced around, making sure no-one was within earshot.

He faced her. 'So what was all that about, back there?' he whispered. 'I don't understand, Ellie. Your mother told me the most ridiculous story, I don't believe it!'

'Let me explain. We didn't plan it; these things just happen sometimes. Walk back with me, will you? My nan's there, it's her birthday and we've made a cake.'

'I can't risk it, Ellie. What were you all thinking of?'

'Please?'

Looking extremely uncomfortable, he nodded, and they started going back. He was very quiet. She could see his brow furrowed, and he squinted through his glasses at the road ahead with his shoulders hunched over. The street was empty, but she drew very close to him and held his arm. 'It all happened so quickly, Rob. We didn't have much choice. Anyone with an ounce of sympathy would have done the same. The man came to our backdoor late one night, in such a state, all bleeding as if he'd been beaten.'

'You shouldn't have even answered the door. There are robbers out there. You could have been killed!'

'It would have been better if my mum hadn't told you.'

'You mean, you were going to keep it a secret from me?'

'All I know is we can't give up on him now, turn him out on the street. The reason I didn't want to tell you is because I knew it would put you in danger too.'

'But also your parents, your nan, probably everyone you know is now at risk.'

'But the man would have died otherwise!'

Throwing his hands in the air in a gesture of hopelessness, Robert walked away, leaving her standing there alone.

Chapter 17

Opening the backdoor quietly, Ellen stepped back into the kitchen and went through into the sitting-room feeling unable to speak. Her mother greeted her: 'Still on your own then, love?'

She nodded. 'I tried to explain, but …'

'And what did he say?' asked her mother. 'That we've all gone mad?'

Albert cleared his throat. 'I would've probably said the same if it was me, to be honest.'

Miserable and confused, Ellen went upstairs to her room. It was probably over between her and Robert. But to try to save a man's life wasn't wrong. How much should we risk our own lives to save others? If no-one ever crossed the German soldiers, looked the other way when someone was in trouble – what sort of a world would it be? It wouldn't be the island community that she had grown up in. She couldn't bear the thought that kindness and generosity could be considered a thing of the past, gone with the invasion of war and cruelty taking its place. In that sense Hitler, and the German Army would already have won. She sat on her bed fighting back the tears. But she refused to cry, to back down under the pressure of Robert's criticism. She and her parents had acted in good faith to save the poor prisoner and she hoped – if it came to it – she would be strong and brave enough to stand up for what she believed in, no matter what. Ellen had been upstairs about twenty minutes when she heard loud voices. It sounded as if someone else had arrived. Alarmed, she suddenly realised it was Robert's voice. Checking her face in the mirror, she went downstairs slowly, listening for the tone of the conversation. If he had returned to argue it out with her parents, she was ready. Robert was sitting on the sofa beside her nan. He had undone his tie and was looking surprisingly relaxed.

'You came back?'

He nodded. 'I'm sorry. I came to apologise. It was a shock, but I shouldn't have said what I did. I've given a lot of thought to what you're doing, and I think you're right. Sometimes we have to stand up and say enough is enough. This occupation isn't even a proper war really, is it, not for us in Guernsey. We've let the Germans do what they want with this island. It's all a bit sickening the way people bow to their every command. There's no fighting going on, hardly anyone's objecting – to their faces at least. We're all accepting their strict rationing and orders as if we've got no other choice. And I suppose we haven't really. But is it right we just stand by while soldiers go barging in, turning defenceless people out of their homes, stealing their food and trashing their houses. They're even arresting our Guernsey people for doing the most trifling things. And what do we do? Nothing!' All eyes were on him. Ellen stood gaping at him in astonishment. 'Rob! I've never heard you speak this way before!'

'Well, it seems to be a day of reckoning for all of us, doesn't it, Ellie.'

Meg got up from her chair 'Right! That's sorted then. Now we've cleared that up and you're all here, let's have our tea!'

Ellen drew him aside. 'Thanks Robert, I'm proud of you, what you said just then.'

'And I'm sorry. Where it will all lead us though, we don't know.' He ran a hand through his thick black hair and sighed.

'It's good of you to come back. Thanks. I'd better go to help mum get the tea.'

While she was gone, Joan turned her attention to Robert with an inquisitive smile. 'Just let me say, dear, I applaud you for what you've decided. I should do more to stand up to them too, if only for my husband's sake who they literally scared to death.' She clasped her hands together and studying Robert with an intense stare she asked, 'So tell me, Robert, how are you all managing at the bank? Can't be easy for you with the German's calling the shots. I hear they can be hard taskmasters when it comes to money.'

'Money, food, petrol, and just about everything else.' The despondency in Robert's voice could be heard from where Ellen was standing in the kitchen, and some of their conversation was drowned out by the rattling of cutlery and clinking of dishes.

'So you're coping alright? You're very short staffed now, so I hear.'

'There's only so much I can do, dealing with the money is the easy part – keeping the customers happy isn't so simple these days.'

'It's a funny old world, don't you think? When there's an enemy in the camp, we all have to keep our wits about us. Some people can't cope with a bit of hardship; they turn to crime surprisingly quickly and have no qualms, funnily enough. But since Max died, I'm not one to bow to the Germans' rules and regulations and why should I?' Meg and Ellen returned with plates, and cutlery but they stopped laying the table when they realised Joan was saying something important. Everyone's eyes were on her. She carried a certain dignity, a reserve which had its base in grief and solid hard work. 'Robert, what you said just now was brave and perfectly true. The trouble is people don't stand up for themselves not nearly enough. They don't stand up for their rights and they're letting those wretched Germans walk all over us. Anything for a bit of peace, I suppose. But sometimes peace isn't enough, eh?' She was addressing all of them now. Robert took off his glasses and rubbed his eyes. He was looking exhausted. Albert began fidgeting with his cufflinks, making a big deal of undoing them and doing them up again. He glanced around with impatience, no doubt wanting his tea but not daring to break the reverence of the speech his mother-in-law was making.

'Well, time's getting on, Mother. Shall we start? I'll pour the tea before it spoils.'

'Thank you, dear, but there's one more thing before we eat, I want to meet this unfortunate man you've taken in. Ask him to join us. We've got enough food. I've brought another spare loaf and some cheese if you need it.' Disregarding the expression of utter fear on Robert's face, Ellen went quickly and rolling back the rug, tapped on the trapdoor. A fierce draught escaped from down below as the door was lifted up, instantly chilling the room. She called to him to come up the steps and his deep voice reverberated from below. They all waited in trepidation as footsteps tramped up the cellar steps. Ellen wondered how Lukasz was going to cope finding so many people in the room staring at him. Her heart was pounding. Lukasz came up looking ashamed and embarrassed and she felt for him, instantly regretting her nan's suggestion. How unkind it was to subject him to this, to be paraded in front of them like some stray dog they had found on the street.

Joan stood up. She held out her hand towards him. He studied her, his gaunt appearance a picture of suffering. Lukasz stared around. 'Your name is Lukasz? Pleased to meet you,' she said, still with her hand held out towards him. Finally, he responded, taking her hand in his, while the expression of bewilderment never left his face. He didn't speak.

'Here, Lukasz, sit down.' Joan indicated where he should sit, and after a brief hesitation he did sit down. Very quickly the atmosphere returned to normal as plates and sandwiches were passed round.

After a while, when the meal was finishing, Joan put down her plate and said, 'Lukasz, I've been thinking. You probably won't understand what I'm about to say but since my husband passed away, I have space in my house. I would like to help you. So I'm inviting you to - '

'No, mother, please!' cried Meg. 'It was our decision to take the risk. I don't want to involve you, it's too dangerous.'

Joan raised her eyebrows. 'Don't you think I'm involved already? Look at us! We are all here. We're all involved. And the more those Germans get away with, the more they'll tighten their grip and the worse it'll be for everyone.'

Lukasz was looking confused, worried by their raised voices and the change in atmosphere. He glanced across at Ellen for reassurance and she gave him a reassuring smile. A smile which didn't go unnoticed by Robert.

Chapter 18

A few people passed Ellen as she waited by the gates hoping to spot Lucy coming up the lane on her bicycle. True enough, within minutes she appeared.

'I wonder what rubbish he's got for us to bake with today,' said Lucy, climbing down from her bike and wheeling it up to the outhouse where she stored it to keep it safe. She wasn't bubbling over with excitement like she had been before but was rather subdued and seemed tired. Ellen was worried. 'Is everything alright?'

Lucy shook her head quickly and looked uncomfortable while they walked through the bakery entrance. 'Don't say anythin' but it's gone past my time of the month,' she whispered. 'Actually, I've missed two months now, or could even be three…' She trailed off, not finishing what she was trying to say.

'It could be our bad diet or worry. They're saying it affects women like that. Cheer up, it's probably nothing.'

'Nothin'! Grow up, can't you? Do I have to spell it out?'

'Lucy! It might not be that!'

'Yeh, right!'

'So, if you're sure … Have you told him?'

A Sea of Barbed Wire

'Told him! You must be jokin'! I haven't told a soul. Let's pretend I haven't told you either, okay? Keep it to yourself or I'm as good as dead.'

Once inside they couldn't talk. George was telling them what to do and pointing out the orders they had to fulfil and the condition of the flour. 'I'm not expecting miracles, girls, but if you produce some decent loaves out of this lot, I'd give you a pay rise if I could afford it.' He rubbed his hands together. 'But I'll allow you an extra loaf each to take home tonight, alright?'

They thanked him. Ellen felt particularly sorry for him as she knew how he used to take pride in his bread. Now it was just a case of 'making do' with what they were given.

The weighing out, mixing and kneading of the dough took them a good couple of hours during which time George was hovering around, clattering tins and cleaning out the ovens. They hardly had a quiet moment together. Finally, he announced that once the first batch of loaves were in the oven, they could stop for their tea break.

They both went to make tea in the kitchen but Lucy, Ellen noticed, was looking increasingly pale and was the first to sit down.

'Are you feeling alright? You don't look very well. Did you have any breakfast? Here, try and have a sip of your tea.'

Lucy shook her head. She had begun looked so ill Ellen was afraid she was going to faint. Lucy tasted her tea and made a face.

'Oh, no, I can't drink that.' Standing up again, for a moment she swayed and steadied herself by holding onto the table. Then suddenly she gasped. 'Oh, no, I'm goin' to be sick!' Diving for the door, she disappeared down the corridor.

Ellen drank her tea alone, barely tasting it. Since hearing Robert talking the way he did, she realised that there were small rebellions, personal ones that were happening behind closed doors everywhere. There was something in the air breathing danger and subterfuge. It was frightening and exciting at the same time. Eventually Lucy reappeared. Her colour had returned a little and she gave Ellen a troubled smile.

'Have your tea, I hope it's not gone cold. I've put some sugar in it. Sweet tea is good, it might make you feel better to have something in your tummy.'

'Oh, I've got somethin' in my tummy alright, somethin' that shouldn't be there!' replied Lucy, regaining her sense of humour almost immediately.

'How do you think Franz will take it?'

'You think I should surprise him? It won't be half the surprise it will be for Pete when he comes home from the war to find me with another baby in my arms!'

It sounded like a joke, but Lucy wasn't smiling.

'If there's anything I can do, just let me know, will you?'

'Okay, if you hear of any old-fashioned remedies for turning back time, like hot baths or drinkin' castor-oil, if you know what I mean, just let me know, eh?'

'Don't go making yourself ill, Lucy. Hurry up and drink your tea, we'd better get back to work.'

'I think I'm better off without it, thanks anyway.'

During the day while they worked, there was little time for either of them to talk. At four o'clock Ellen walked with Lucy to collect her bicycle. They had a few moments together and as Lucy had confided in her, suddenly Ellen felt an urgent desire to share her secret about Lukasz too.

'Lucy, before you go …'

'What? Are you goin' to tell me I've been stupid and should never have let him -'

'No, it's just that if you need any help, you know, don't forget I'm here.'

'Thanks Ellen! You always were the sensible one. I know you'd never do anythin' so stupid, get yourself into a mess like I have. See you tomorrow, eh!'

'Take care, won't you!'

'I never have so far!' she called back as she cycled off. 'You should be tellin' me I shouldn't be riding a bike in my condition!' She giggled and her bicycle wobbled precariously. 'It seems to be gettin' dark already an' I haven't got any lights. Let's hope I don't meet any lorries along the road, or it'll be curtains for me for sure.'

Ellen looked around the yard; she shivered and retreated back into the light of the bakery. There she waited for Robert to come and walk her home. But she was so preoccupied thinking about Lucy's predicament that when Robert arrived about ten minutes later, she felt tongue-tied. There were too many secrets. Sharing another one with him would have been more than enough. But Robert didn't mention the previous night. Instead, he began describing various events that had occurred; some customers' complaints that were becoming extremely difficult, when he stopped mid-sentence.

'You're quiet, Ellie. Had a hard day?'

'Yes, I suppose I have but no more than usual. I'm just tired.' She glanced at him. After the revelation about Lukasz, she wasn't expecting him to sound so normal. She had been afraid, once they were alone, that he might start asking questions about it again.

'Have you got something else on your mind that you want to talk about? We should be sharing our problems.

'No, I'm alright, Rob, honestly! I was just thinking about last night, and how kind you were towards Lukasz.'

He squeezed her hand. 'I'm sorry about how I reacted. It was the shock, that's all. Once I'd met him, I felt sorry for the poor chap, standing there in the middle of us all.'

'Yes! Me too, especially as he can't even understand half of what we are saying. It must have been awful.'

Robert smiled, glancing at her quickly. 'Not half so awful as being a prisoner though. You were very kind and brave to take him in.'

She thanked him, mulling over how polite and formal he always was. They were walking hand in hand back to her home. They had been going out together for a few weeks, but she still didn't really know that much about him. He never truly put away his business suit and professional manner. They were so much part of him she wondered if he would ever relax into being more than just a friend. What was it about him? Even though he was always kind, there was something cold about him, a barrier, as if the shiny polished counter in the bank was still an obstacle between them. When they entered the back door, Ellen heard voices.

'Ah, you're home! Hello Robert, come on in.'

'Listen, Nan has something to say. We haven't discussed it with your father Ellie, he's not home yet, but I'm sure he'll agree it's for the best.'

Ellen sensed trouble. Glancing at Robert and looking from one to the other, she said: 'What is it, Mum?'

'Just listen to your nan.'

Joan's expression was direct, her eyes a cool grey. Nothing phased her for long, even after the sudden death of her husband; she rallied quickly. With a quick nod to acknowledge Robert's presence, she addressed Ellen directly.

'I want to help your young friend.'

'Who, you mean Lukasz?' For a second Ellen thought she meant Lucy and her stomach did a somersault.

'I think he would be better off staying at my house. I have more space, more food and room for him to move about. He could even do a bit of work to help me. It would do him good to have some fresh air and exercise.'

Something like panic rushed through her veins. 'But he's been alright here!' she protested, and then blushed at her sudden outburst.

Joan gave a sad smile. 'I'm afraid he isn't alright, dear. He doesn't have room to stretch his legs, there's no light down there and you can't spare the extra food. Be practical, Ellie. If he stays down there much longer he'll wither up like an old pot plant.'

Ellen caught Robert staring at her, looking vaguely surprised. Fighting her inner turmoil and in spite of all her senses screaming the opposite, she had to agree. 'Have you talked to Lukasz about it?'

'He doesn't have a choice I'm afraid. It's what's best for him, and for us. We'll tell him what we intend to do when the time comes. It's a matter of how to move him safely without the Germans spotting him, but I have a plan.'

Chapter 19

In the dead of night, the presence of Lukasz in the house filled Ellen with a sense of excitement as well as fear. But now he was being torn away from her, the spark of attraction she had felt towards him exploded into a fire. She couldn't stop thinking about him, the way his dark eyes met hers, his quiet pondering presence, his mysterious past. She recalled again how he had held her, how he had gazed into her eyes. *Oh, if only I could sleep!* she whispered to herself. But suddenly she really was crying. The tears erupted and her throat ached with trying to suppress her choking sobs. It was agony trying to be quiet; if her mother heard her, she would want to know why she was upset. But under the covers, stifling her cries in the pillow, she wept as if her heart would break. Her heart was beating so wildly she had to sit up and force herself to calm down. Taking deep breaths, her pulse gradually slowed, her tears subsided and then listening out for any movement and hoping she hadn't disturbed her parents, a sound caught her attention.

There was a muffled noise, just the odd scuffle. It could be a mouse, but it could be someone was moving around downstairs. Perhaps it was her mother, still up after all. None of them could sleep well, they were all worried and hungry. Slipping out of bed, she put on her dressing-gown and crept down. Perhaps her mum was making tea and sitting up for a bit as she sometimes did when she couldn't sleep. She reached the bottom step and looked for the light from a candle in the sitting room. There was none.

Ellen knew, when everyone went to bed, that they drew back the blackout curtains so they could see their way to the stairs. That night, the moonlight was sharp and clear as it shone in through the window. She could hear breathing. Her heart skipped a beat.

'Mum?'

Someone stepped forward out of the shadows.

'Lukasz! What on earth are you doing here? You frightened me!'

'Sorry, so sorry. I come for water.'

'It's okay.' Taking a glass from the kitchen, she filled it for him, and he drank thirstily. How she wished her heart would quieten down; it was pounding so hard she thought he might be able to hear it.

'So couldn't you sleep?' she asked in a whisper.

'No, I not sleep. I hear people talking. I listen. The lady say she will take me away. I don't want. I stay here, please. I not go.'

Ellen was amazed that he had understood. 'It's for your own safety, Lukasz. My nan has some land and a vegetable garden with lots of space. You'll have fresh air and daylight; you'll like it there.'

'No, no, I not go with the lady. I stay here. I safe here.'

Drawing her dressing-gown tightly around herself, she perched on the side of the settee. With the shock she had just had, she was having trouble controlling her voice.

'My nan will be careful. You'll be fine.'

He shrugged, struggling to accept the new arrangements they were making for him.

'You must trust us, Lukasz. You can depend on my nan; she knows what she's doing.'

Sometimes he appeared to understand her more than she expected, but to this he didn't reply.

'Have you been writing in the notebook I gave you?'

'Yes. I write the letter. I write to my sister. I tell her not worry. I tell her soon I come back for her.'

'But, Lukasz! Where is she? Is she safe?'

He looked away. 'I not know. Maybe she dead.'

Ellen went to the sink and drew a glass of water for herself, and they talked for a while longer. Any moment she expected her mother to hear them and come downstairs complaining, but no-one appeared and finally he returned to the cold cellar while she crept up to bed.

*

In the morning, muddle-headed from lack of sleep, Ellen set off for work soon after six o'clock. It was going to be a long day too as she had agreed to do some extra hours overtime and she didn't know how she was going to get through it. The night before, reasoning with Lukasz, she had tried to explain that there was no way he could post his letters as they were all inspected and censored – but it had been difficult. A single letter in his handwriting and written in Polish would be seized upon immediately. Whether her parents had heard them talking she didn't know but it was with some relief that she was able to leave for work before her parents were awake. Reaching the bakery, she was thankful for the warmth from the ovens as she was chilled through. Lucy came in while she was in the kitchen boiling the kettle for tea. She looked extremely pale.

'I feel so ill! I don't get it. I never got mornin' sickness when I was expectin' Charlie. Oh, honestly, I've been up half the night bein' sick and it's not as if I've even had much.'

'Was Franz with you?'

'Not last night, I told him I had a tummy upset. He said I'd probably eaten somethin' that was off. It happens all the time.'

Ellen poured the tea. 'I'd put some sugar in it if we had some. They say sweet tea is good for that.'

'Oh, here, I've got some!' Delving into her pocket she brought out a paper bag and twisted in the corner was some white sugar.

'Lucky you! We save ours up to make a cake.'

'I don't have that problem. I've never baked a cake in my life.' Lucy sprinkled a generous amount into her cup of tea and reached for a spoon.

'Steady on, you might need some tomorrow morning!'
Lucy giggled. 'Oh, I'll have some more tomorrow. Franz gets me all I want.' A smile of satisfaction spread across her face. You know, he brought me round a whole basket of fruit, just for me! I don't know where he gets it all from, but I'm not goin' to complain am I!'

Ellen suddenly found the tone of her voice distasteful. Lucy sounded so cocksure of herself, smug even.

'Does he really though? I mean, get you all you want?"

A Sea of Barbed Wire

She took her time replying, tying on her apron and drawing her hair back into an elastic band until Ellen grew impatient.

'I mean, does he bring you lots of stuff that everyone else has to pay a fortune for?'

Lucy looked up quickly, her eyes flashing. 'You sound as if you're jealous!'

'No, of course I'm not!' Ellen blushed. 'I don't want you to get into trouble that's all. You sound as if you're becoming dependent on Franz, and it can't last. At any moment he might be sent off to France or the Russian Front or the war might end or anything.'

Suddenly there were footsteps heard coming down the corridor and Ellen put her finger to her lips. There was a rustle of packaging, a cupboard door closing, and the footsteps receded once more. When it was quiet again, Lucy whispered, 'Soon as the war's over, he's takin' me away with him, if you must know – me and Charlie. We're all goin' to live in Germany! I'm so excited! I can't wait!'

'What do you mean? You can't go off just like that! What about Pete when he comes home? That's if he's lucky enough to survive.'

Lucy shrugged her shoulders, 'It's too late to worry about him! He shouldn't have gone and left me in the first place should he.' Saying that, she put down her cup and disappeared out of the door. Staying where she was, Ellen tried to absorb what she had told her. It was an extraordinary change in their relationship. A few minutes later, afraid George would be coming after her to see why she wasn't working, Ellen sighed and went to start unloading the oven. But there was an awkward silence between them. How relieved Ellen was that she had resisted the temptation to share her secret about Lukasz. It had been close, but now she knew she was on her own.

When Ellen got close to home, she was exhausted. The lack of food, the hard work and now the strain of coping with Lucy's attitude were all taking their toll. However, when she came in sight of her house, she saw her nan's horse and cart were outside their gate. This was nothing to be alarmed about except she saw her mother and her nan were carrying several boxes and stacking them up in the cart. All her energy flooded back like a thunderbolt as the adrenalin kicked in and she started to run.

'What's going on?'

Meg looked up and was surprised to see her. 'Oh, you're here! I thought you were going to be late back from work tonight, love.'

'No Mum, he let us go early after all. What's Nan doing?'

But she didn't stop to hear the answer. In the sitting room she found the cellar trapdoor open and some scuffling sounds coming from down below. She could hear Lukasz. His deep voice was reverberating from the hollow interior of the cellar, while Joan was answering as if she was contradicting him. After a few minutes she came up the steps shaking her head.

'The man's a fool. I have the cart ready. I've packed some supplies and made a space to hide him. Everything's ready and he refuses to come.'

'But Nan, perhaps he's right. He's safe enough here. Supposing you're stopped and they search the cart! He's got no ID papers. At least at night it would be safer, please, at least take him after dark.'

A Sea of Barbed Wire

Joan told her to sit down, and she fixed her with a long stare. 'Do you think I don't know what I'm doing? They're used to seeing me driving the cart to and fro to town every day making my deliveries. They've already stopped me three times. They won't bother me again. They're bored with me. In daylight, at this time of day, he'll be safe. You worry too much, girl.'

Desperately trying to calm herself she knew deep down, if it worked, it would be for the best. Lukasz would be safer out in the parishes, away from the town. He would be in a better place and have room to stretch his legs. Her mother had gone back through to the kitchen when suddenly she realised her nan was watching her with a softening almost sympathetic expression.

'Don't worry, Ellie. I'll look after him for you.'

To her horror, she blushed scarlet.

'You care for him a lot don't you. I do understand. Your mother, well, she's a good soul, but she doesn't always notice things the way I do.' Reaching out, her nan squeezed her hand. 'The war brings with it a lot of unforeseen problems, doesn't it dear.'

All Ellen could do was smile faintly and nod as the tears flooded down her cheeks.

'It changes us, Nan. I don't know what I feel these days.'

'Come on, dry your eyes. You can come over and see him whenever you like.'

When Lukasz finally emerged from the cellar he paused and looked at Ellen. Their eyes met briefly before he walked on. With a quick check up and down the street before he stepped out onto the path, he followed Joan outside. As he went climbing up easily onto the cart, it was noticeable how strong he was now, a different man to the one who had collapsed at their backdoor that night. Ellen watched her nan standing up on top of the cart rearranging potato sacks as Lukasz, with one quick glance over his shoulder, dropped down among the boxes and disappeared from sight. When Joan had finished shifting stuff, she got down and bolted up the side of the cart. Ellen watched as, raising a hand of farewell, her nan climbed up onto the driver's board, and with a flick of the reins the horse moved off. Within a few minutes they were round the corner and out of sight.

The hours went by, and they still hadn't heard from Joan. Ellen went about the house in a kind of stupor. Suddenly the phone rang. As she went charging across the room to answer it, it was her mother who got there first.

'Hello?' A few moments of silence followed.

'So you won't be needing any shopping tomorrow then? Well just let me know if you need anything, eh?'

She replaced the receiver and looked directly at Ellen. 'All's well. She told me if she says she doesn't need any shopping then they got there safely.'

'Oh, thank goodness! But Mum. He will be alright, won't he?'

'He'll be fine, love, safer than here.'

Her mother smiled and drew her into her arms. 'You worry too much, darling. We can't do any more for him. Time will tell. If only this wretched war would be over soon.'

The next day, at work again. Ellen was, despite herself, feeling relieved that her nan was taking care of Lukasz. 'I feel so tired, I hope we're not working late tonight,' she told Lucy and sighed. 'I've hardly the energy to knead this dough let alone prepare a couple more batches ready for tomorrow. We certainly earn our keep don't we.'

'Don't we just. Wish I could chuck it in. You seein' your Robert after?'

'I suppose so.'

Lucy was measuring flour which she took from a large paper sack with a scoop. The texture of it resembled coarse oatmeal and occasionally as she worked, she picked out bits of what appeared to be threads of sacking or possibly stems of straw. These she chucked over her shoulder, clicking her tongue and turning up her nose. Neither of them bothered any more to comment on the quality of the flour. Now it was a blessing if they had any at all.

'You don't sound exactly bowled over with excitement.'

'No, you're right, I don't do I. Sorry!'

'You needn't say sorry to me! You haven't gone off Robert already, have you?'

'No, I don't know, it's just the war, and I feel so lethargic.'

'Don't suppose you've eaten enough, have you. I'm lucky really, Franz brings me nice cuts of red meat that he gets from the barracks. He says I need it now, to build my strength up.'

Ellen looked at her in astonishment. 'You mean you've told him, about ...you know! I thought you didn't dare tell him, or anyone!'

'Well, he's not daft. He saw the signs straight off. I can't hide nothin' from him!' She giggled.

'Lucy, don't you think it's a bit, well, risky, carrying his child?'

'Probably, but not much I can do about it now, eh? I've given up carin', Ellie. He's nice to me. I eat the food when he brings it for me and I help look after him, wash his clothes and that. He doesn't have anyone else to do it for him. I like to take care of him, he appreciates it. Some of his mates stink! They hardly ever have their clothes washed. The state of some of them!'

All this was too much for Ellen. She was puzzled, and even envious of her friend's relaxed attitude. There she was, a married woman with a little boy, with a husband out fighting in some godforsaken place trying to beat back the Nazis, and all she was interested in was Franz. She seemed to have forgotten about Pete, who she imagined would be looking forward to returning home as soon as the war was over. That is, if he's lucky enough to still be alive. It didn't seem to occur to Lucy that he could already have been killed, his body lying in some foreign field. She knew how other wives and girlfriends waited anxiously for news of the men, mothers for their sons, dreading the arrival of a telegram. She thought for several minutes before speaking again.

'So you've met some of his soldier friends then, have you?'

A Sea of Barbed Wire

'Yeah, I've met some of 'em a few times. Oh, they're a funny lot, honestly, they pretend to be so strict and particular but then you see them off duty and -'

'You mean they're not? Their orders are pretty grim sometimes. Look how they grill people when they stop us in the street and demand our papers! Look how they're requisitioning houses and turning people out! Even elderly couples have had their houses taken, told to move out with only twenty-four hours' notice. They're heartless.'

'Some of them do that, yeh.' She turned her nose up. 'But most of them are alright though actually, as long as people keep on the right side of 'em. They don't often cause the islanders no trouble.'

Ellen was consumed with rage. 'Don't cause us no trouble? Who do you think you are, for goodness' sake? Anyone would think you were on their side!'

But Lucy laughed, she was defiant. 'Look, Ellie, get a life, will you and stop picking on me. I'm only making the most of what I've got. If Franz wants to make a fuss of me and look after me and my little boy, what have I got to lose? He might be sent to the Russian Front any day. He's terrified of that. Judgin' by what his mates have been tellin' him he won't stand a chance there. So leave me alone! We could all be dead tomorrow.'

Chapter 20

A few weeks later

After work one day, Ellen started walking to Robert's flat. The days were shorter now and Christmas was approaching. It was already getting dark and as she passed old granite cottages, people were drawing their curtains. Several houses stood empty and locked up, abandoned when their owners had fled to the safety of England. Others looked cosy inside and through some of the windows she could glimpse the faint glow of candlelight and the flickering shadows of flames from a warm fireplace. Buttoning up her coat right to the chin, she shivered as she walked on, facing into a cold east wind. The month of November had seemed like years, it had dragged by so slowly. Suddenly she was surprised to see Robert coming towards her. He was wearing his suit as usual and carrying his briefcase. With his studious, plodding way of walking, he appeared older than his years and when he greeted her, he kissed her so timidly she longed for so much more. Without knowing why or what was happening, suddenly she was in tears. The relief of letting go flooded out of her. She didn't know which way to turn. Robert put his arm round her and appearing rather confused, told her not to worry. "Don't upset yourself, my sweet. I'm sorry, you must be over-tired.' They walked on to his place hand in hand. Once he had switched on his electric fire, and she had warmed her hands she followed him into the kitchen, where he was putting the kettle on.

'I'll try to find us something to eat,' he said, peering over his glasses into the pantry for some food, fumbling about among the tins, his dark hair flopping over his eyes. 'There's spam, this old cauliflower and these potatoes might be alright. He held up two potatoes; they were badly pock marked with scabs and he pulled a face. 'Not much to offer you, I'm sorry. You didn't happen to bring any nice bread with you, did you?'

She shook her head. 'I've had my share this week already. George didn't dare let us have any more, although I know he wanted to.'

Looking around his room, which was no bigger than her bedroom at home, she couldn't help thinking how it needed brightening up. She knew she shouldn't expect anything smarter, but the frugal shabbiness of it all depressed her even more.

'Ellie, darling, please tell me, are you ill? Do you have a pain? I wish I had some nourishing food to offer you.'

She put her finger on his lips. 'It's not the food. Well, it is partly, and I'm not ill honestly.' She sniffed, drying her eyes and blowing her nose. 'I'm feeling especially worried today, that's all.'

'But why? What's happened?'
She told him then, about Lukasz. How her nan had taken him away without any warning. If Robert detected anything other than genuine concern for Lukasz, he didn't show it. Kissing her, he held her hands and tried

his best to warm them between his own, cupping them in his like two baby birds.

After returning to the kitchen to start on the cooking, he told her about how his working day had been. He had encountered a German soldier who, while waiting in the queue, had suddenly become impatient, shoved the customers in front of him aside and demanded to be served first. One of the customers, an elderly man, fell to the floor and was badly shaken.

'So, I ordered the German off the premises. I can't have my clients being treated like that!'

Ellen stared at him in amazement. 'You did what? Oh, you mustn't, Rob! You shouldn't have, I mean, you're not allowed to speak to a German like that. He could have had you arrested and charged!'

'They wouldn't dare. I told him I'd report him to his superior if he didn't leave the bank immediately.'

'And did he leave?'

'Yes, he did, and as he marched out of the door all the customers clapped! Oh, don't look so pale and scared, sweetheart. I showed him who was boss. They can't walk all over us, not here – it's our island, and as far as that particular German is concerned, it's my bank. I never wanted to deal with his dirty money anyway.'

It was Dora who broke the news to Ellen as she was walking past her shop the next day. Dora rushed out and asked her if she had heard. German soldiers had been to the bank, arrested Robert and taken him away. Word was out everywhere in the street that the senior bank clerk had been charged with insulting the German Army. The bank was closed. Caught completely off

A Sea of Barbed Wire

guard, and already feeling weak with hunger, the shock almost caused Ellen to faint.

'Oh, no! I was so afraid that would happen!'

Dora steadied her. 'Come on, love. Here, lean on me. I'll help you into the shop and make you a cuppa. Don't worry about him. I can't see Robert doing anything to annoy the Germans, he's always polite to everyone, he's the perfect gentleman.'

But the tea failed to revive her and Ellen hadn't fully recovered when her mother arrived half an hour later. The incident Robert had told her about kept running through her mind. To show any German soldier disrespect was considered treason. It was printed on the posters that the soldiers had put up around the island. It was just one of their many rules and regulations – and threats. She couldn't think straight, her thoughts were everywhere. Somehow, she knew she had to warn her nan. Now that Robert knew what he knew, not only his life but all their lives were in danger. If the Germans questioned him too severely, tortured him as she had heard, they might extract the truth from him. It would lead to an even more serious charge. Being accused of being rude to a German soldier was one thing; harbouring an escaped prisoner was another matter entirely. He might be forced to tell all.

Her mother came and knelt at her feet. 'Look at me, Ellie,' she said, peering up into her face. 'Robert is a sensible young man. He'll apologise and knowing they need him at the bank, they'll let him go. You mark my words. The German soldiers like their money too much to risk getting on the wrong side of the bank.'

'Oh, I hope you're right, Mum! Poor Robert!'

'More tea, love?' asked Dora, hovering between the shop counter and the back of the shop. Normally, there used to be scarcely room to move in Dora's shop. It used to be piled high with boxes of biscuit tins; tinned soup; sardines; flour and rice; crates of vegetables and breakfast cereals. However, the food they used to take for granted was now a dream. The concrete floor was bare, scuffed where boxes used to be. Her shelves were almost empty and there were second-hand goods in the shop window arranged on faded newspaper. There were children's clothes, shoes, the odd cotton reel and other small items which people could bargain for or exchange for other items. Whatever gifts might be given that Christmas, they would be cherished, even if they were second-hand.

'We ought to start walking home, Ellie. Do you think you can manage it?'

She nodded and stood up, pulling her coat tightly about her. 'Mum, what if Robert …'

'Never mind what if …Let's get you home.'

'Tell you what, dears, since I'm about ready to close the shop now anyway. I'll give you a lift back in the van.'

Their house was even colder than the shop. Ellen couldn't help wondering what Robert was going through. They had heard so many things, such cruelty, so many harsh sentences for small trifling misdemeanours. The thought of what could happen to him terrified her. People had been imprisoned for such minor discretions, deported for the most trivial of offences to German internment camps.

A Sea of Barbed Wire

'Everything's changed, Mum.' Ellen sat down, keeping her coat on. 'What can we do?'

'Not much we can do but wait and hope they're lenient with him. He's been pushed a bit too far perhaps. The bank's a huge responsibility for him and he's been working long hours. It's enough to make anyone a bit short-tempered in the end.'

'But Robert's never short-tempered. I've never known him be rude or challenge anyone.'

'He was ready to challenge them the other night, wasn't he? Don't you remember how he spoke up about no-one ever standing up to them? Well, it sounds as if he stood up to them yesterday.'

'He'll hate it being locked up in a dirty prison cell or worse. Suppose they sentence him to hard labour?'

Her mother looked at her steadily. 'People have had to put up with worse, Ellie. Take your nan: she's lost Gran'pa just because he was stopped and searched. If they'd known he had a weak heart I doubt that would have made any difference; they literally scared him to death. We've been lucky so far. We must thank God that your nan has got the presence of mind to carry on the way she does.'

When Albert got home, he had heard about Robert. Some news travelled fast on the island even though communications were limited. That evening after blackout they sat and talked, huddled round a single candle. Meg warned that they all had to be extra vigilant and hope the Commandant would be lenient with Robert.

'He'll stand up to them. If I know Robert, he'll be polite and respectful even if he doesn't feel it,' she announced. 'What happened must have been a one-off – perhaps he was over-tired or anxious about work. I'll go up there in the morning and ask after him, put in a good word for him.'

Ellen looked up in surprise. 'Mum!'

'Yes, of course I will. He doesn't have a mother on the island, or any other relative. They've got to hear what I've got to say – we can't lose a good man like that just over one trifling misunderstanding.'

'But it's on the posters and it was in the Press: to let the German soldiers move to the front of the queue and give them priority. Robert knows that!'

'And do other shopkeepers comply? Does Dora serve them first when they come barging in demanding what they want?'

'You know she does, Mum. She's half-terrified of offending them, like most others are around here.'

'Well, I'm not afraid of them. I can see right through their bullying ways. I'll go up there and speak for him. They don't scare me. I'd take them a present if I had anything to give them.'

'A present? You mean a bribe?'

'Look Ellie, I'm not going to let them send him off to some Godforsaken prison camp just for asking a customer to wait his turn. This is a civilised country!'

Albert spoke up. 'It used to be love, but times have changed somewhat.' He cleared his throat and in the candlelight the others could see the muscles in his throat working. 'You can't treat folk like them with common decency, they don't abide by the rules anymore. And I'll tell you something else – you're not going up there to speak to no Commandant in the morning, I won't allow it.'

A Sea of Barbed Wire

Meg left her seat, and she stared down on her husband defiantly. 'Well, if you don't want me to go – you go yourself!'

Ellen interjected with her own challenge: 'Neither of you needs to go. I'll go. He's my boyfriend and I can say what a good man he is. I know him more than either of you.'

'No dear, I'll be worried sick something might happen to you. You've heard what they're like with pretty young women. It wouldn't be right either of us letting you go up there. Robert wouldn't want that; I know that much. He'd never forgive us for letting you go. He would expect us to keep you safe while he's away.'

'Then what can we do?' cried Ellen, feeling that her world was collapsing around her.

'Your mother's right, I'll go. God knows a man must stand up for his friends and see that justice is done. It's a small wonder I haven't said something similar to them myself, the way they behave in the pharmacy. I'll go up there first thing tomorrow.'

Chapter 21

The next morning, Albert called in at the pharmacy to put someone else in charge and then he set off for the German Headquarters at the Grange Lodge Hotel. Wearing his best suit, the one he reserved for funerals, and a white shirt and tie, he called round to the house of his old friend, who was a well-respected advocate. Together they planned to try to mediate with the Commandant, hoping to appeal to his sense of responsibility to the island. Albert would explain that Robert had been under a lot of strain to keep the business running smoothly when the bank was so short of staff. He hoped Robert would be let off with a warning.

'Forgive me, Arthur, if this seems a crazy idea. Trying to reason with the Nazis is like wrestling with a hungry tiger.'

Albert's companion was more philosophical. 'I'm of the opinion that with a wild animal it's best to play the submissive part, the equivalent of a bitch, rolling over on one's back and exposing one's belly,' replied the old man who was more experienced in the book of Law.

'Then we make it easy for them; you mean, hold our hands up and apologise for the young fellow's behaviour?'

'In a way, yes, Albert, but we don't want to give them any excuse to punish your man. Let's make them stop and think: what's in it for us?' He tapped the side of his nose mischievously. 'We lay out our stall, we compliment them on what we might call their smooth-running occupation and present them with certain advantages in letting him go.'

'Such as? I don't follow you, Arthur.'

'Banking plays an important part in the economy of the island. I can bet you not one of those German soldiers knows a fig about the financial world. But they do have to report back to people who do, officers who have to report their progress on to a certain person, namely Hitler. So, they have a vested interest in how valuable their new acquisition is.'

'So we can persuade them that Robert plays a part in looking after the island's economy?'

'Exactly, well almost.'

Albert looked at his wise friend with a hopeful expression.

'We can, how shall I say it, encourage them to believe that Robert is an essential link – even if he isn't, eh?' Arthur was smiling and evidently feeling quite pleased with himself.

*

'You're not dressed! Aren't you feeling well?'

'How can I go into work, Mum, when all this is happening?'

'Life has to go on, love. We need bread, the whole island needs bread. So I suggest you get yourself ready girl and get going. Apart from anything else, if you don't, we'll have no bread ourselves for our tea. If your father comes back with some good news, we'll be able to tell you when you get back. There's no use both of us moping around all day.'

'No, I suppose you're right.' She sighed and tried to relax. Her head ached. Refusing breakfast, such as it was, she went back upstairs and got dressed. Her mother wrapped up a slice of bread and dripping for her and gave it to her to eat in her tea break. Fifteen minutes later she was on her way, and when she arrived she was almost an hour late. George was furious. Lucy had failed to turn up altogether and he was all behind. So over the next three hours she barely had time to worry about Robert, or her father. With the work of two people to do, the mixing and kneading, the dividing up and weighing, it soon taxed her strength. Without food and hardly any sleep, it was no wonder that by half-part eleven George came to find out how she was doing and found she had fainted and was lying semi-conscious on the floor.

Meg had been looking out for her husband and became worried when she saw the baker's van draw up outside the house. She rushed out to the van and saw George helping Ellen and supporting her as they came down the path.

'Whatever's happened?' she cried. 'Has there been an accident?'

'I don't think so, dear. Let's get her indoors and we'll see how she is. You might need to call the doctor.' They both helped her up the step and eased her down into an armchair. She was extremely pale. Her mother fetched a blanket and put it round her.

A Sea of Barbed Wire

'She just fainted I think, dear. Perhaps you could pop the kettle on. I think a nice hot cup of sweet tea might bring her round. I've had another girl off today as well. They're all going down like flies. Not enough to eat probably, that's the trouble with these young women, they need a bit of boosting up and some decent protein. Who would have thought it, eh? The war going on for over two years and still no sign of it ending. We'll all be dropping where we stand at this rate.'

Suddenly Ellen opened her eyes. 'Oh! Where am I?'

'You took a funny turn and fainted, lovey. I thought it best to bring you home to your mother. There's not much an old man can do when a young lady's poorly.'

Meg brought the tea on a tray and set it down, sighing with relief on seeing Ellen awake.

'Thank goodness, you're looking a bit better. How are you feeling?'

'I've got a splitting headache, Mum. I don't know what happened. George, I'm sorry. I was trying to get a batch in the oven and suddenly …'

'It doesn't matter now. You're getting your colour back already, so that's something.'

'You'll stop for a cuppa won't you, George?'

'Thank you, but now I can see she's feeling better, I ought to be on my way back to the bakery.' He looked at Ellen. 'You take the rest of the day off, dear and I'll try to get the last of the bread baked before tonight. I'll do it, even if I have to do the whole lot myself. How are you off for bread? I've got a spare loaf in the back if you'd like one. Ellen here could do with a nice bit of bread and butter, I'm sure. It would do her the world of good.'

Meg thanked him and he went to get the bread from the van. When he returned, he insisted she didn't pay for it.

'But how are you managing up at the bakery, George?'

'It's a hard slog, to be honest. I used to enjoy my work but there's no pride in it now. The flour's nothing like as good as I'd like it to be and I'm so short staffed. No fault of our Ellen here. She's a good girl and she works her socks off. Between you and me, I suspect one of my girls is expecting a baby and that'll be all I need.' He raised his eyebrows at Meg. 'It's a wonder I manage to keep going, but I do. You have to, don't you, eh?'

Whether it was the way George looked at her, or Ellen's funny spell, Meg looked as if she was bursting to ask a question. 'Surely you're not suggesting our Ellen here is - ?

'Oh, no, no of course not!' he chuckled. 'But there's someone who might be in the family way. I don't like to say who, but time will tell.'

'Well, thank you for the bread, George. It's very welcome.'

After he had left, Ellen was lying back in the chair with her eyes closed but she looked up at her mother when she came back in. 'Your boss is so generous. He's such a nice man.'

There was only one question on Ellen's lips. 'Mum, has there been any news about Robert?'

'No, nothing as yet, love. Your dad will be back soon, I hope.' Curiosity appeared to have got the better of Meg, however. 'George was saying, he thinks one of

A Sea of Barbed Wire

the girls at the bakery is expecting a baby. I thought he meant you at first. My goodness, that did give me a turn!'

Ellen was taken aback. Firstly, that her mother should suspect it was her, when the closest she had ever got to Robert was a brief kiss on the lips, and secondly, how could George possibly know that Lucy was expecting? She had to be careful how she responded.

'What on earth gave him that idea?'

'He said he only suspected, and he wouldn't say who it was, but, darling – you would tell me if, that is, if you …'

She had to laugh. 'Of course I'm not pregnant Mum! Who do you think I am! What did he say to make you think that!'

'He didn't say anything more but he's not one to make up a story, love. George is as straight talking as anyone I know. He always has been. I've known him since I was at school.'

'Oh Mum,' said Ellen, 'I was sworn to secrecy. How on earth did he find out?'

'So you know who it is?' Meg could hardly disguise her surprise. 'I don't expect anyone told him. He's not daft, I guess he just noticed something.'

Ellen reflected on this for several moments, sipping her tea and trying to collect her thoughts. Her gaze came to rest on her mother's face. Gradually realisation seemed to dawn on her because she began to giggle.

'And you really did think it was me, didn't you!'

'Oh, the relief, Ellie! Well, I …' She blushed and struggled to regain her composure.

'You did! Oh, Mum!' she cried. 'Of course, with me fainting at work and – seriously though, Mum. You wouldn't have minded that much, would you?'

Meg appeared to consider the question longer than Ellen expected. She picked up her knitting and put it down again. 'I wouldn't be very happy about it, and neither would your father, but I suppose, darling, if Robert did the honourable thing and said he would stand by you, it wouldn't be the end of the world.'

Ellen sighed. 'I've only been going out with him a few weeks Mum, it's a bit soon to be thinking about that.'

'Well, strange things happen in a time of war.'

They heard the sound of Joan's horse and cart arriving outside. Already feeling better and anxious for news, Ellen stood up and hurried to open the door. She saw a bag of potatoes on the doorstep. Her nan, Joan, was tying the mare up and lifting some more bags from the cart.

'Well,' she said. 'Let's hope your father has more luck than I've had with that lot this morning.'

'Why, what happened, Nan?' Her heart turned over.

'Oh, my dear, come indoors, Mother,' said Meg, taking the bags of shopping from her. 'Come inside and tell us all about it.'

Chapter 22

The news Joan brought drove all other concerns from their heads. Joan looked at each of them with a look of despair. 'Early this morning, I was out feeding the hens and collecting the eggs. Eggs from the few that I still have left, most of the hens have been stolen now. Then I saw two soldiers marching up to me and to be honest I was afraid the game was up. That some informant had told them about, well, you know who.' She sighed as if the news was too much of a burden for her to share. 'They informed me that my house is required by the German Army for billeting troops. It's to be requisitioned immediately. They don't ask, you know, they just demand what they want. Apparently, it's a suitable size and in a desirable position for them.' She raised her eyebrows, as if losing her husband to a heart attack wasn't enough. 'They ordered me, yes, ordered me, to leave my house. They have given me just two days to pack. Their instructions are for me to leave all my furniture and provisions behind. The only compensation they have offered me is that I can keep my horse.' She clicked her tongue. 'To think I should feel grateful for that, but I am. Poor old thing, there's not much meat on her these days. Probably that's why they've let me keep her.'

She gazed around at each of them, at the room, the pictures on the wall and her hands which rested in her lap. Finally, those red worn hands covered her face. Her old shoulders began to heave. Then she was weeping openly.

'Oh, my Goodness!' gasped Meg, putting her arms around her mother and staring in horror back at Ellen with fear in her eyes. She had never seen her defeated by anything. 'Then you must come here and live with us. You can bring everything you can manage. We'll help you. We're all in this together.'

Joan looked up, her eyes blood red. 'Your husband. You must ask Albert first. I wouldn't want to impose. And there's …you know. He will have to come too. I can't think at the moment what else I can do with him.'

'Mum, dear, I'm still waiting for Bert to get home. There's been no word from him, but there's no question of him saying no – he will understand. You can sleep in the back bedroom and,' she continued, lowering her voice to a whisper, 'and Lukasz will go back to the cellar.'

Meg and Ellen began busying themselves with household chores while Joan sat with her back tense and straight as she sat at the table, writing a list of things she wanted to bring with her. All their senses were raw. While waiting for Albert, no-one had mentioned Robert at all. Neither did they discuss Joan's predicament. It was like they were still digesting all that had happened that day. The way her jaw was set, Joan looked determined to remain strong. The day drew on, and there was still no news of Albert or of Robert's fate but then a sudden shuffle on the doorstep alerted them. They sprang into action and went to open the door. Albert came in looking like a long-distance traveller, his coat hanging open, his shirt and tie undone, his hair windswept.

'Bert, my dear! How did you get on? Is Robert with you? What did they say?'

'Let me sit down, woman! Let me get my breath back first!' He spoke gruffly, as if he had almost lost his voice. 'Pop the kettle on, will you, Ellie? Make your dad a nice cup of tea.'

Gladly she did as she was asked, with the tension ringing in her head. She couldn't bear it. Tuning her ears to any conversation that might be going on in the sitting room, she filled the kettle, put the cups and teapot out quietly and crept back, keenly listening while the kettle hissed on the hob. What she thought she heard filled her with dread, but she went back, waiting for the kettle to boil. Finally, the tea was made, and she carried the tray through.

'Dad! Did I hear you say they wouldn't believe him?'

Albert sighed. 'It wasn't a case of them believing him or not. They weren't very impressed with his version of events. They don't think anyone would be fool enough to tell a German Officer to get out!'

'But they won't deport him, will they?'

Meg poured the tea, handed a cup to Albert and he stirred his tea thoughtfully before continuing: 'I heard them saying about it going to trial, and I tell you, if I hadn't had Arthur with me, I think he'd have been thrown in prison by now.'

His colour was returning. He untied his shoelaces, complaining about the distance he had had to walk, eased his coat off his shoulders, and relaxed back in his chair. Then he winked at Meg and raised his eyebrows at Ellen with the teasing expression he used to use when she was a little girl. 'Robert's back at home, love. Arthur and I left him there only half an hour ago. He would have come on here, to see you, but he was exhausted, poor lad.'

'Oh, Dad! So you got him out!' Ellen rushed to hug him.

Meg didn't react so obviously; she merely sighed in relief and said, 'Well done, dear,' before topping up his tea. However, just for a moment, she gazed down on her husband with an expression of sheer pride.

The next day was Sunday and Ellen set off to walk to her nan's house to help her pack. She was apprehensive at the possibility of meeting Lukasz again. Since he had left their house, life had begun to feel a little more normal. As normal as it ever could be since the occupation began that is. Setting her shoulders straight with determination, and a certain amount of resilience, she approached the house with more a sense of sadness than excitement. As a child growing up, she had enjoyed so many happy summer days there helping her grandparents in the garden, feeding their chickens, picking tomatoes and strawberries. Dead leaves covered the drive and there were a few hens scratching around in the soil under the trees, but she was filled with sadness. To think the whole place would soon be overrun with German soldiers upset her. She had heard so many stories of how they had messed houses up, burnt the furniture, and held drunken parties late into the night. Her nan may never be able to live there again. But there was no time for reminiscing; there was work to be done.

A Sea of Barbed Wire

Everything her nan and gran'pa had cared for was in that house. Her nan could only select the most necessary clothes, and documents. She could take towels and bedlinen, photographs and other personal items. These all had to be packed up, carried away and stored safely in the space of a few days. Some of their furniture her gran'pa had made himself but it was no use even attempting to save it. Joan had been told to leave furniture, beds, mattresses and kitchen cooking utensils for the Germans to use.

When Ellen walked round to the back of the house, the door stood open. Joan was calling her from the sitting room, so she went through and found her kneeling on the floor surrounded by letters, books, documents and boxes spilling papers. Joan raised her head and met Ellen with a stern expression, her reading glasses balanced on the end of her nose.

'Ah! Good you're here. Perhaps you could help me load this lot into boxes and put them on the cart.'

Ellen found herself staring around the room in dismay. Books had fallen from their shelves to the floor, and many were heaped on the sofa. Gran'pa had loved his books. Surfaces now covered in dust held the shapes of Nan's treasured ornaments and photo frames that once stood there. Some boxes already stood by the door. All kinds of things bulged from cardboard boxes and tomato crates. There seemed to be no order about it at all.

'Where's Lukasz? Is he still here?' She bit her lip, stealing herself for what her nan might say next.

'Lukasz, Lukasz, you worry your head too much about that man, love. Lukasz is alright. He's out in the stable loading the cart; I've asked him to pack it in as tight as he can.'

Ellen sighed in relief and gazed around at the chaos that surrounded them.

'Nan, it's impossible, isn't it? I mean to pack everything up in two days?'

'Impossible or not, it has to be done. At least I have to save the things your poor gran'pa would have wanted me to look after. There are several boxes on the cart already. We were up half the night.'

'Oh, Nan, you'll wear yourself out. Shall I make you a cup of tea?'

'Thank you dear, but let's get this done first.'
Looking at her more closely Ellen could tell she had had little sleep. The news had aged her already. She began packing items into the box as fast as she could and continued filling the box until it was full.

'This one's full but it's very heavy. Will you help me carry it into the stable?'

Joan took one look at the box and said, 'Leave it and fill another. I'll call Lukasz shortly to carry them out.' She said this so matter-of-factly that Ellen looked at her in amazement. 'Is that safe? I mean, out in the daylight?'

'Safe!' Joan almost exploded. 'Nothing's safe now! Nothing and no-one is safe, do you understand me? We do what we can, when we can, Ellen. They're stealing my home and there's nothing I can do about it.' She gazed around her room at all the chaos. 'What are these things of mine anyway, but a few books and old bits of wood. I don't know why I'm bothering. I've got no time for sentimentality.'

A Sea of Barbed Wire

'But Nan, when the war's over, you'll feel differently though, you'll be sorry if you haven't kept some of these things.'

'Perhaps I'll be in my grave by then, who knows.'

'Nan! Don't say that!'

'Well, I'm doing two trips, but there's a limit to what your poor mother can fit in. My next-door neighbours will store some boxes for me and a few bits of furniture. What the Germans don't see, they don't get, eh?' Her lips were firmly closed into a thin mean line. 'When I get the house back, if I ever get it back, Ellie, dear, I suppose I'll be glad of what I've managed to save. Thank you for helping.'

Joan's outburst was uncharacteristic and when she saw tears forming in Ellen's eyes, she hugged her, apologised and told her that whatever happened they would get through it. Her resilience apparently having returned, she soon put on her business-like self again. Turning abruptly, she led her out the back door to the stable. There, they found Lukasz shifting boxes, heaving one up on top of another onto the cart and strapping them on. He paused as he heard their approach, and the horse, tied up on the far side, snorted and stamped its foot impatiently. The strong pungent smell of the stable, the soiled straw and sweet hay in the hayrick enveloped Ellen and it immediately took her back to her childhood once more when she used to help her grandfather muck out the stable.

Lukasz nodded to them both but didn't speak.

'Lukasz, has my nan told you what's happening?'

He shrugged and didn't speak but his expression was filled with fear.

'It's not exactly easy to explain anything to him, dear. When the time comes, he'll understand soon enough.'

But Ellen wanted to reach out to him.

'Lukasz, we're taking you back home, you'll be okay. You'll be with us. Where is your notebook?' She made the sign of scribbling on her hand. 'Would you go and get it, please?' He began to shake his head. 'No, no. I keep. I keep.'

'It'll be okay. Don't worry, just bring it here please?' She tried to restrain the sudden urgency in her voice and smile reassuringly. She realised she had frightened him, but it was difficult as her nerves were in shreds. When he left, she sighed, trying to relax her shoulders. She felt so tense. Joan stopped what she was doing and looked at her curiously.

'What's going on?'

'A while ago now, he asked me for some paper; he wanted to write to his family.'

'We can write the briefest of messages through the Red Cross, but a letter from him? And in Polish? It's impossible!'

'No Nan, he's not expecting to post them. I've told him. It's more like a diary I think. It's just something for him to do when he's stuck in such a small space all day and night, to keep himself from going nuts probably.' She smiled, genuinely, as it occurred to her what a crazy time they were living through when even writing a letter could mean arrest, imprisonment or death if it was found.

'Don't you see? It gives him something to look forward to.'

A Sea of Barbed Wire

Joan gave a quick nod of her head. 'I understand Ellen, but you watch yourself young lady. You can sometimes be too kind for your own good.'

'I know what I'm doing Nan.'

'I hope so.' She resumed packing the cart. Within a few minutes Lukasz returned with the notebook in his hand.

Ellen smiled, giving him a thumbs up. 'Hide it inside your shirt, like this.' Taking the book from him she tucked it under her cardigan. 'Now you, like this!' she said, and handing it back to him she started to undo the buttons of his shirt. 'Keep it here, close to you. Do you understand?'

He nodded, tucking the notebook safely against his chest.

Joan stood watching them, muttering under her breath. 'What it is to be young and foolish.'

Several hours passed, with much sorting and packing, the rooms began to look bare. Many boxes had been packed and carried out, and the cart was fully loaded. They had left a small space in the centre of the load for Lukasz to hide. Joan announced she was ready to harness up the horse, deliver the load and return for the night. It was dusk and before too long it would be blackout time. They would have to hurry.

'At this time of day,' she said as she came out carrying more blankets, 'the soldiers are tired and hungry. They lose interest in what's going up and down the road and start making their way back for something to eat.' Turning to Ellen with serious concentration, she said, 'Would you explain to Lukasz he's got to lie down and hide between the boxes like he did before? You seem to have a way with him. You're riding back with us are you, dear?'

'I'll come with you to the end of The Queen's Road, Nan, but I've arranged to meet Robert in town. I'm going to tell him what's happening and just want to make sure he's alright.'

'That's kind of you, love, but do be careful.' Tears rushed into Joan's eyes as she spoke to her granddaughter with an intense urgency. 'Don't take any risks protecting other people. If it all goes wrong for me tonight; if I get stopped on the way and they find Lukasz on board, remember me and your gran'pa won't you, that we loved you very much.' This sudden emotional response was so unlike her nan it stopped Ellen in her tracks.

'Oh Nan, you'll be alright, won't you? You said yourself they're used to seeing you going up and down the road. They won't stop and search you, not now, will they?'

'Who knows? There's always the risk but look – listen to me. You know, you remind me so much of myself when I was your age – torn between two worlds. You've got my independent streak, I can see that now. Your mother was different, intent on getting married and settling down from the start. She was more than happy to stay at home and cook and do the ironing, and she had no other ambitions, bless her. But I was always restless. I had dreams of leaving the island and going on a big adventure. I wasn't sure I should marry at all, let alone a man like your gran'pa who was set in his ways, growing tomatoes like his father before him and never wanting to do anything else. But Robert seems a kind man and if it's meant to be, and you stay together, he'll

A Sea of Barbed Wire

make you a good husband. When the war ends, and God knows we hope it will finish soon and the Allies will succeed, don't be too tempted by the wider world. You'll need some home comforts after all this. You might feel like settling down. You know, Ellie, when your gran'pa first proposed to me, I lay awake for night after night wondering whether to accept him or not, but in the end I wouldn't have given myself to any other man – not in the whole world.'

'Thanks for telling me that, Nan. You know, it seems sometimes you can see right through me. What helped you decide, in the end, to stay and marry Gran'pa?'

'He was my best friend, dear. The best friend I could ever have. I could be myself when I was with him and I grew to love him very much. A friend for life is better than any man who spells excitement and adventure and who might be more handsome, but that kind of relationship doesn't last.' She turned her head momentarily to the place where Lukasz was stowed away in the cart. 'I never regretted my decision.'

'I'm so sorry we've lost him, Nan. Everything's changing.' Ellen looked back at her nan's lovely house, grieving for the past, the childhood memories she had there.

Before they left, Ellen and her nan walked through the house once more together searching for any remaining items they might have forgotten or any tell-tale signs of Lukasz being there. It could be, perhaps, a razor, a man's shirt, a shoe, but the rooms were bare, stripped of any personal items. A few more bags and a suitcase stood by the door, ready for Joan's final trip in the morning. Soon they switched off the lights and stepped outside. The dog was waiting for them. He wagged his tail and bounded towards the cart as if he knew what they were doing.

'It'll be late by the time I drop this lot off and get back here so we must hurry. I want to spend just one final night here on my own, to remember old times. It's better it happened this way, that your gran'pa didn't live to see our beautiful home ruined and the war destroying everything we worked for together. He worked so hard for this place, Ellie. And he loved this house so much. I'm stronger now. I can take anything they throw at me.'

She smiled sadly before moving back to the cart. Checking the horse's harness, tightening all the straps, she gave the horse an affectionate pat. With everything ready, she said, 'Right, girl, let's get going. Giving Ellen a hug, she whistled the dog, climbed up onto the driving board and Ellen clambered up beside her. With a flick of the whip, the old horse moved off. The cart swayed as it clattered its way out onto the road. Whatever thoughts were going through her head, there was nothing she could do but hope and pray for her nan and her precious cargo.

At the junction, Joan brought the horse to a standstill just long enough for her to climb down. Slightly concerned that it was already getting late, and that she still had to walk back, she set off down The Grange towards the town. However, pausing briefly, she stood still to watch the horse and cart continue up the road, and bit her lip at the vulnerability of her nan and the task that lay ahead of her.

Chapter 23

Meg and Albert's house was near to The Rohais, there was still enough time for Joan to get there, deposit Lukasz safely, unload the cart, and drive back to the farmhouse before the curfew hour. The journey to Meg and Albert's house usually took her about thirty minutes when the weather was fine, but the roads were becoming more uneven by the day and in fading light it could be treacherous. Joan's old mare was used to the route, a journey she had been making to and fro for years. The streets were virtually deserted.

Suddenly the horse stumbled. 'Whoa, whoa!' yelled Joan urgently, bringing the cart to a halt and securing the reins. She climbed down, muttering to herself, 'Oh dear, Oh, dear!' as she found the mare lifting her front hoof. This meant trouble. If the horse was lame, she was stuck unless she could sort it out quickly. The last thing she wanted to do was attract unnecessary attention. If they stayed there too long, they could be in serious trouble. As she stooped to examine the hoof, the mare neighed, rearing back slightly and breathing heavily through her flaring nostrils. 'Easy! Easy!' cried Joan. She tried again but the hoof was extremely sensitive. The minutes ticked by. At any moment a German vehicle might come thundering along the road, or a soldier might take a scout around and find her. As a matter of routine, he could demand to see her identity papers. Her imagination went into overdrive. He might summon other soldiers, strip down and search the cart, and then they would find their missing prisoner. She took a deep breath trying to calm herself. 'What to do …what to do?' she whispered. Suddenly there was a scuffle behind her and Lukasz was there by her side.

'I look. I find problem.'

'No, get back on the cart, now! Get out of sight!' hissed Joan, panic rising in her chest.

Lukasz put a hand on her arm. 'Please. I help. I know horses.' He stared into her eyes.

She nodded and moved aside reluctantly. Lukasz sprang into action. He ran his hands down the mare's leg, crooning in a babyish, sing-song voice deep from his throat. The sound fascinated Joan. He was speaking in Polish, but his gentle tone seemed to sooth the mare as he eventually seemed to find the inflamed spot. The mare suddenly kicked out and whinnied. Steadily he brought her back under control, his fingers apparently investigating something lodged in the frog of the hoof. But darkness was descending rapidly. Hunting in the front of the cart for the torch she kept for emergencies, Joan realised there were German soldiers on duty nearby so she didn't dare switch it on. Waiting, while Lukasz worked on the horse, she could hardly breathe.

'It here. I find problem. A rock,' he said, raising his head to Joan. 'I do it. Okay?'

'Yes, yes, whatever you can.' She looked around anxiously. A few minutes passed and she was listening for the slightest sound of an army vehicle approaching or the heavy footsteps of a patrol.

A Sea of Barbed Wire

Within a few more minutes, Lukasz whistled quietly to himself and murmured, 'Ah, it come loose. It is done.' He passed a sharp piece of stone to her, and continued his crooning song, stroking and breathing onto the mare's nose. Then Joan saw him put his face down and put his mouth near to the hoof, sending his warm breath onto the tender part. 'Ssh, ssh,' he murmured. Again and again, he breathed on it. Finally, he placed her hoof carefully to the ground and she stood firm.

'She okay,' he said. 'We go.'

In seconds he had jumped back up on the cart and ducked down between the boxes as before. Sighing with relief, Joan climbed back up onto the cart, picked up the reins and with a soft, 'Walk on,' the mare moved forward. Her pace was steady again.

Until that time, she had been so preoccupied with the reality of losing her home, Joan had scarcely given a thought to Lukasz, hidden away under the blankets. But when she realised how close they had come to being discovered by the soldiers – it was all she could do to regain her composure and calm down. Ten minutes later however, their destination came into view. She pulled up, climbed down and holding the mare's bridle, walked the final stretch. She wanted their arrival to be quiet and hardly noticeable so tying the mare to the post as usual, she tapped gently on the door. Albert appeared and immediately turned back to the interior and called to Meg. Unloading the cart as quickly as they could between them, Lukasz was smuggled indoors, covered in a blanket. Soon the cart was unloaded, Lukasz was back down in the cellar and Joan's boxes were stacked high in the sitting-room.

'Tonight will be my last night in my own dear home,' she said. 'Tomorrow morning I'll bring the last of my things. What happens to the rest will be up to them.'

'Won't you stay here now, Mother? It's got so late and you're tired.'

'And go without spending the last night in my own home? You won't deny me that, will you, dear?'

'But you've managed to move your most important things, surely tomorrow will do?'

'The most important things to me can't be moved. My memories, the years I shared with your father in that house. No, I'll be back first thing in the morning, dear. Don't worry. If it hadn't been for Lukasz, we may never have made it here tonight. He has a gift, that young man, a wonderful way with horses.'

'But why is that I wonder?'

'You'll have to ask him, but his skill saved us tonight. I must get going again; it'll soon be curfew.'

The journey back was uneventful. With a sense of finality, she drove on, not hurrying too much, feeling philosophical about how things had turned out and how unexpectedly her life had changed. Familiar aspects of her everyday life were being stolen away. To evict a woman recently widowed seemed particularly cruel but Joan wasn't a woman to feel sorry for herself.

However, when she came within sight of her home again, she couldn't believe her eyes. The lights were on, all the lights, and the windows were thrown open. There were loud voices, shouting, laughing, and there was singing. The singing of German songs. Joan stopped the mare and just sat there, up on the cart,

A Sea of Barbed Wire

feeling completely stunned. She was silent for several moments. Finally, the mare grew restless and without hesitating any longer she pulled steadily on the reins and turned her around. A neighbouring farmer had offered a stable for her and there she would be looked after until such a time as Joan was able to take her back. With one backward glance she said goodbye to her home, her lifetime security and the few possessions she had kept till last. Her nightwear, toothbrush, change of clothes and a few last-minute mementoes were as good as lost. She had no intention of going to her own front door and asking for them, subjecting herself to yet another indignity.

Reaching the rough track to her friend's farm, she halted the cart and climbed down. After a brief discussion with her friend at the door, she walked the mare the rest of the way across the yard to the stable. There she unharnessed her, rubbed her down, gave her some hay and putting on her rug, wished her farewell. Stealing herself for whatever the future might bring, she manoeuvred the empty cart to one side and set off on the long walk back to her daughter's house.

Chapter 24

On Monday morning, Ellen was the first up. It was still dark, and the house was silent. Everyone was still sleeping. Her usual breakfast, a slice of rough bread with a scraping of dripping, didn't appeal but she ate it anyway, the fat clagging in her mouth, but she washed it down with hot tea. Her mother had made blackberry jam in the summer, and they still had some left but she didn't want to use any. Her nan's store of delicious homemade strawberry jam, pickled onions and tomato chutney, that were all stored in her pantry ready for the winter, had unfortunately been left there, by strictest orders.

It was too early to wake anyone or attempt to speak to Lukasz, so she set off for the walk to work. She hardly noticed the distance because her thoughts were elsewhere. When she got there George was shifting sacks of flour and she greeted him before going to put the kettle on. George was a good boss to work for, sympathetic, understanding and not too demanding. He had even left some oatmeal biscuits out for the girls as his wife had been able to make some.

'Help yourself, love. There's a drop of honey to spread on them too. Don't ask me where she got that, just enjoy it while we've got it.'

Carrying her cup of tea through to the area where the dough was mixed, she saw Lucy already working up at the far end; she had been toying yet again with the idea of confiding in her about Lukasz.

'How are things, Lucy?' she asked, casting a curious eye over her friend.

'I'd be better if I wasn't stuck in here workin' but...' She shrugged her shoulders. 'Perhaps it won't be for too much longer.'

'I suppose you'll be leaving, because of the baby?' she whispered.

'Because of a lot of things,' replied Lucy, tight-lipped.

Ellen looked at her quickly but didn't reply. The bakery was no longer the cheerful place it used to be. She put on her apron and began kneading the dough, measuring it out in chunks and popping each portion onto the large baking tray ready for proving and baking. Each tray took ten loaves, and they would have to keep up a steady stream of mixing, kneading, measuring out, leaving to prove, and putting in the oven – throughout the day. By three o'clock the last of the loaves would be baked and distributed and their task would be done.

'How's little Charlie?' Her question hung in the air for so long she wondered if Lucy was going to answer at all.

'I don't know actually. He's gone.'

Ellen stared at her. 'What do you mean, *he's gone*! Where? Oh, come on Lucy, what's happened?'

Suddenly Lucy's defences crumpled. She slammed the dough she was kneading down on the counter but her eyes didn't move from it. Ellen stepped forward and asked again, gently. 'What's happened? Where is he? Are you okay? Here, come and sit on this stool and tell me what's going on.'

It was as if her friend was a different person to the girl who had been so philosophical about life before. She had been so carefree about her affair with Franz, so happy, so fun-loving. She turned to Ellen in despair.

'Last night, my mother-in-law came to the house with two other women. They demanded to see my Charlie. I told them he's fast asleep in his cot and I asked them to come back today when he's awake. But they pushed past me and tore up the stairs. They nearly knocked me over, they were so rough, and you should have heard the things they called me! And that's apart from the usual *Jerry-bag*!'

The reputation of so-called 'Jerry-bags' had been the talking point in the local shops for months. They were considered the worst of women, cheap whores who were sleeping with the enemy. They were accused of being collaborators, traitors, people who would betray their family and friends to seek their own ends.

'Oh Lucy, I'm so sorry!'

'Those horrible, evil women! He was fast asleep, my poor baby!'

Lucy's words were blurted out in spite of the fact that both of them were aware George could be around. 'He was so happy after his bedtime story, and he was so frightened he started cryin' like mad. They just grabbed him up out of his cot and I pleaded with them to stop but they didn't care, they just carried him downstairs. Scared him half to death, with him screamin' his poor little head off, and calling "Mummy, Mummy!" He must have thought he was bein' murdered.'

'And they took him away? Just like that? How awful!'

She was weeping openly now, her eyes swollen and red. Reprisals were common, Ellen knew of many, but she just didn't think decent women, especially the boy's own grandmother, would behave in such a way. The war, she thought, was turning good decent people into monsters.

'There must be something you can do! He's your child, whatever they think of you. They shouldn't be allowed to steal your little boy. It's against the law.'

'And whose law would that be? English, Guernsey or German?' Lucy fired back that question defiantly, sniffing and blowing her nose.

Ellen took a mental step back. Lucy's antagonism towards her hadn't exactly been dispelled, even with this drama unfolding. She must be careful. The girl's rebellious spirit was returning fast. 'What do you suggest I do?' she said haughtily. 'Go to the big chief, Ambrose Sherwill, and tell him how wicked they are takin' my child away? What do you think he'll say to me? He'll probably tell me to go to hell!'

It was time for Ellen to collect her thoughts. What hope did Lucy have of winning support? Would the police help her? She wasn't sure. She wasn't sure of anything anymore. Who would be prepared to speak up for her when she was sleeping with a German soldier, pregnant with his child and hanging out with him and his fellow soldiers openly? They were both discussing the mother-in-law's actions when George walked in and found none of the dough ready and both girls deep in conversation.

He scratched his head as he stood there and said, 'Look, you two, I don't know what's been going on in here, but I need that dough proved and ready to be put in the oven in an hour and it's not even in the tins yet.

You'll both be working overtime if you don't catch up, and I'm warning you, there are other people who would be glad of your jobs.' He looked at each of them with a long hard stare. Then, with a tired, almost exhausted expression, he added, 'Come on, girls, help me out, eh?'

'Sorry George, we'll get going straight away,' said Ellen, standing up. 'Lucy's had some bad news, that's all.'

'Bad news?' he said over his shoulder. 'We all have our share of that, I'm sorry but that's the way it is right now. And there's plenty more where that came from. As for you, young lady,' he said, looking directly at Lucy, who still sat where she was, sniffing and mopping her eyes with her handkerchief. 'If you don't get on with your work and stop causing me trouble, I'll have something else to say to you soon but …' And before finishing his sentence he turned abruptly and walked off.

Chapter 25

The house was empty when Ellen got home, that is, apart from her nan's old dog who wagged his tail, turned round once in his basket and settled down again. Lukasz, she knew, must be down in the cellar but where her mother and Nan were, she didn't know. She was anxious to speak to Lukasz alone before they returned. Changing quickly out of her working clothes, she went back to the sitting-room and pulled the rug away that concealed the trap door.

He must have heard something moving because he was there on the steps when she began to lift the door, pushing it upwards to help her as it was very heavy. The cool air rushed up towards her as the door was lifted and thrown back. Lukasz said something which she didn't catch. How she wished she could speak Polish.

Looking over her shoulder and listening to check there was no-one coming, she began to step down and immediately he reached out and took her hand firmly to help her. The light was dim down there as the only daylight and air came from a small slit of a window that was open to the back garden.

'Do you still have your notebook?' she asked, almost in a whisper, making the scribbling sign with her fingers as before. Lukasz nodded, retrieving it from the inside of his shirt, snug against the bare skin of his chest. 'I have here,' he said, watching her. 'It alright, yes?'

She smiled. 'Yes! That's good! I was worried because if you lost it along the road, or left it on the cart, the soldiers could find it. Then they would come after you – after all of us. You must be careful!'

'I very careful. I keep it here, okay?' He gave her a reassuring smile. 'The lady, she say to me - you marry soon, to the Robert?'

Taken aback, she replied hastily, 'My nan told you that! How dare she! No, no, it's not true!' Lukasz looked away from her, staring out towards the tiny window, a muscle flinching on his jaw. He didn't speak. Perhaps he didn't believe her. When he looked back at her his dark eyes were fiery. 'I sorry, that is all. I not want you marry the Robert.'

She shook her head. 'Listen. When the Germans came to Guernsey, took over the whole island and told us no-one was allowed to leave, they made us feel like prisoners. We know if we try we would be arrested or even shot. So, we're all prisoners, all of us, not just you. I feel trapped too. I'm not going to settle down and marry Robert or anyone. When the war's over, I want to get away and explore and see the world! Tell me about your country, Lukasz! What was it like when you were at home, before this horrible war started? Tell me about your farm and the countryside, how it was for you then, please? I want to dream! I want to think about you and imagine what it was like when you were free.'

Seeming surprised by her sudden change of mood, he said, 'We sit here. I tell you.' He sat on the steps and taking her hand he indicated for her to sit on the next step down. She settled herself on the step and rested her chin on her arm.

A Sea of Barbed Wire

'My country very beautiful. There is much sky. Mountains. It very big place, much sea, plenty space. I work with horses in the fields, when sun rise in sky to when it dark. Very tired but good, it very good work. We have plenty crop to sell. My father, he good farmer, he teach Lukasz when small boy. He say he only have one boy. Me, Lukasz. He have no other sons. Only girl, Irena. He say I have the work of two men. Then he say, I good worker! My father, he take me to my uncle house. I hear him say he proud of me!'

Ellen senses a surge of emotion flow through him as he talked. He went on to describe the sea-fishing trips he took with his uncle at night, the farmhouse where his mother spent most of her time in the kitchen and how his sister helped her to prepare the food and preserve the fruit. There were the times he took the horse and cart to market, the weather and how the crops suffered in the cold winter blizzards. Gradually a picture of life back home as he had known it became real to her.

And then: the thing she had never dared to admit even to herself, the feelings she had, the unspoken feelings she imagined they had for each other had suddenly become a reality.

'I sorry that I am here,' he said, and his eyes flashed around the small confinement of his hiding place. 'I here in dark, it dirty place. I ashamed. In my home I work hard. I good man. I be proud. You not like me here. You not like this man, he hide away like animal. 'I feel, inside Lukasz, here.' He placed his hand against his bare chest where the notebook had been lodged only minutes earlier. 'I feel – Lukasz and Ellie – in here, we be together.'

'But how can it be possible?' she cried. He was saying all that she felt in her innermost being, what she had never dared admit even to herself. Suddenly she was crying, overcome. All the tension of the day, Lucy's outburst, the war, the danger, the Germans, and her own weakness, came down on her and she covered her face with her hands. She could hear him speaking in Polish, not a word of which she could understand, but she understood the meaning behind them, nevertheless. He was apologising, attempting to comfort her. She felt his strong arms come around her, his warm manly scent enveloping her and lifting her up. Gently taking hold of her face in both his hands, he kissed her softly and passionately on her hair, and then on the lips. He kissed her wet eyelashes and that brought fresh tears, and a sense of yearning came over her. Never had she experienced such warmth, such passion in a kiss before. His closeness, his breath on her face, his physical warmth thrilled her.

'Oh, Lukasz, we mustn't! I have to go.'

'Please! You feel it too? You feel it here, for Lukasz!'

She nodded, 'I do, Lukasz, I do very much but I can't …' The tears came and unable to explain, she turned away.

'Ellie, I sorry. Lukasz sorry.' Helping her back up the steps, with a sad smile he retreated, lowered the trapdoor back over his head, shutting himself underground again in the darkness. Ellen pulled the rug back across the cellar trapdoor and rushed upstairs to her room. There she flung herself down on the bed, sobbing as if her heart would break.

A Sea of Barbed Wire

It was half an hour before her mother returned with her nan. They had been into town, queuing all afternoon for food. Cold and hungry, they came carrying what appeared to be a meagre amount of provisions for the time they had taken to obtain it.

'Two tins of sardines,' said Meg, taking them out of her bag. 'They'll be handy for making fish cakes since we've got the potatoes to mix with them.' She was unpacking her shopping basket, laying her goods out with a certain amount of satisfaction. A cabbage, a cauliflower, a few shrivelled up carrots and a tin of apricots. 'The butcher gave me a few bones for the dog and I managed to get a double ration of cheese! I think Dora's been saving some extra for us.' She smiled at Ellen. 'Pop the kettle on, will you, love? We can have one of these biscuits.'

Joan hadn't said anything about her purchases, but she had carried in quite a heavy bag. It rested on the floor beside her while she herself lay back in the armchair with her eyes closed. Ellen fetched cups and saucers. Having had a good while to compose herself there was no sign that anything had been amiss an hour before. Even so, her hands shook as she put the cups out.

'What did you buy, Nan?' she asked, trying to make her voice sound normal even though her heart was still fluttering.

'Oh, you have a look for me, Ellie, would you, dear? I'm too tired to remember. I don't know how you are all going to manage with me here. I can't contribute much now. I suppose they'll kill and eat my laying hens too. They don't have the brains to keep them and not wring their necks.'

'We'll manage, Mother. We'll make the most of the rations we're getting. It could be worse – everything could always be worse.'

'Huh! Hark at that daughter of mine!' said Joan, chuckling and catching Ellen's eye. 'It's just as well I had Lukasz with me last night you know. I doubt I'd be sitting here now if I hadn't. He has a special way with horses, that one, for sure. He must come from a family who kept horses, eh?'

'We don't know much about his background, Mother. It's another mouth to feed, that's all I know. But we're all in this together. We'll get by. We can't do much about it but keep our heads down and stay out of trouble. Come on Ellie, that kettle's surely boiling by now; let's have that cuppa.'

Chapter 26

The life they had known, the beauty of the island Ellen had grown up in, was lost, it seemed, forever. Guernsey was being transformed by the ugliness of what the Germans were building to defend their newfound territory. The soldiers accompanied by the Nazi Organisation Todt guards, drove the exhausted and emaciated Todt workers and prisoners-of-war to toil away all day. They were ordered to mix, carry and pour tons of concrete into structures, creating massive bunkers, thick-walled bomb-proof buildings which were situated along the coast in strategic positions. The guards were cruel, and they showed their captives no mercy. Whatever shreds of hope the men themselves had for the future were soon abandoned as they struggled simply to survive. An end to their suffering could come only when the war came to an end, and only if the Allies could claim victory. Then they might be given their freedom at last. However, for some of them the only freedom they would find would be in death.

More barbed wire defences, and more concrete bunkers were appearing on the skyline around the coast every day. More and more beaches were declared out of bounds. In the building of the fortifications, a huge amount of manpower was being used. All of the workers were deprived of food and clothing, sleep and cleanliness. Their faces were drawn with pain and anxiety, their skin and clothing covered in cement dust and dirt. Rumours spread that they were infested with vermin, head lice, fleas, and contagious disease like tuberculosis. Their living quarters were said to be so unhealthy they were attracting rats. Many islanders tried to steer well clear of them. Local people watched in dismay as groups of men were marched through the narrow lanes to their places of work. Some were incapable of marching, some had such little strength left, some had no shoes on their feet and their trousers were hanging in shreds even though the winter was now upon them.

One of the prisoners however, had still managed to evade capture. Sheltering Lukasz from his German captors was now part of the family's way of life. They no longer questioned the wisdom in doing so, the danger involved or the moral of it. Lukasz was simply another human being who needed looking after. He had become almost one of the family. When he first went missing, soldiers were everywhere. They searched fields, barns and greenhouses and then searched houses too. They were angry, humiliated more than anything, that a prisoner had escaped them. Fed no more than a crust of bread and watery cabbage soup, if a man collapsed out of weakness, they might kick him, order him to get up, and failing that, they might shove him aside and shoot him.

From time to time, it was revealed that some islanders had attempted to escape, usually in small boats, and mostly resulting in failure. Some enterprising and fearless young men had even drowned in their attempt. In revenge, and to deter others from trying to get away, the German Commandant issued an incentive: a notice of rewards for informants among the islanders to supply information while at the same time threatening anyone foolish enough to harbour any fugitives. Throughout it all, the family managed to remain comparatively calm. They hadn't been able to plan ahead or think how they could manage if the war continued longer than they had ever imagined. But weeks passed and since then, others had gone missing. Some were later found lying dead out in a field somewhere or in a ditch, having died of sheer exhaustion, hyperthermia, malnutrition, or a combination of all of those things. Prisoners, the Germans seemed to believe, were expendable. The soldiers, it appeared, barely bothered to count them anymore. True or not, rumours spread of bodies being buried where they fell.

When possible, Ellen tried to avoid seeing Lukasz. Since he had kissed her, her thoughts were all in turmoil. There was something between them which confused and excited her. If she could only switch off her feelings, then she thought she could fool herself into thinking she would be alright. Even telling herself she would get over it, grow out of it, or whatever it was that drew her to him as if it was her destiny. She told herself it was only the war, and what the war had done to her.

Robert was being as kind and attentive as usual, and it would soon be Christmas. She didn't know how many times people had said the occupation would be over by then. Somehow, they were all determined to celebrate with some simply made decorations. They planned to pick some fresh branches of evergreens and bring some festive cheer into the house. There was plenty to do in the kitchen while it was still light although it grew dark soon after four. Ellen and her mother would make soup for the next day, if there were enough ingredients available, and even a cake could be made by substituting mashed potato for some of the flour, blackberries instead of currants and sweetened with saccharin which was still available in the shops. There were always clothes to wash with or without soap powder. But their weight had dropped dramatically and most nights they all went to bed hungry.

Walking to work early in the morning was becoming a journey Ellen dreaded. There were hardly any people about that early in the morning – apart from the German soldiers. She dressed to look as inconspicuous as possible, with her hair tucked inside a grey woollen hat, and keeping her face averted whenever soldiers passed her. It was worse for her when she had to walk the length of an empty street when there was a band of soldiers standing on the corner, or a troop of prisoners being marched to work, taking up the whole road.

The stories she heard about soldiers enticing women to talk and offering them gifts was something she had become wary of, especially knowing Lucy's situation. Many women had been tempted to accept the advances of a soldier through hunger alone. Their offer of food or chocolate, presented with a smile, tempted many a young woman to accept a gift. Often it was simply because some soldiers were polite and friendly. There weren't many young men left on the island and it was tempting to respond to them. It cheered the girls up to be flattered, to receive a wolf whistle or a compliment. Ellen didn't blame her friend Lucy, or some of the others, for being persuaded. Life was very

A Sea of Barbed Wire

hard and they had no idea how long it would continue to be that way.

When she got to work, she didn't mention to Lucy how keyed up she felt about her nan's house being requisitioned. She had to be on her guard. None of her anxieties could be shared with Lucy and it was hard. But it was just too sensitive a subject. In a way she didn't trust herself to talk about it in case she said the wrong thing and accidentally opened up about what was happening at home. However, on that particular morning, the first thing Lucy said to her instead of the usual, "The kettle's on" or "There's some tea in the pot" was: 'Those bloody Germans!'

Ellen was still taking her coat and hat off and she looked at her in amazement. She had to be very careful how she responded.

'What's happened now?'

'They take what they want from us and then -'

'Ssh!' Ellen drew closer. 'Is George around?'

'No, he's off across the yard getting the van loaded up. I don't know, it's just men perhaps, how they blow hot and cold with us.'

'Why, Lucy, what's happened? I thought you and Franz were okay.'

'I told him last night about how those awful women came and took my little boy away, eh? I know he was only trying to comfort me, but he said I should remember we would have our own baby soon and I'd do best to forget about Charlie. Can you believe that? It's not like I can give up one child and just turn around and have another.'

'Well, I suppose I can believe it actually, in some of them. They seem so heartless, but they can't all be bad. I'm not saying your Franz is like that, but I don't trust any of them.'

'Franz isn't like them though!' she cried. 'It's this war, that's all. It's this bloody war! It turns men into monsters!'

'Don't upset yourself again, Lucy, come and sit down. It's not good for you or your baby to get all worked up. You're worried and it's understandable. But Franz will realise when he sees how upset you are, I'm sure.'

'Oh, Ellie, you're always so level-headed. I wish I had your sense. You're so good to me.'

Ellen wasn't sure she deserved this compliment, but she suggested they went to share her mother's cake which she had brought with her to cheer themselves up. When they reached the kitchen, Ellen watched Lucy for a few minutes, thinking about her situation. Should any of them be taking so many risks? Her own life was turning into one big helter-skelter, and the direction she feared was downwards. But in spite of having her usual common-sense, she wanted to help her. She knew it was a dangerous game but she was already up to her neck in a situation where there was no going back.

'Lucy, I've been thinking: would you like me to help you get Charlie back?'

Her head shot up in surprise. 'Do you think you could?' She was holding her teacup, with the other hand resting on her growing tummy. 'My mother-in-law was like a mad woman when she came and grabbed him.'

'We could go together and talk to her, reason with her.'

A Sea of Barbed Wire

'Huh! I know what she'll say. She'll tell me to repent, have done with the German boy, finish with him and then she might think about it.'

'Could you do that? For the sake of getting Charlie back, give Franz up I mean?'

'No! Yes! Oh, I don't know! I don't know what I think any more. I'm scared, Ellie. I've got myself into this mess and I can't see a way to get out of it. It's fun being with Franz, he makes me laugh. Honestly, he does! He's bored and hungry and he complains that all he does is carry out stupid orders, takes part in drills and the rest of the time just tries to keep his head down. They work them so hard. They drive them to the limit. Some of the lads, Franz told me, they actually hate their corporal so much they're talkin' about doin' him in. He said they'd pull their guns on him rather than on us Guernsey people. It didn't sound like a joke either.'

'I believe you. The army must know they're being told lies. Their government propaganda is ridiculous. They must know the war isn't really going as well as they make out.'

'I'm afraid for him, Ellie. You mustn't tell anyone, but I'm more afraid for Franz than I am for my own husband. I don't want to lose him. One of these days he might just step over the line and land a punch right in the middle of his sergeant's face.'

Ellen hoped she was exaggerating, and she tried to bring the conversation back to reality.

'But you don't want to lose Charlie either though. It could be worth trying to do a deal with your mother-in-law. You don't have to make any promises, but at least she should allow you to see Charlie sometimes. It's not fair on the poor little boy.'

'I'm ready to try anythin'. What could I say to her?'

'I haven't had time to think about it yet, but I will.'

The girls sat drinking their tea. Multiple thoughts went flitting through Ellen's mind. As far as she was concerned, Franz had filled Lucy's head with a fantasy future. What future could there really be for them both? With Pete away fighting on the Front Line, most wives would be missing him, writing to him and looking forward to when he returns. That's if he does return. But she hadn't forgotten the tales Lucy shared with her before the war. She had told her then that Peter had never been the love of her life. Once the excitement and novelty of marriage had worn off, and domestic problems had taken their place, the spark had fizzled out. Their marriage was in trouble even before Charlie was born. Lucy was lonely and unfulfilled, even before Pete had left the island to go to war. She deserved some happiness but at this rate she risked losing her little boy, and Franz, and possibly Pete as well. Lucy's love life was even more complicated than her own.

'When are you seeing Franz next?'

'Tonight, but I told him I might not come. We didn't leave on very good terms actually.' She began to sniff and took out her handkerchief. 'I made a bit of a fool of myself, beggin' him to help me get Charlie back. Of course, he couldn't do that anyway. '

'But you know why his grandma has taken him, don't you, eh?'

'She doesn't think I'm fit to be his mother, 'cos I'm sleepin' with Franz and havin' his baby. But I wasn't thinkin' about Franz being a German, about him being the enemy, I just fancied him. When I met him, he was off-duty and he was just a kind really good-lookin' man. I don't know what he's like when he's on duty with his unit, but at least he's nice to me. Oh, I don't know, Ellie, it's all a mess.'

The more Lucy opened her heart to her, the more she longed to share her own troubles in return. The tears backed up in her throat like rocks and at any moment she thought she was going to cry too. If Lucy thought her situation was a mess, how much more of a mess was her own life? If she put a step wrong, Lukasz and the lives of her parents, her nan and Robert would all be in danger, not to mention her own. It would be heartless and unreasonable to involve Lucy too. Perhaps it was this justification for keeping her own secret back that gave her the confidence to attempt to help Lucy. Next to her own problem, a disagreeable mother-in-law taking care of a grandchild when the mother had been disgraced seemed an easy task to deal with.

'Should I go and talk to her?' suggested Ellen. 'What's she like? Has she been bad-tempered with you before?'

'I don't think she likes me much, but she's usually alright. You know she has him for me when I'm at work. But I certainly won't be leavin' him with her anymore when I do get him back!'

'Have you thought what you'll do if you can't though?'
Lucy looked a bit shocked for a minute. 'You mean ... Well, of course I'll get him back! She can't hang on to him forever, can she?'

Ellen pulled a face. 'I don't know.' Her guess was that the woman could, and quite probably would, if

Lucy's circumstances didn't change. But judging by the expression on her friend's face, she didn't want to sound too pessimistic.

'Could you take Charlie with you, if you do go to Germany to be with Franz?'

Lucy raised her shoulders. 'Of course!' But she gave Ellen a despairing sigh. 'I'm all confused. I can't think straight, and I've hardly slept. What's Germany like? I've never been there and I can't speak German.'

Ellen found herself wondering about Lukasz, his home life and his country, Poland. It was all mysterious and intriguing and she felt impatient to ask him more about it. So much of life in the wider world had passed her by. Living on an island and never having travelled, Lucy's talk of leaving and moving to a foreign country with Franz startled her. Her friend's ability to be open-minded about the future, in a strange way, impressed her.

While replying to Lucy, her mind was still racing ahead to form questions that she could ask Lukasz next time they were alone. She pulled herself together and thought about the dreaded mother-in-law. Then she had an idea:

'Shall we go and see her together tomorrow after work? We could take her a loaf of bread and some clean clothes for Charlie as an excuse.'

Lucy caught her eye and nodded. 'We could try,' she replied but she was looking anxious. 'I'm dyin' to see Charlie again. Poor Charlie! He must be missin' me so much! I miss him too; I couldn't sleep last night for thinkin' about him. How can that woman be so cruel?'

'I don't know,' replied Ellen, although in fact she did know how despised girls were who slept with

A Sea of Barbed Wire

the enemy. Even though she was afraid of the situation she was involving herself in, she wanted to try to help. But who knew what reception they would receive when they knocked on that woman's door?

Chapter 27

That evening, after their meagre dinner, Albert said, 'That poor fella down there, we'd best do something about him stretching his legs. What d'you say, love?'

'I don't know that it's safe, Bert. If anyone were to -'

'Later on then, eh? When the blackout curtains are drawn and most folks nearby are in bed, let's light a candle and have him up here for a bit. He'll be going round the bend stuck in that cellar all day and night without company.'

Meg was knitting and she clicked her tongue in disapproval. 'Why should we take risks, dear? Isn't it enough that we feed him and hide him?'

'If you say so, love.' He sighed and picked up his paper.

However, Joan spoke up. 'I don't see what harm it could do. Bert's right, dear. He'll be going cuckoo locked up in the half-dark in a small space like that. I know I would.'

Ellen held her breath, her heart quickened. 'I think we ought to. He needn't stay up here long.'

'Well, I think he's better off down there than where he was,' insisted Meg. 'Some of them have to put up with a lot worse.'

A Sea of Barbed Wire

'When he was with me at the house,' Joan admitted, 'to be honest I used to have him in to sit by the fire every evening. I couldn't leave him out in the barn all the time on his own. He was company for me too. You know, he's a well-behaved young man. You've nothing to fear on that account.'

This remark seemed to sway Meg's opinion and she glanced at her husband guiltily as if she felt she had indeed been a bit harsh. Half-an-hour later, the room was lit only by candlelight. Ellen sat at the table with the book she had been reading now closed before her. It was too dark to do anything other than talk. They had two of their precious candles burning, one was next to Meg, and one was flickering in a candlestick on the table. When Lukasz came tramping up the steps from the cellar his figure loomed above then as his giant shadow cast weird shapes on the wall. Ellen felt excited, his presence sent her pulse racing, but she kept her eyes cast down, opened her book and pretended to read.

Lukasz sat down next to Joan, perhaps encouraged by her confident smile and her gesture of welcome. There was still a fire alight in the grate, but its flame was poor. Evidently, he was more at ease in her company and because they had shared many an evening in conversation together at Joan's house, she knew him better than any of them.

'Lukasz,' she said. 'I'm glad you're here. I want to thank you for helping me with the horse. You have a way with horses, don't you. Was it your father who taught you?'

Lukasz raised his shoulders and gave a brief shrug. 'Horses? My father, yes, he show me. From when I was boy, I do horses. I work land, you understand.

Hard work, but good. We had food, wheat, corn. Plenty grow.'

'You were happy working on the farm then, lad?' said Albert. 'Did you work just with the horses or drive a tractor?'

Lukasz looked to Joan as if she would interpret for him and sure enough, Joan answered for him. 'His father couldn't afford a tractor, Bert.'

Ellen remained quiet, watching Lukasz, how his strong hands moved with expression when he was talking, and how his jaw flexed when he was thinking. Everything about him thrilled and fascinated her.

Joan helped him to talk by prompting: 'You didn't always have plenty to eat though, did you Lukasz. You can tell them, dear, it's okay.'

His eyes turned to the fire and there was emotion in his deep voice when he spoke about his life at home. 'My father. My Mother, my poor sister, Irena. The hunger very bad. The Nazis come. They take our farmland. The soldiers - they kill my father, they take my sister. My mother, she couldn't...she didn't ...' he stopped speaking. He hung his head, and the room was silent.

'Oh, Lukasz, what happened to her?' cried Ellen.

Joan intervened. 'Let me explain. It's okay, Lukasz, I'll tell them.' She spread her hands on her lap as if she was figuring out how to say it. 'He told me how the soldiers came and attacked them. Already his neighbour's farm had been invaded but there was nothing Lukasz or his father could do so they kept working in the fields. The Nazis arrived, shot his father dead where he stood and attacked and raped his sister but his mother ...well, he doesn't know what happened after that. Lukasz was beaten, tied-up and dragged away. They threw him in a lorry with a lot of other prisoners.'

Ellen gave a sharp intake of breath, but her nan smiled at her. 'You have a lot to learn, dear, about what the Germans are capable of. There is a lot more to his story. Leave it for now. In time he might tell you himself.'

They continued to talk about other things, gossip they had heard in the town, and news being spread from those who had access to a wireless. The intimacy of the candlelight and them all huddled together in the fading warmth of the dying fire, brought a new bond of togetherness. In a lowered voice, Albert revealed that a colleague at the pharmacy had discovered a means of finding out what was going on in the outside world and what was really happening in the war. During his lunch hour, he told them, his friend would walk up to the Priaulx Library to take out a book. But not any book. Between the pages of a certain book, would be concealed a copy of GUNS The Guernsey Underground News Service. It was a daily typewritten account of the latest BBC World News.

'People who print this are taking a huge risk, they'll be arrested if anyone betrays them,' said Albert, his eyes travelling round the room fixing each of them with a meaningful stare. 'This is a deadly secret, you understand, you mustn't tell a soul.'

There were several murmurs of agreement.

'But what does this news actually say, Bert?' demanded Meg.

'It tells us that the Germans are failing, the war isn't going their way, and certainly not half as much as they like us to believe. They're losing hundreds of aircraft every day, thousands of men and their morale is very low.' He looked up keenly. 'You know, the chaps who type it out – they really believe our boys are going to win!' His eyes shone as he looked round at each of them with a confidence none of them had seen for a long time. Meg, however, appeared unimpressed. 'Well, I hope they're right, dear. Shall I make some tea everyone? Lukasz, would you like some tea?'

The intimate atmosphere evaporated. While Meg took one of the candles, leaving them almost in darkness, Ellen said, 'Lukasz, if this is true the war might be over soon.'

He raised his head and looked directly at her for the first time.

'I hope so. I say to myself they safe, they wait for me. Maybe they go to my gran'mamma. They stay there, but I not know.'

'Try not to worry,' said Ellen. 'One day you'll be free to go home and see them again.'

Lukasz shrugged. 'My sister, Irena, she very beautiful. I see Nazi man take her. He hurt her. He tear her clothes. She scream. You know, I can do nothing!'

Joan frowned at Ellen and shook her head. 'No more talk of this. We think of good things, Lukasz, remember how I told you?'

Chapter 28

There was so much on her mind that night, Ellen tossed and turned her way into the small hours. The next morning, having to be at work by six-thirty, she was glad of the fresh sea air which helped to clear her head. When she arrived at the bakery, there was a bit of a panic going on. News gained by certain underground sources, according to George, who Ellen presumed had access to such things too, was that something had caused excitement among the locals. Twelve British commandos had invaded Sark and gone ashore secretly, killing two German soldiers and escaping with a third who they had taken prisoner. Climbing the cliff at the Hog's Back, they had gained information from a local woman as to the whereabouts of the Germans, crept up on a guard and attacked. George told the girls that he had heard Hitler was furious.

'Well, gossip won't win the war for us quite yet,' scolded George. 'If we don't get on with some work, there will be no bread baked here today. Come on girls, let's be having the first batch ready in double quick time, eh?'

Lucy finished weighing out the flour and was dusting herself down. Her expanding waistline could no longer be disguised by the apron she wore.

'So this news, it's all over the island, is it?' whispered Ellen.

'Who knows! The British must be mad trying to land anyone on there when the place is crawlin' with Germans. I'll try to find out more from Franz tonight.'

'Did you see Franz last night?'

'No, he was on duty. Am I glad he wasn't in Sark! Anyway, I decided to go to my mother-in-law's house to see Charlie, see if he was alright.' Lucy was kneading some dough and throwing all her energy into it. 'She wouldn't even let me in, the old bag. I could hear him cryin' at the back of the house, but she wouldn't budge. She said it's for the best, I'd only upset him. But it's not right! How can she steal my child and get away with it? Can't anyone stop her?'

'We could try again this afternoon. I'll come with you. But you know what you'll have to do. You'll have to apologise and promise never to see Franz again. I can't see her agreeing to let him go back with you otherwise.'

Lucy stopped what she was doing and stared at her. 'You're tellin' me I've got to choose between Charlie and Franz, the father of my unborn baby?'

'Well, yes. I suppose I am. But what about Pete? That woman's only thinking of her son too, and probably worried sick over him. I bet she's longing for him to come home safely.'

'I've got no sympathy for her. If Pete was here now and not out on some battlefield none of this would have happened. It's all his fault for leavin' me and goin' to sign up for their stupid war. There's no right answer to it now, I might as well go and throw myself off a cliff an' be done with.'

A Sea of Barbed Wire

'Don't say that Lucy! Nothing's ever that bad, you shouldn't even think that way!'

'But I hate this war!' she wailed. 'Why did Franz ever have to come to Guernsey and show me his beautiful blue eyes and cuddle me and make a fuss of me like he does? No-one's ever cared for me like he does, not Pete, nor my mum and dad, nobody, never!'

Ellen couldn't reply. It was heart-breaking to hear her say that. Even if Lucy did give Franz up, there was no guarantee she would be forgiven in the eyes of her mother-in-law, or the rest of the island. Her baby would be born, fathered by the enemy. Gossip and idle words were poison, especially when they were cut off from the rest of the world. They were isolated, and watched all the time by the German soldiers, not to mention the local spies who were out to earn a few extra pounds for betraying their friends and neighbours.

Mid-afternoon, Ellen hurried home. 'I'm going out again Mum. Just going to do a bit of shopping with Lucy.'

Meg chuckled. 'Shopping? You'll only be stuck in a queue until closing time. What are you hoping to buy?'

'I don't know, anything sweet perhaps. It depends on what's there. Is there anything you need?'

'Something tasty for tomorrow's dinner would be nice. I doubt there'll be anything worth having this time of day though.'

Changing out of her work clothes quickly and once out in the fresh air again, Ellen went to meet Lucy feeling apprehensive. Putting herself in danger by attempting to defend her friend was probably a huge mistake. Now she began wishing she had never got involved let alone offered to help and intervene in a tug of love between a mother and a grandmother over a little boy. As if that wasn't enough without the complication of Lucy being pregnant with the German's baby. As if she wasn't in enough trouble!

A German army vehicle, with rifles bristling out of every window, came careering towards her along the road. It was going much too fast for the narrow road and quickly she pressed herself up against the granite wall as it shot past, missing her with only inches to spare. Dust and petrol fumes smothered her. What worried her more though was where it was going. She stood staring after it, her heart thudding, hoping that it didn't draw up outside her own house. But it sped on past and disappeared round the corner. A seagull, crying its raucous call, soared overhead as if in warning and she hurried on.

When she reached the place where they had arranged to meet, Ellen looked around thinking Lucy hadn't arrived. Then she spotted her sitting on a wall, very small and huddled, with her arms wrapped around her body protectively and her hair half-covering her face.

'Lucy?' There was no response. She walked up to her slowly.

'Hey, Lucy, are you alright?
Looking up briefly, the girl shook her head. 'I'm in such a mess.'

'Oh, no, what's happened?'

'I don't know if I'll be seeing Franz again. I've been getting him down, he said, going on about getting my little boy back all the time.' She sniffed, pulling her handkerchief from her pocket. 'He told me he's got enough of a headache with his corporal, without me moaning all the time.'

'I'm sorry. He probably didn't mean it, perhaps he was just having a bad day.'

'I don't know, maybe.'

'If you finish with him, at least your mother-in-law might soften up a bit at least.'

'Oh, I doubt it. If I wasn't expecting his kid, she might have but not now. Whichever way I turn I'm stuck, really.'

She looked up at Ellen with her tear-stained face all pink and puckered. 'I don't want to lose him, Ellie! And look at me, I can't come with you, not in this state. It won't do any good anyway. As soon as she sets eyes on me, she'll start shouting. Really, I daren't go again. You don't have to go either. Why should you speak up for me, eh?'

'I promised I would go, Lucy, so I will. I could try at least.' What had come over her? She didn't quite know because the chance was there to walk away and not become involved. But it was almost as if another mindset had taken over. She wasn't sure at all what she was going to say and not knowing the woman, had no idea how the mother-in-law would react, but she felt a new strength welling up inside her. 'At least let me go and see what she's got to say, eh? She's a mother too, after-all, just like you. And I can check that Charlie's alright while I'm there. Have you brought some of his clean clothes?'

'Yes, they're here,' replied Lucy miserably, handing over her shopping bag. 'But Ellie, be careful!'

'I will! Wish me luck!' she called over her shoulder as she went striding away.

Lucy waved back, crossing her fingers.

It was a pretty granite cottage where the woman lived. There was no pavement, so she walked along on the other side, keeping close to the wall in case any vehicles came hurtling past. When she saw the name of the cottage, she crossed over, her heart pounding at double speed, as she opened the rusty gate. Approaching the front door, a dog started barking from somewhere indoors and realising that her presence had been announced, Ellen took a deep breath and tapped on the door. She heard some bolts being drawn back and it was opened by a kindly looking woman with a weather-beaten face and sharp eyes which betrayed a rather guarded welcome. There was understandably an element of fear if any unknown person called at the door. It wasn't like the old days before the war, when doors were left unlocked, and no one felt insecure. The lady had the door open just wide enough to frame her face. The dog was barking frantically behind her.

'Could I come in a moment please?'

'What's it about? I'm not buying anything.'

'I'm sorry to disturb you. It's about Charlie.'

'You're from the Welfare, is it? I don't want no one interfering, he's doing alright.'

'No, I'm not, nothing like that. My name's Ellen, I'm a friend of his mum, that's all. She sent me with some of his clean clothes. She thought you would need them.'

'Mmm... she's right there. Certainly, hard to get hold of any baby clothes at the moment. She's not with you, is she?'

'No, she's not feeling too well today.'

'Huh! Isn't she! Well, I suppose you'd better come in.'

Ellen found herself in a practical kitchen, where some vegetables were in the process of being cut up on a large pine table. Attempting to stroke the little dog, a Jack Russell who had quickly quietened down and was actually quite friendly, she glanced about for signs of Charlie. There were some toy cars on the stone floor, but no child.

'Is he well? I'd love to see him, just for a minute or two.'

'He's upstairs, having his nap. Where are the clothes then?'

'Oh, here!' Ellen reached into the bag and retrieved the small pile of little boy's clothes, rompers and vests. These she placed next to the chopping board on the pine table. They were neatly folded, and Ellen imagined how Lucy had so lovingly washed and dried them.

'Thank you, dear.' She clicked her tongue. 'Huh! I can see there's some good in her then. What the girl's playing at I don't know.

'She loves her little boy and misses him you know.'

'Does she now! Poor little mite, he's got a lot to get used to.

'The thing is, I work with Lucy at the bakery you see. She wanted me to tell you how sorry she is the way things have worked out. Couldn't you consider giving him back to her? She misses him so much. A baby boy needs his mum. She doesn't want to lose him, and she's so upset. She'd do anything to have him home.'

'Anything, eh?' replied the woman, regarding Ellen sceptically.

'She's been crying her eyes out. Please, won't you - '

'How does she think I feel, the little madam? And now you come to mention it – how does she think Charlie is feeling? It's bad enough him losing his daddy, going off to war, without his mummy going off with a flaming German!'

Ellen blushed. It was all true. She knew her argument was hopeless. Looking the woman in the eye, she said, 'Between you and me, I don't think Lucy realised what she was getting herself into.'

'Huh! She's a right one; the little hussy! Always has been. I've heard all about her goings on, y'know. How she leaves him on his own of an evening to go mooching around with her lover boy. So, you work with her, do you? What do *you* think of her? Forgetting her husband's away fighting for his country and there she goes, flirting about with them soldiers, eh? She's told you she's pregnant by that man, eh?'

'Yes, she has. She's got herself into a bit of a mess. I just wish -'

'You wish what? That she'd seen more sense? Seen what her behaviour looks like to us decent folk. I know why they do it, those girls, getting themselves all dolled up and flashing their eyelashes at the soldiers. The soldiers spoil them rotten, give them luxuries we can only dream about. It's my Pete I feel sorry for. How's he going to feel when he comes home – if he ever

A Sea of Barbed Wire

comes home, poor lad. Can't go away without his wife going off with the likes of people like that.'

'I understand, but just so that I can put her mind at rest, do you think I could see him? Just for a minute.'

Without replying, but sighing in despair, the woman gestured for Ellen to follow her. 'You can see him, just so you can tell her he's kept clean and comfortable, and she can't go reporting me to the welfare. But she's not having him back. Not after what she's done.'

Following her up the stairs, Ellen peered in through the bedroom door to see Charlie and he was fast asleep. Rosy cheeked, with his little hands clutching a teddy bear, he looked so tiny tucked up in an adult's bed it brought the tears to her eyes.

The woman told her, when they were back downstairs, that it had been his father's bedroom when he was a boy, and that Charlie was now sleeping in his own father's bed. This thought gave her a lump in the throat. To think that the war had all come down on the tiny shoulders of this poor little boy. When they were standing by the front-door, Ellen asked: 'Have you heard from your son, Peter?'

'No, dear, nothing. Not a letter, not a Red Cross message, nor a telegram, nothing. And God help me if a telegram comes.' She made a sign of the cross and her eyes moistened in an instant.

'I'm so sorry about everything. I hope you hear from him soon, really I do.'

The woman nodded. 'Thanks. Bye, dear, and thanks for bringing the clothes.

Her departure was one of sadness for both of them, knowing they were at a loss as to what would happen next. Leaving the cottage and beginning to walk back, she was feeling a complete failure, no longer sure whose side she was on or what she could report back to Lucy.

Chapter 29

The islanders' rations had been cut again. There was now virtually no protein in their diets. The lack of fats, oils, and meat resulted in their skin becoming dry and sore, their nails brittle and they had little energy. Tired and bored of the relentless diet of vegetables, their stomachs felt pinched, having little of substance to eat.

Meg was cooking in the kitchen when Albert came in the backdoor.

'You're home early, dear. Something wrong?'

'Not really. We're just running so low on supplies of medicines there wasn't much more I could do today. Even basic things like eardrops are gone. I don't know how the hospital is managing.' He took off his coat and hanging it up on the door, lowered himself into the armchair with a deep sigh. Meg sprinkled more flour on the table and continued rolling out her pastry.

'What's cooking? I'm looking forward to my dinner tonight, that's for sure.'

'Turnip and cheese pie, if this turns out alright. That's the last of the cheese now.'

'You do well, coping with so little, love. It'll be good to eat I'm sure, whatever it is.'

'Oh Bert, it's so difficult feeding you all, it's as much as I can do to keep going.'

'I know, but you're doing a grand job, love. You do your best, and that's all any of us can do, eh? Now, where's your mother?'

'She's gone to visit one of her farming friends. She's hoping to get a few eggs or some meat. Mother's bearing up very well I must say, after losing my father and now their home too. She's made of stronger stuff than me.'

'Meg,' he ventured, anxious to voice the question which had been on his mind for days. Lowering his voice deliberately in case he was overheard by the subject of his concern. 'Is it too much for you with Lukasz here? Should we try to move him again?'

The mood changed instantly.

'And where could he go? Tell me that!' she snapped. This obviously wasn't the reaction he had been expecting.

'Ssh! I just wondered if there's somewhere else. If he could go and stay with someone, just for a while. It would take the burden off your shoulders, dear. I don't know, perhaps one of your mother's friends would -'

'And put even more souls in danger? No dear. I'm sorry but it wouldn't be fair. We took him on and we have to see it through. Either that, or we turn him out on the street to the mercy of the soldiers.'

Albert turned away, defeated by the determination of his wife. But it didn't alleviate the feeling he had lately that they were all sinking slowly into oblivion, without any notion of when the occupation would cease and bring an end to their anxiety.

That evening, Ellen was out walking with Robert. It was dark and cold and there weren't many places they could go where they could relax and talk. The couple wandered hand in hand along a lane close to the coastal path, keeping an eye out for soldiers and signs declaring 'not entry'. Their mood was sombre. As usual Robert was tired after his day at the bank, but he slipped an arm around her waist and told her things would soon get better. But the uneventful grinding on of the war, the relentless propaganda issued by the Germans and the monotonous diet was taking its toll. When Ellen mentioned their struggle to obtain enough food, Robert said he would see what he could do. He told her he didn't use what rations he was allowed, but she thought he was exaggerating especially as he was looking so pale and thin.

No amount of consoling from him would set her mind at rest. She felt restless and anxious and finally had to say what was on her mind: 'You know, Rob, if my parents didn't have Lukasz to feed,' she whispered, 'it would help make the food go a little further.'

Robert looked at her and pushed his glasses up into place as they constantly worked their way down his nose. He swept a hand across his forehead, clearing away his fringe of flopping hair the way he always did when he was thinking.

'If you didn't have him, yes, where else were you thinking he could go?'

'Rob! I know it's risky but would you be able to take him for a while?'

'Me? Where on earth would I put him?' he clapped a hand over his mouth, realising he'd spoken so loudly. 'But I've only got a couple of rooms, you know I have.'

'Yes, I know, stupid of me. I'm afraid, that's all. My parents are under so much pressure. It's so worrying.'

'Ellie, the war won't go on forever. There's talk of it coming to an end in a few months. Just hang on and I'll try to get you some more supplies. You can't give up now. Look at it this way. If he was still a prisoner, I doubt he'd still be alive. The pitiful state those men are in, you've seen them, haven't you? It makes me sick to see them, they're treated worse than animals.'

He began to talk to her about their future, when the war was over, they could do this and do that. Instead of cheering her up it almost made her cry. He told her about how friends and neighbours would return from England after the occupation was over, how they would be full of stories about their lives in the houses they had been sent to. How the schoolchildren would arrive back, looking so much older and taller, and how their parents would barely recognise them. The picture he described was of everything returning to normal, of Guernsey being free of the Germans at last and the war being over. Finally, he said how happy Lukasz would be, being able to return home to Poland. The finality of it all took her by surprise. Of course, Lukasz would be gone. He was right. Lukasz would be gone out of their lives, safe and free; that was how it should be. However, suddenly she was weeping openly. She couldn't stop.

'But it won't happen, Rob! Don't you see? It won't be like it used to be, we won't be the same people, we won't be able to just snap back to how we were before the war. Everything will have changed. Look at us! How can we pretend we're a normal courting couple and everything is going to be alright when it can't be! How can it be? We'll never be the same. How can we be, after all that has happened?'

'Darling! Don't upset yourself. We'll be alright, you'll see. Trust me. Once the war is over, we'll soon get back on our feet again. The island will start to recover and –'

'No! No Rob! It won't ever be the same!' Ellen cried, rushing away from him, a tumult of emotion choking her. She just had to get away. She needed time to think, to be by herself and get a sense of perspective. The trauma of Lukasz shut up for hours on end in the cellar, the danger of giving her secrets away. The tension she felt made her unable to talk naturally and it had all built up until she felt fit to burst. Leaving him behind, she went hurrying on alone down the coastal path, the sea and the waves crashing against the rocks below her. Without heeding the danger, let alone the thorns and brambles tearing at her clothes, she was running, just running. It was so dark she could hardly see where she was going.

'Ellie!' Robert's voice came above the wind, 'Wait! Listen to me!' He was running after her and when he caught up with her, he grabbed her. Desperately holding her firmly by the arms, he pleaded, 'Forget the war. Forget the future. Forget Lukasz and everyone else! All that matters is that we have each other, doesn't it? I'm in love with you, Ellie! Can't you see that? I'll look after you. We'll be alright.' He released her, panting and catching his breath. 'Marry me, darling! Will you marry me? I'll look after you and everything will be alright. I promise!'

But something had died within her. She couldn't explain it. She looked at him through her tears and it was as if he was a million miles away. It was as if he was a stranger to her. And she found herself shaking her head. 'I'm sorry,' she said. A new energy, a feeling of being a new person, had entered her soul – so much energy she couldn't contain it. She felt she could have run and run away from him forever.

'I don't know, Rob, I don't know how I feel at the moment - about you or anything.' He staggered back as if he had been struck. He was staring at her, looking utterly shocked. The wind whipped around them, stealing any last fragment of warmth. Robert took a deep breath and appeared to draw on his professional manner when he said:

'I apologise. You've been under a lot of strain lately, of course you have. Let me walk you home. You'll be better at home. It's no wonder you're upset. Come now, you're overtired and hungry, I understand. I should never have said that, not now.'

He came forward, put his arm around her and drew her to him, holding her tenderly. It was the closest they had ever been. She felt the warmth of his body through his shirt and pressed her face against his shoulder. His embrace reminded her of her father, of what it meant to have security and the innocent childhood she used to enjoy, where there were no problems, and nothing was complicated. So she relented, but her mind was blank. It was as if she was so alone in the world she felt as if no-one knew her. Then she thought of Lukasz, quiet, strong, passionate Lukasz, who was hidden away in the dark cellar and waiting, waiting for her. Waiting for his life to begin again.

Waiting interminably for his freedom, like a caged animal.

'The thing is, Rob, I don't know who I am anymore,' she said, stepping back. 'It's the war I suppose. I don't know what it is.' Hardly daring to look at him, in one swift glance she saw him straighten his tie, compose himself as if he had been insulted by a customer at the bank. She knew she was being unkind, but she couldn't help herself. Honesty, truthfulness had taken hold of her.

'I don't know if I'm ready to think about getting married. When the war's over, we'll all be free to do things again, to go where we want, to start our lives afresh. It doesn't feel right just to get married and settle down when we've been given our freedom back.' There was nothing she could think of to say that would make it sound better. But a sense of relief came over her. 'I'm sorry. I suppose it's just all the worry. Everything's so difficult. Life isn't like it used to be. You do understand, don't you?' Even with those few words, she was able to stop crying and began to feel herself again. She felt stronger.

Robert stood with his hands in his trouser pockets, regarding her with an expression fluctuating between sadness and confusion. Their walk abandoned, he wandered away. It occurred to her how much he must depend on her. She was, she realised, apart from the bank and his work, the only source of joy in his life. Overcome with shame, she was filled with pity for him. Going after him, she gave him a hug and said she was sorry; she kissed him on the cheek as if he was the big brother she had never had. He smiled sadly, and told her not to worry, that they were both feeling the pressure and that everything would be alright. But having opened her heart to him, she didn't want it all to slip back, for it be to him like a lover's tiff and for everything to go on as normal. Terrible as it may seem, she realised that at Robert's expense she had just made herself feel a lot better.

They found themselves walking back the way they had come. Where their paths crossed, he stopped. 'I won't walk home with you after all, if that's alright. I've got some paperwork to do but I'll see you soon, eh?'

She stood watching him walk away and was ready to wave but he didn't once turn round.

When he had gone, she dried her eyes. Took a deep breath and looked up, hearing a plane soaring overhead. All she could see were the lights twinkling. It could be a German plane making for the airport or an RAF plane risking a flight low over the island and dropping some leaflets. The war was continuing, the world was still spinning. And for the first time in ages, she felt in control of her life again.

Chapter 30

Rumours were becoming spiteful and dangerous. Because the Occupying Forces were offering rewards for information, informers among the local island community were more a danger to the family than the soldiers themselves. At least they could see the soldiers and hear them coming. Islanders were tempted by the Germans' enticements, for example they were given cigarettes, chocolate, meat, and money in exchange for information which would betray people. A note, a letter posted through the German Headquarters' door, or an anonymous tip-off could mean the end for all of them.

Such incentives unfortunately were very tempting to some and, if taken up, made life easier for them. Everyone needed extras to add to their meagre rations, as many were at starvation point. Revealing secrets to the enemy however: the location of black-market traders, names of those who stole supplies from the German stores or fuel from the Germans' vehicles, or those who concealed wireless and crystal sets – for these unscrupulous islanders it offered rich pickings. Since listening to or owning a wireless set had been banned again, and all the wireless sets on the island collected up and stored, it was difficult to believe that the world news they read in the German controlled and censored local newspapers was true; in fact, they knew it wasn't. So much of the news about the war, and the advance of the German Army, and their success in battle was pure fiction, fabricated by the Third Reich. The truth was that the German army was losing men by the thousand, and their planes suffered huge losses under fire from the Allies. But tragically, many lives were being lost on the Allies' side too, not only soldiers but also civilians who were suffering bombing raids on English cities. When such news filtered through, the fact that so many islanders had sought refuge there and sent their children away to what they believed was the safety of England, filled them with dismay.

A few days after Ellen and Robert had had their heart-to-heart, and she had refused his proposal of marriage, she was at home quietly sewing a button on her skirt for work when her mother said: 'So what do you make of what they're saying now about Dora?'

'That she won't be able to stay open much longer, you mean?' asked Joan. 'Stock is so low in there now, it's pitiful to see.'

'Worse than that, Mother. I thought you might have heard. Someone's reported her for keeping some stuff back under the counter, for, well, you know, like she has for us. Anyway, some bright spark has informed on her, and the Germans were everywhere when I went past, searching her shop and storeroom, turning everything upside down.'

'That poor woman! Why? What were they looking for?' Joan looked alarmed. 'And who would do such a thing? She's got a heart of gold.'

'They won't find anything, will they Mum?' asked Ellen. 'You know, sometimes she saves us a few eggs or a tin of custard powder. And she gave me a lovely bar of soap once – but they're such small things. That wouldn't be enough to make them go and arrest her, would it?'

Meg looked at her with raised eyebrows. 'They'll dream up a reason and exaggerate it out of all proportion. It's their idea of setting an example; good behaviour, obedience to the Commandant, whatever they like to call it. In actual fact they're bored and glad of something to do probably. It doesn't take much to rub a German up the wrong way, does it. They can charge Dora with dealing in black market goods but if she's innocent, how is she going to prove it? You can't expect to get a receipt from a thief! The soldiers can say and do what they like really.'

'But she's such a dear lady! I hope she's alright. Who would do such a thing as to report her?'

'Walls have ears, as they say! There are plenty who would drop a note into the German HQ if it meant there was something in it for them. People aren't just becoming suspicious, they're bored too, and envious. In fact, they're bitter against anyone who gets a bit extra.'

'But who though?'

'Just people. There are more on the island than you'd imagine writing those sorts of letters. Dora probably has her enemies like anyone else, especially in business. A lad who's been caught thieving, perhaps, or someone with a grudge who thinks she's making a bit of money on the side. Who knows?'

Ellen felt nervous. Danger, it seemed was around every corner. 'What will happen to her, Mum, if they do discover something that they think she shouldn't have?'

'She'll be arrested, taken away, and the next we'll hear – if we're lucky – is there'll be a trial. Let's hope it doesn't come to that.'

The room fell silent. As she sewed, concentrating on threading the needle, her hand shook slightly. She grew increasingly afraid. If anyone informed the Germans about Lukasz … Her heart nearly missed a beat. Laying aside the skirt and mumbling that she'd forgotten something, she rushed upstairs. But she hadn't been in her bedroom for more than a few minutes when she heard her mother coming up the stairs and a slight tap on the door.

'Is everything alright, love?' she asked, coming into her room. 'Don't go worrying yourself over Dora, she's an honest woman. I'm sure they won't find anything she would do deliberately that they could accuse her of. A few extra bits held back for her customers doesn't mean she's trading on the black-market.'

'But you admitted yourself, they can invent things. We don't know where we stand if there's no truth in anything anymore!' Ellen was standing looking out of the window as she often did when she was thinking. Her room was at the back of the house and from there she could look across the back gardens to the fields. Beyond them, the sea ran like a blue ribbon and although it was misty that afternoon, on a fine day she could see the dark shadows on the horizon of the island of Sark. Memories of happier times, when she was a child free to play outside, to explore the beaches for tiny creatures and treasures washed up by the tide seemed such a long time ago.

A Sea of Barbed Wire

Her mother was sitting on the edge of the bed. 'Ellie, you haven't been yourself lately, I can't help noticing. Is anything wrong?'

Ellen turned and saw the concern in her mother's face.

'No, Mum, nothing's wrong. I'm fine honestly. I was just upset hearing about Dora, that's all.'

'But you've been so quiet. And you haven't seen much of Robert at all lately, have you?'

Sometimes her mother knew her more than she knew herself.

'No, we went for a walk the other day but …' Ellen was fiddling with her hair, twisting it round and round on her finger. 'I'm not feeling very happy, but none of us are. We don't know how long the war is going to go on for and everything's so …so uncertain.' She bit her lip. If only she could pour her heart out to her mum about what she was really feeling.

'You've had a row with Robert, haven't you.'

'No! I mean, yes, well not exactly a row but sort of.'

'We're all under strain at the moment. It's only natural for a young couple like yourselves to have a tiff occasionally. Don't worry, in a few days you'll have forgotten all about it.'

But Ellen was shaking her head. 'I've got to tell you. He proposed to me, Mum. I didn't expect it, it's much too soon and I hardly know him really. Honestly, I didn't mean to hurt him; it was just so sudden.'

'So you turned him down, darling?'

She nodded. Putting her arms around her, Meg tried to comfort her. 'Haven't you always said you should follow your heart? Well, you did. Don't feel bad about it. Robert's an understanding young man, he'll come round.'

'I don't know, maybe.'

Several minutes passed and she hadn't realised how long she had been deep in thought while Meg all the time had been watching the expressions flitting across her daughter's troubled face.

'Knowing Robert, he'll be anxious too, I expect. He's probably thinking he's blown his chances. The best thing to do is for both of you not to think about the future too much until the war is over.' Saying this, her mother smoothed her hair and hugged her again. 'It's alright, love, I understand. You will have moments like this, but it will pass. Don't worry, you'll feel much better tomorrow.'

Chapter 31

At the end of the day, it became a custom for Lukasz to join them in the sitting-room. He usually sat passively, listening to them talking but rarely attempting to speak himself. Albert often complained about the shortage of medicines, insulin and first aid equipment in the pharmacy and at the hospital. Their usual conversation was about rumours they had heard and food, or rather the lack of it. Food was a topic returned to again and again as almost everyone on the island, even the German soldiers themselves, were always hungry. Sometimes the locals had news to tell each other, for instance: where to buy certain items that they sorely missed like washing-powder, thread for mending their clothes, candles and tea. There was a thriving black market for certain unobtainable goods, but the family weren't tempted, neither could they afford the prices being demanded which were astronomical. Various remedies and substitutes were discussed, quite imaginative ideas emerged for things like toothpaste, hand cream, and coffee. These ideas and recommendations often made them laugh. Albert seemed to enjoy having Lukasz present, and he would cast an appreciative eye towards Lukasz occasionally. He liked having some male company "in a house full of women" as he often referred to it. Lukasz was beginning to pick up a few more words and was sometimes able to join in the conversation or at the very least, understand a joke.

Ellen sat apart, under the light of a candle, mending some clothes or reading. From there she liked to watch Lukasz, while her mother, father and Nan chatted away about various domestic problems and gossip they had heard. Joan often mentioned her house, what it looked like now as she went past, and wondering if she would ever get it back. Sometimes she went to visit her horse which was being stabled with her friends, Jack and his wife, on the neighbouring farm. There she could check her over, muck out the stable and take her out for exercise. On such visits she learnt a lot of what was going on at her house, as her friends lived only a short distance away.

'So Lukasz,' Albert began one night. 'What did you grow on your father's farm at home?'

His command of English was improving and he smiled, his eyes growing distant, as if the question brought back memories of happier times. He spoke slowly, thinking through every word.

'We grow wheat, barley. We have much land. I do the fishing. My uncle, he help us. He have boat. We go at night. Plenty fish. Plenty, plenty fish. My uncle live near forest. He cut big trees. I work hard, timber, load on wagon with horses. Big horses. They very strong.'

'That sounds like hard work, eh?'

'Yes. It hard. Sometimes the sea. Sometimes the land. I like very much to work.'

Ellen wanted to know more. 'Do you live near your uncle?'

A Sea of Barbed Wire

He shook his head. 'No, no, we live city, Kolberg. I get train. We go together. Me, my father. Early morning.'

'Then the Germans came?' asked Albert. 'A rough business, eh?'

'Yes, yes. One day we work the land, we hear soldiers come. We run. Straight away they shoot my father. They take my sister, tear her clothes. I hear she cry.' He clenched his fist and hammered it down on his thigh and such a dark shadow came over his face Ellen could see the anger and terror in his eyes.

'I not see no more. They throw me in lorry. They tie me here, and here.' He wrapped a fist around his wrist and swept his hands across his ankles. He was choking on his words and Ellen put down her sewing. Getting up, she lay a comforting arm around his shoulders.

Meg cleared her throat. 'Lukasz is alright, Ellen. Go and sit down.'

She did so, hating to be spoken to like a child.

'We there in prison long time,' he continued, fighting back emotion. 'One day, they come - shout at us, get up. We go on ship. Sick on there, very bad. It dark, it cold. No food. No water. My friends die. Many friends die. I come here. We work. No sleep. We hungry. If we not work, they beat us. If we not strong to work, they shoot, they kill.'

Lukasz stopped talking abruptly. It was silent in the room as if they were all holding their breath.

'In Poland, you said they shot your father?'

'Yes. Dead, yes.' He nodded, scraping a hand across his face.

'Well, you're here with us now,' said Meg, abruptly. She evidently didn't want to hear any more.

Albert frowned at her. 'We'll do what we can for you, lad. But we can't guarantee to keep you safe. The Germans could come at any time, you know that.'

Lukasz nodded. 'I thank you very much. But it not safe for you. I go soon. I swim, I go back.'

Meg pulled a face, stood up and said it was time for a cup of tea. As she passed him, she patted him on the back, a gesture of reassurance but also in a way indicating the end of the conversation. But Ellen was distraught to hear his story and impatient to learn more. She asked him to describe the house where he used to live, and about his mother.

To her surprise, Lukasz turned to her. 'You have sister? You have brother?'

'No,' she replied. 'There's just me.' She smiled at her mother who had returned with the tray of cups and even a few dry biscuits on a plate.

'You and Irena, you like my Irena. My sister, she teacher. She go to the work in – how you say –?' He demonstrated with his hand, indicating the height of a small child.

'A nursery perhaps?'

He shrugged and nodded. 'If she safe, I not know. I write the letters. One day. I give her the letters.' He turned and looked at Albert. 'Thank you, Sir. I stay here. If not for you, I be dead. I think, soon I go home.'

'Lukasz, listen to me,' said Meg, who stood there waiting for the kettle to boil with her arms folded. 'It won't be possible for you to go home. Not until the war is over.'

A Sea of Barbed Wire

'It okay. I go – it alright – I swim. I strong now.' He smiled. Ellen saw such a genuine warm smile full of hope for the future and it tore at her heart.

Joan had been quiet all this time, but suddenly she spoke up. 'There's a lot of sympathy for men like Lukasz.' She looked at Albert, almost fiercely. 'I've been making some enquiries. You're not the only ones who want to help people like him. I think I know someone who could be prepared to have him and look after him for a bit and give you all a break. My friends, Jack and Myrtle, have the space. And more importantly, I trust them.' She turned to Lukasz. 'It would be better for you, dear, they have a farm and they're good people.'

Lukasz looked confused.

'Would you ask them? That would be a help, wouldn't it Meg? And no risk to him, you think?' asked Albert.

'No more of a risk than you're taking yourselves.'

Lukasz had been excluded from the conversation. He looked on, while they talked about him as if he was no longer in the room. He was glancing from one to the other, aware that whatever they were saying involved him. Ellen sympathised, understanding his fear but unable to do anything. She was struggling to work out what this might mean for him. The implications were dangerous. Meg was busy with dishes in the kitchen, and the relaxed atmosphere of companionship had evaporated from the room. Contemplating moving Lukasz between houses yet again was the last thing Ellen wanted.

An hour or so later, when Albert had retired to bed early, Lukasz had returned to the cellar and Meg and Joan were upstairs getting ready for bed, Ellen heard a noise outside. She peeped round the blackout curtain, and by the light of the moon she saw Robert coming up the path pushing his bicycle. Being during black-out and after the curfew hour, he had no lights. Rushing to open the door, she gasped as the clatter of it falling against the wall shattered the still night air. He came in breathless and flustered.

'Oh, Rob! What are you doing out at this time of night?'

'I thought I might as well use the bike while I still had it.' His voice sounded strangely aloof.

'But now? You've come so late. You could be arrested, Robert!'

'Well, apparently the Germans have demanded a hundred and fifty bikes, and if they don't get them there will be reprisals.' He sank into an armchair, sighed, and dragging off his thick glasses, he mumbled, 'I'll take mine down in the morning.' He was looking utterly exhausted.

'But they must make allowances for people like you. Your job is important.'

Robert shook his head. 'I don't think they care.' He put his head back and closed his eyes.

'Have you eaten? You look pale, Rob and look at you; you've lost weight again.' His suit no longer seemed to fit him properly at all, and his shoulders looked so small as to be almost feeble. Robert usually dressed smartly for his job, but his tie was thin and knotted too tight, his shirt collar frayed, and his hair had grown long over his collar. Whatever else was happening, he was faithful to the bank, punctual, hardworking, and committed. However, for the first time Ellen saw his vulnerability.

Robert still had his eyes closed and was breathing heavily; she thought he was asleep. As she passed by to go to the kitchen, she patted his head as she would an old dog. 'Shall I make you a cup of tea?'

He opened his eyes suddenly and looked up at her. 'Ellie, do you love me?'

Caught completely off guard, she felt as if he had read her thoughts. She blushed. Instead of answering straight away she sat down next to him and took his hand in hers. His was a pale hand, accustomed to holding a fountain pen, sorting files, counting out notes, typing. His fingernails weren't well manicured as they once were, his fingertips were stained with ink and the cuffs of his shirt were scuffed and dirty. When she glanced up at his face, he was looking at her intently, his short-sighted eyes unfocussed and bloodshot. He was staring at her.

Wanting to love him as much as he needed her to, she replied quietly and without conviction, 'Yes, of course I do, Rob, it's just that …' She didn't finish the sentence. He leant forward and kissed her on the cheek. 'Then everything will be alright,' he said, 'trust me.'

'It's so late, Rob, why did you come here tonight when you're so dead tired?'

'I needed to see you, to hear you say that. I feel better now. Tomorrow I'll hand over my bike to the Germans. Then it won't be so easy for me to see you in the evenings, but don't worry, my sweet, I'll work something out.'

Standing up quickly, as if his mission was accomplished, he went straight to the door. Barely wishing her goodnight, he was outside, picking up his bicycle and pushing it down the path. She stood there in the darkness, watching him go and shivering. He never even looked back.

Chapter 32

The following day, when the girls arrived for work, George told them the deliveries hadn't arrived. There was such little flour left he told them to do what they could and if no more supplies came, they could take the rest of the day off. The work kept them busy all morning but by noon the ingredients had virtually run out. They had baked less than half of what was required but, with nothing else he could give them to do, George sent them home.

Ellen, arriving back much earlier than usual, found the house empty. She was relieved. Running upstairs, she changed hastily and went to lift the carpet so she could talk to Lukasz about what the family had been discussing the night before. Rolling the rug aside she tapped on the trapdoor, calling his name and waiting for him to push on the heavy door from below. There wasn't a sound.

'Lukasz are you there?' she called, lifting the door an inch and calling down the cellar steps. A cold draught met her. She opened the door, lifting it back, heavy as it was, and she didn't have the strength she used to have. Was he ill? 'Lukasz! Lukasz!' she called urgently. Then she stepped down slowly onto the steps, shining the torch into the darkness. He wasn't there. It was not only empty, but there was no sign that he had ever been there. She stood and stared in amazement and shock. He had gone but it didn't make sense. Trying to calm herself and stem the rising panic she felt inside, her thoughts went back to the previous evening. There was no sign that the Germans had ransacked the house. It was all neat and tidy. She took a deep breath and sighed. It was Nan! But so soon?

When her father came home a few hours later, Ellen was in the sitting room, sewing. She pretended to be totally absorbed in what she was doing but her heart was racing.

'Hello love, no work today then? Where is everyone?'

'I don't know Dad. George gave us the afternoon off because the deliveries haven't arrived. You're home early.'

'Same problem George has, love. No point in hanging around waiting for a ship that hasn't come in, is there. I could do with something to eat though. Where's your mother?'

Ellen paused before she answered. 'With Nan probably. They'll be out trying to buy something for dinner perhaps,' she replied. She waited, wondering if her father knew what had been going on.

'Shall I put the kettle on? We can have a cup of tea while we wait.' Putting her sewing aside she got up from her chair and was walking into the kitchen when her father said,

'Go and see if the lad wants one too, will you, love?'

Ellen stopped and turned. 'So you don't know? Lukasz isn't there, Dad.'

'Not there? Are you sure? Where the devil's he gone?'

A Sea of Barbed Wire

'I went to see him when I got home, and the cellar's empty. There's no sign of him; all his stuff has gone too.' It was all she could do not to burst into tears. Going into the kitchen to make the tea, she noticed there was a slice of cake on a plate. It wasn't a cake her mother would normally make; for a start it had icing on it. Real icing! It had that delicious golden colour that sponge cakes used to have. Also, it wasn't on one of their own plates, but on a pretty, decorated plate. She hadn't seen anything so appetising for years.

'Dad, look at this!' she said, carrying it through.

'Well, that's a vision, eh? Whoever baked that must know something we don't – or should I say someone...'

'Mum must have had a visitor. It could have been one of Nan's friends maybe.' By this time her heart was thumping. They had been and taken Lukasz away, she knew it.

'I don't suppose we ought to eat it,' said Albert, eyeing the delicacy.

'I'm not hungry,' replied Ellen. In fact, she felt sick. Gradually piecing together a story, she concluded that Lukasz had been taken and in his place they had left a piece of cake. A sort of weird exchange. What a strange thing. 'I think Nan's been and taken him, Dad.'

'Well, they could've let us know,' Albert complained. Those two must have taken it on themselves to move him; well, would you believe it! Women!' He didn't sound very pleased, in fact he sounded annoyed. Filling the kettle, Ellen's mind was entertaining all kinds of possibilities. So many questions ran through her head. Where would they have taken him? Who would be sympathetic enough to risk it? How would they have transported him now Nan didn't have easy access to the horse and cart?

When she came back into the sitting-room with the tea, her father was sitting in the armchair flicking through the Guernsey Evening Press. 'Be a fine thing if the Germans have been and taken him. Oh, I don't know, who can you trust these days? There are enough fools out there who'll do anything for a few cigarettes or a nice cut of meat!'

Ellen tried to steady her nerves. 'I think we would have heard if the Germans had come, Dad. None of his things are down there, even the old clothes he was wearing when he arrived.'

'You're right. If they'd been in, all hell would've broken loose. And they wouldn't leave us a nice slice of cake either.' He was shaking his head. 'Oh, it'll be your nan, meddling as usual.'

'I expect she was only trying to help, Dad.' Ellen was stirring the teapot thoughtfully. 'Nan usually knows what she's doing. She wouldn't put Lukasz or any of us in danger.' She surprised herself as words of reassurance poured out of her, which reflected nothing of the tumult of uncertainty she was feeling inside.

An hour went by and neither her mother nor nan had returned. The tension in the house was palpable. On an impulse Ellen decided to go for a walk. There were plenty of people about, soldiers and locals alike. Some soldiers appeared to be off duty, and a group of them were hanging around talking to some locals and chatting to the children, handing out sweets. She hurried on past, but a shout went up and as Ellen turned her head Lucy came hurrying towards her.

A Sea of Barbed Wire

'Ellie, wait! Come on, let me introduce you to Franz. He'd like to meet you.'

'Oh no, I don't think I should.' Her face flushed with embarrassment, and she stepped up her pace and carried on walking.

'Please,' pleaded Lucy. 'I've told him you're my best friend. He won't believe me if you don't come over and say hello.'

Seeing her look so offended made Ellen feel awful and she hesitated. In that moment, Lucy assumed she had changed her mind. Within minutes, she found herself chatting on the street corner with them as any gathering of young people would. Franz was dressed in his uniform, but he was evidently off duty; he had his shirt open, and his jacket was slung across his shoulder even though the weather was cold. His piercing blue eyes struck her as amazingly shrewd. As he draped his arm across Lucy's shoulders affectionately, she could do nothing else but utter a greeting. Lucy began to chatter in the light-hearted way she had, and it was easy for Ellen to forget that she was standing conversing with the enemy. He didn't look like an enemy, she had to admit.

Franz didn't say much, but when he introduced himself, his English was precise even though his accent was sharp. It didn't surprise her that Lucy had fallen head over heels in love with him. His blue eyes were captivating, and with his fresh complexion and ready smile he was the opposite of everything she associated with the cruelty of war. If he hadn't been wearing the German uniform, he could have been any handsome young man visiting the island. There wasn't a hint of malice in him that she could detect. He had a good sense of humour and all he seemed interested in was his girl – Lucy. His eyes danced in merriment when she was talking – he seemed absolutely besotted with her.

After a few minutes, Ellen made an excuse and left them, but as she walked away, she found herself envying their fun-loving relationship. So all Lucy's earlier fears about losing him were unfounded; you could feel the affection between them. There was much talk about how such girls will be punished when the war is over. But she couldn't join the locals in condemning their love. They were young people, forced together by circumstances in an attempt to forget their hardship, and discovered each other as a source of comfort when there wasn't much else to bring happiness into their lives.

She was walking further and further away from the town, longing to escape the situation at home for a few moments. Ahead she noticed there was a bit of an incident going on. She heard loud voices and suddenly, realising what was involved, she became alarmed. A group of soldiers on sentry duty were questioning people who had stopped in a lorry. Suddenly she realised the people the soldiers were shouting at were none other than her mother and Nan.

Turning sharply down a narrow lane, she stopped and hid behind a wall, she tried to observe what was going on. The angry voices of the German military were interspersed with a woman's hysterical voice. But it was a voice she recognised – it was her mother's! Sounding so shrill, Ellen dreaded to think what had happened. She couldn't bear it. How she longed to run out there and help her, but she knew it would be stupid to intervene – anything she said could endanger them

A Sea of Barbed Wire

even more. Without knowing what their story was, the fear of making things worse stopped her in her tracks.

She tried to breathe deeply, calm herself and concentrate on the distant sound of seagulls soaring overhead. The Germans were shouting and demanding something. There was a scuffle and a rush of voices, and then – gunshots. A scream! More shouting and Ellen gasped, forcing her arm against her mouth to muffle her own whimpers of fear. Then vehicles were moving, and the noise of their engines reversing, Ellen didn't wait to see what had happened, but she turned and fled back the way she had come. A sense of unreality had taken over.

She had run quite a long way before she could slow down to catch her breath and pull herself together. Unable to bring herself to face the facts, she just wandered on and on, hardly knowing where she was. It began to get dark. Weak with hunger and anxiety, still she wandered on. Vehicles passed her, driven crazily as usual by soldiers who didn't care. They went speeding by, careering around corners and throwing up dust and debris as they went. There was an old man ahead pushing his bicycle up the hill as the road had grown quite steep. He acknowledged Ellen by nodding and tipping his cap.

Crossing over to speak to him, she asked, 'Could I walk with you a little way? I think I'm lost.'

'I was wondering what a young lady like you was doing out here. Them'll be out lookin' for you. You have to be careful these days, a pretty young lady like yourself, eh?'

She thanked him and they walked on together. His company calmed her, making her doubt what she had witnessed had been real, and whether she had actually seen her mother there at all. He had a large basket attached to his handlebars, loaded with freshly dug potatoes, turnips and bunches of fresh carrots. They had dark moist soil clinging to them and she could smell the goodness in his burden. This was probably why he was pushing his bike rather than riding it. The fresh fragrance of his loaded basket took her mind back to the days when she would go shopping in the marketplace and see the stalls piled high with abundant fruit and vegetables.

'Them are so heavy I can't pedal 'em uphill, eh, not with my old bones.' He winked at her, his weather-beaten face crinkling up in a cheeky smile.

'You grow them yourself?' she asked, not having seen so much good food for a long time.

'Yes, I grow 'em, dear, an' if no-one pinches 'em before I get a chance to dig 'em up then they'll give me an' my dear wife our dinner for a week or two. I'm takin' these to my sister, she's been poorly these last few days.' He paused and looked at Ellen. 'You're lookin' a bit peaky. How far is it till you get home?'

'It's not far, thank you. I know where I am now. I just have to go down there and round the corner.'

'Right then, thought I knew you. You be Albert's child, eh? Here,' he said, reaching into his basket and pulling out two potatoes and a bunch of carrots, 'Got room in that bag of yours, have you? Take these home for your dear mother. You look like you could do wi' somethin' nourishin'.'

Choking back the tears, she thanked him and hurried away.

A Sea of Barbed Wire

When Ellen finally drew near home, she saw with much relief the blackout blinds were drawn so someone must be home. By now she had almost convinced herself that what she had seen earlier wasn't anything to do with her family, that she had been mistaken. But feeling so weak, she could hardly manage to carry her bag, which was weighed down with the vegetables the old man had given her. Opening the back door, she held her breath, listening…

'Is that you, Ellie?' came her mother's voice.

'Oh Mum, you're here! What happened? Are you alright? I saw the soldiers. I heard all the shouting and gunshots! I thought they'd arrested you, Mum, and I …'

'Ellen! Darling, how do you know all this? Where have you been?' Her mother's eyes were alive with astonishment.

'But I don't understand, Mum. Are you alright? And Nan? Where's Nan? Where's Lukasz?' Ellen tried to slow her breathing and calm herself. Then she explained how she came to be walking along the road when she witnessed the scene before her and how she ran to hide. Drying her eyes, she looked around and saw that her father was there in his usual chair. He wasn't reading his newspaper; he was watching her with such a sad expression it brought new waves of fear.

'Where's Nan?' she pleaded, staring at her mother in anguish.

'She's alright, love. We're all safe, don't worry.' And she wrapped her arms around her. Nan's gone to have a lie down. We took Lukasz over to Jack's house and we were on our way back when we were stopped. It's all over now. We're home safe and everything is okay. We would have been alright, but the soldiers waved us down and asked us for our ID. Nan's friend Jack was driving. We all had to climb out. They demanded to see our papers and while we were getting them out one of them started poking about. Jack had his ready to hand over straight away. Nan had hers in her handbag and then mine … I couldn't find mine! I was so nervous.' She trailed off, catching her breath. 'I told the soldiers I must have left my ID card at home but could bring it up to the Grange Lodge tomorrow morning. I even told them they could call at our house later, but they started shouting at me. The more I pleaded, the more irritable they became, you know what they're like. Then suddenly I found my ID and papers. They had fallen out of my pocket onto the floor of the lorry! What a relief!'

'Oh Mum! So wasn't that enough?'

'They were angry at us for wasting their time, they said, or something to that effect. They snatched my papers, looked at them, and flung them back at me – in a temper. One of them raised his gun and fired into the ground at our feet. It scared us half to death. We climbed back in the lorry as fast as we could and Jack started the engine.'

'So they let you drive on?'

'Yes, they waved us on with their rifles. Just as well I don't speak German, I expect the words they were using weren't very polite! Well, it sounds like you witnessed a lot of what happened. I'm so glad you had the sense to stay away. Good girl! We had to laugh about it afterwards. Just think if Lukasz had still been there hiding in the back! She chuckled, the relief so evident in her laugh.

A Sea of Barbed Wire

'But Mum, why did you move him at all? He was alright here, wasn't he?'

'Maybe, but we thought he's better shifted between houses, safer for us, just in case any bright spark has noticed something and feels like reporting us. There's more room on Jack's farm, he'll have some space and get a bit of exercise and daylight. You know Jack does a lot of odd jobs and he's a fisherman too. He'll find Lukasz some work to do too, it'll do him good.'

'But is it safe, Mum? Jack's farm is so close to Nan's.'

Suddenly serious, Meg said, 'As safe as any of us are, love. We have to live. We get by one day at a time.'

Ellen admired her mother then, the way she looked so defiant. These last few days she had been pale and exhausted, defeated, her face drawn under the strain. But she still had her common sense, even though she had aged so much over the last two years; as they all had. Picking up her bag to put it away, Ellen felt the extra weight in it and remembered. 'Oh, I met an old man along the road, and he gave me these to give to you.' She began retrieving the vegetables from her bag and placing them in her hands, soil and all. The fragrance of freshly dug carrots burst into the room.

'Oh, Bert, look at these! Thank you, Ellie. But how kind of him! Who was he? Did he give his name?'

'I didn't think to ask. But I think you must know him Mum, he mentioned dad's name. He had loads of vegetables in his bicycle basket, stuff he'd grown himself. He said he was taking some to give to his sister.'

'I think I know who that was,' she replied but without explaining any further she took the vegetables into the kitchen, and they heard her humming to herself. Perhaps just the prospect of some fresh food to cook had cheered her, or maybe, Ellen wondered, it was the relief of having the responsibility of Lukasz lifted from her shoulders.

Chapter 33

Signs of Christmas began appearing in the shops. The resources of local people were limitless when it came to making the best of things. Paper chains were made by cutting up strips of newspaper and old wrapping paper. Old toys were washed, repaired and displayed on the shop shelves so children wouldn't miss one of the most exciting days of the year. In true island spirit, life continued as close to normal as possible. Gifts for the children were displayed in a colourful array of dolls, building bricks, wooden trains and toy cars. Worn they might be, but cleaned and polished, they looked bright and cheerful, especially if they had been repainted. People collected sugar rations to make toffee and sweets; old teddy bears were washed and spruced-up, and dolls were bathed, and dressed in new clothes handmade from scraps of material.

Fortunately for Dora, and everyone who loved her and depended on her little shop, no evidence was found by the German soldiers who ransacked her premises. After an anonymous tip-off accusing her of trading in black market goods, the shop had been raided, but the soldiers had left empty-handed. But as she said to one of her concerned customers, 'I think they were rather disappointed, in more ways than one, eh? I bet they'd love to have found a stash of cigarettes or a few bottles of brandy!'

So, in her usual cheerful way, she proceeded to decorate the shop with Christmas wrapping paper, dug out from attics and left over from Christmases in the past, and covered the dull wooden shelves. Party clothes and hats had been found and put up for sale. Although her husband no longer had his racing pigeons, all of them having been destroyed, he was there too, busy putting handmade sweets into jars. Among the items on display, set apart from the other second-hand clothes, was Meg's beautiful wedding dress. Dora had strict instructions from Meg that on no account should it be sold to any German soldiers as they were inclined to send luxury goods home. Its presence prompted many a conversation as people could look forward to the spring when traditionally weddings would be a time of celebration.

It was an understanding among the locals that no matter how long it took, they were confident of victory. In spite of what the Germans wanted Guernsey people to believe, with all their propaganda and so-called 'news', no-one believed the stories they published on the front page of The Star and the Guernsey Evening News. Tales of triumphant victories on the battlefield were a bluff; the locals knew differently. Through various means including the secret distribution of GUNS, or a crystal-set which was a home-made radio called 'The cat's whiskers', islanders got to know the truth.

Time had moved on since Ellen went to visit Lucy's mother-in-law, to appeal to her to give little Charlie back to his mother. But the woman had been adamant. Her opinion was that if Lucy chose to mess around with the

Germans and get herself pregnant, she wasn't fit to be a mother to her grandson. War changes some people, makes them bitter and resentful; in others it brings out the camaraderie, the generosity and kindness of heart. Nothing would ever be the same again for Ellen. She was becoming more philosophical, perhaps it was through lack of food, but she didn't feel able to decide about anything. One minute she could see one side, the next she could see the other. Her confusion was showing itself when she least expected it, when those around her were becoming more indignant and resentful. If any serious question was raised, with a shrug of her shoulders she would probably say she didn't know and walk away. In truth, she wasn't coping very well at all. She was torn in her feelings about Lukasz and now it was virtually impossible to go and see him. But one day she heard from Lucy that her mother-in-law was softening.

'I've been up to see my Charlie again. I went last night 'cos Franz was on duty.'

'I'm glad she's come round to letting you visit him at last. That's progress! But it must be hard coming away and leaving him. It can't be easy for him to understand what's going on either.'

'I know, he cried again when I left him,' she said, her face puckering as she sniffed, driving back the tears. 'I keep telling Daisy a little boy's place is with his mummy, but she won't listen. I pleaded with her, I said she must be able to imagine what I'm going through, honestly!'

'But has she heard from Peter yet?'

'No, she said she hasn't – but actually…' Lucy paused, lowering her voice. 'I got a Red Cross letter from him at the weekend.' Her face took on a haunted expression and she was no longer the defiant girl of a few minutes before. 'I'm finished, Ellie. He's in a field hospital somewhere out the back of beyond in France.' She stopped what she was doing and stared. 'He says he's been injured. He trod on a landmine and got his leg blown off. And …and he said he misses me.'

'Gosh, Oh my goodness, I'm so sorry!'

'I don't know how to deal with all this, Ellie, really, I don't. I haven't told his mother. I daren't. I don't know what to do.'

Lucy was never usually beaten by anything, she always rallied whenever she was put down. Ellen went over to give her a hug. 'Don't worry, Lucy, they'll be looking after him. It's better he's in hospital than on the battlefield and he's a strong man. He'll be okay.'

Lucy turned a pale face towards her and showed tears streaming down her cheeks. 'What have I done to him, Ellie? Where do I go from here? What the hell am I going to do now?'

'When was the letter posted?'

'The third of June.'

'That means it's taken over five months to get here. He'll be recovering well now, probably having physio. I wish I could say something to help, but it's you who'll have to make the decision.'

'Decision! What decision? Look at me!' she cried, throwing her arms wide and revealing her huge baby bump. 'I can't let him see me like this! The baby's due in a few weeks. Oh, Ellie, what have I done?'

As the friends parted to go their separate ways, Ellen's thoughts were dominated by Lucy's dilemma. When she got home, she flopped down on the settee,

A Sea of Barbed Wire

hardly having the strength to go upstairs and change. But she didn't want to be drawn into a conversation. Lucy's situation wasn't something she could discuss. That Lucy was pregnant by a German soldier was no longer a secret, but no-one would know about Peter. The worst thing would be that his mother got to hear about it from a rumour. That poor lady, she couldn't help feeling sorry for her.

Chapter 34

That evening, the sky was filled with what appeared to be hundreds of RAF planes flying overhead from England and heading for France. The roar of their engines was deafening. Their target, according to news on the grapevine, was the city of Cherbourg. As they stood out in the garden looking up into the sky, Robert spoke loudly to make himself heard above the drone of their engines.

'Those guys up there. Some of them are only young lads. Their lives have hardly begun, and there they are, likely to lose what short lives they've had.'

'You mustn't say things like that Rob. It doesn't do you or anyone any good. They're very brave and proud of what they're doing.'

He turned and looked at her. 'Are they though? I bet they didn't know half of what was expected of them when they signed up. Poor lads.'

She took his hand and led him back indoors, unable to bear the loud drone and the smell of aircraft fuel any longer. The war was fighting itself out across the sea and there was nothing they could do about it but wait and hope. Robert was having a run of bad luck, forever complaining about the arrogant behaviour of the German soldiers in the bank, as well as the new regulations they kept announcing. He wasn't, she knew, coping well with the responsibility he held or the hardship he had been put under. Now, being denied his bicycle, he was growing thinner and more miserable by the day.

When Ellen was at work the next day, however, Lucy had some more news for her. As soon as she arrived, she whispered that she had something to tell her, drawing her aside with a cheeky look on her face. She appeared to have forgotten her devastating news of the day before.

'Franz was moanin' about his corporal and what the officers have done to a house they'd taken over. They had a drunken party apparently and they've made a right mess of the place. I thought right away it could be your nan's house they were talkin' about, but I kept quiet of course.'

'It could be.' Ellen was cautious. 'But they've requisitioned loads of houses, we'd be very unlucky if it happened to be my nan's.' The possibility captivated her thoughts though and she was hardly listening when Lucy continued talking about the soldiers.

'They were having a right laugh about all the rubbish they'd left, sayin' they were on the lookout for a nice clean place again. Honestly! Franz told me he nearly punched one of them! He's livid!'

She forced herself to reply. 'But he didn't, did he?'

Lucy didn't miss a trick. 'Oooh, hark at you! Worrying about a German soldier getting himself into trouble! He was thinkin' of you, silly! And your poor nan. He is human you know. He says he's ashamed of some of the things his lot are doin' to the locals.'

'That's nice of him. But I've never said they're all terrible.'

'No?' Lucy looked at her quizzically, raising her eyebrows and giggling. Having apparently kindled her interest, Lucy didn't hold back when she described how frustrated Franz was by the orders he was given to carry out, the relentless drills and manoeuvres he had to undergo. She went on to describe how he complained about his officers keeping the best food for themselves, drinking whisky and smoking cigarettes they'd plundered from houses, and how some were getting fat and drunk, and being entertained by 'ladies of the night' shipped over from France.

Putting aside her hopes for the house that her nan feared she may never have again, she had to ask: 'So, have you heard any more about Pete and whether his mother knows?'

Lucy's face clouded and her mood changed abruptly. 'No, and I don't want to be the one to tell her either, she hates me enough already.'

Ellen had noticed Charlie's name was mentioned less and less. Neither did she talk about her visits to see him much. If questioned, she often managed to change the subject. Not wanting to upset her however, she didn't pursue it. But as it turned out, Lucy's hunch that it might be her nan's house that had been abandoned by the Germans was true. When Ellen got home, her mother told her that Joan had received the news in a letter put through the door informing her that the house had been vacated and the keys could be picked up from The German headquarters in the Grange.

A Sea of Barbed Wire

Filled with excitement, Ellen got to her nan's later that day and found the front-door ajar, she pushed it open a little more, and called out nervously:

'Nan? Are you there?' Scared that it was a trap, that a soldier might jump out and grab her, made her heart thunder away in her chest. But nothing stirred. The silence and the smell hit her as soon as she stepped inside. The overwhelming stench of old beer and rotten food caught in her throat. She ventured further in.

'Nan? Where are you?' Strewn across the carpet in the sitting-room were papers, bits of food, leaflets, newspapers, all crumpled and covered in muddy footprints. There were cigarette butts littering the floor, some stamped on and burnt into it. The furniture was either broken, soiled or missing altogether. The remainder of what looked like her dining-chair legs were half burnt in the fireplace. Going further, and into the kitchen, she found a complete mess. It stank of bad meat, sour milk and general rubbish which had been piled up in the corner. Pressing her sleeve against her nose and mouth she crept upstairs. The transformation from cosy bedrooms to a dirty billet was shocking. In the three rooms they had presumably housed twenty or so men, judging by the number of the mattresses and old blankets left on the bedroom floors. In the small bedroom at the back, where her late Gran'pa used to sit under the window and do his accounts, his books had been torn off the shelves and the wooden bookcases were missing. Presumably the soldiers had chopped them up and burnt them in the fireplace. His collection of encyclopedias and gardening books were scattered haphazardly on the floor. The curtains were hanging down and there were empty beer bottles on the windowsill.

Retreating hastily back down she rushed out into the garden for some fresh air. There, quite a way from the house, she found her nan building a bonfire. Her dog was by her side. Joan looked up and gave her half a smile and a nod of welcome when she saw her coming. Ellen ran over to hug her, to comfort her as best she could. But there was nothing she could think of to say that could come near to cheering her up or express how she felt. All the memories of her childhood, her gran'pa, the warmth and happiness she had always experienced when she spent time in that house had been destroyed. But for her nan it was so much worse. The house had been what was left of her family life. It wasn't just a cigarette butt that they had stood on and stamped into the carpet, it was their lives together. However much she could restore the house it would never be the same. It was so much worse than being burgled but amounted to the same on a grand scale. All personal things that may have been touched by the intruders seemed soiled. Joan, however, looked extremely pale and hardly said a word.

'It's okay, Nan, we'll all help you get it cleaned up. Robert said he'll come along later.' She hugged her, and whispering, 'Don't worry,' she went back to the house. There was no time to delay. Finding an empty potato sack in the kitchen, Ellen set about gathering up dirty newspapers, socks, shirts, propaganda leaflets and stuffing them in until it was full. They would make a grand fire with all the rubbish left behind, the broken furniture, torn books and soiled discarded German paraphernalia. Heaping what they had gathered into a

A Sea of Barbed Wire

pile, Joan used one of the last few matches she possessed to set light to it. Flames spread hungrily, roaring with the power of tinder dry papers and stumps of table legs and broken chairs. They had to hurry. It was getting late and they couldn't risk the flames being spotted after the blackout. To save time, Ellen got the wheelbarrow and wheeling it to the kitchen door, she filled it time and again with rubbish before pushing it down the path to feed the fire. Fortunately, Joan had chosen a place which was well away from the house so steadily the fire grew, engulfing all the rubbish they could bring. As dusk fell it grew colder and already Ellen could see her breath rising in clouds of vapour in the damp air. It was going to take a long time to restore the house to anything like its original state but they both felt desperate to remove every trace of what the soldiers had left behind. Finally, she knew it was too late to continue. Joan seemed thoughtful and wasn't speaking much at all.

'We'll have to go home now, Nan. It'll be dark soon, but we'll come again tomorrow.'

Joan looked at her; she seemed in a bit of a daze. 'I thought I remember you saying your Robert was going to come and help.'

'I expect he's been held up at work. But we've a long walk back, Nan. Let's cover over the fire with the ashes and let it die down now. We can't risk it being seen.'

'You go ahead, dear. I'll just do a bit more. You've been an angel, thanks for helping me.'

'I'm not going without you, Nan. Anyway, I'd rather walk with you than on my own.'

Joan seemed to be playing for time, poking the fire with a stick and sending up cascades of glowing particles into the sky that crackled and danced like glowworms. Then she picked up the shovel and began turning some soil over the fire, causing huge plumes of smoke and sparks to rise. It was very obvious they were having a huge fire and close to panicking, Ellen begged her to leave it. 'Let's go back now, please, Nan!' she cried, taking her arm.

Suddenly they heard a vehicle. Ellen nearly died of fright when it pulled up with a screech outside. But it wasn't the Germans.

'Rob! Where did you get this?' asked Ellen joyfully as he emerged from the driver's seat of a builder's van, dangling the keys and looking pleased with himself.

'I borrowed it, no time to explain now. I've got loads of detergent in the back, buckets and scrubbing brushes. No idea where he got it all from, but he said don't ask! This will help us to get the house clean. If it's anything like what I've heard, it'll be a filthy mess.'

'It is that alright. We've burnt lots of rubbish already but there's still more. We can't do any more tonight though, Rob.'

'You're right. If you could just help me unload this detergent and cleaning stuff, I'll drive you both home.'

Joan was standing still in the doorway watching them. Robert explained to her what he was doing and what he had brought with him. She began shaking her head and looking confused.

'We've got to unload the stuff and go now, Nan,' explained Ellen, 'or we won't be home before dark. Let's hurry!'

A Sea of Barbed Wire

'Yes, yes, but I'm not going back with you, my dears. I'm not leaving my house again. They'll have to drag me out of it this time.'

'You can't stay here, not with the state it's in. Please Nan! Rob will drive us back.'

'No, no, I'm alright, Ellie - you go. Leave me.'

'But they won't come back, Nan. They'll have found another house to take over by now; what they've done here is all behind them. They're not interested in this place anymore. But quickly, we must get going.'

'I'm staying, love. It's not just them,' she whispered, peering around. 'There are some people, local people, who can't wait to get their hands on anything that's left unattended. I'm not giving them that pleasure. What I've got left, pathetic as it is, is mine and I'm staying right here even if I have to sleep on that filthy floor. I've got the dog with me for company.'

'But it's so dirty, Nan, and there's no bedding or anything!' Ellen was close to tears. There was no way she could imagine anyone sleeping there in its present state. While Robert began unloading whatever cleaning materials he had been able to find, she begged her nan to change her mind. But Joan wouldn't budge. Leaving Ellen, she went off back down the garden in the half-dark to check on the bonfire. Ellen knew when she had an idea there wasn't much that could be done to dissuade her. She was a strong-minded woman.

'Nan's refusing to leave the house again, Rob, she's afraid of what might happen. She won't come back with us. But we can't leave her here on her own, in this mess. What can we do?'

He stopped and thought for a moment. 'I see. She didn't look very happy when I arrived. What's it like in there anyway?' He walked past her and went inside. A few minutes later he emerged. 'It's worse than I thought, sweetheart. But if she insists on staying, I'll stay with her.'

'Stay with her? No, Rob! There's nowhere to sleep. How will you manage?'

'I'll take you home first and if your mother could find us some spare blankets and pillows, I would be grateful. There are limits to my generosity you know,' he added, pushing his glasses back into place on his nose and grinning at her. She had to laugh. She had never known him being reckless before. Hours later, as she lay safely in bed at home, she kept thinking about Robert who, so heroically, was staying with her nan in the house. All the dangers that could befall them kept her awake for hour after hour. She might as well have stayed with them for the sleep she was getting.

In the morning, as it was Saturday, she started out early to walk there. The dog barked when she tried the door and it opened. When she stepped inside, calling their names, she didn't find them in the house, but the transformation was amazing. The soiled carpet had been ripped up, the floorboards scrubbed and the piles of rubbish in the kitchen had gone. There was a fresh smell which she could see was due to the wet mop, the bucket of water and disinfectant.

'Robert? Nan?' she called, before she looked through the window and saw them both outside by the bonfire. They told her some passing Germans had seen the smoke and come to the door, ordering them to keep the fire down low. 'They gave us two hours to burn everything and finish with it,' said Robert. 'I didn't argue with them. They know me now.'

A Sea of Barbed Wire

'Two hours?' said Ellen. 'But there's loads of stuff to get rid of!'

'They wouldn't listen. I'll take the worst of it away in the van and lose it somewhere.'

Ellen chuckled at this new side to Robert. Dressed in old flannel trousers, with his sleeves rolled up and wearing an open-necked shirt, he had a day's growth of stubble on his chin. Even his crop of untidy hair, which was usually so well combed, made him look years younger.

'How did it go? Did you get any sleep?'

'We've been up half the night cleaning, love,' explained Joan. 'Your young man here has done me proud.' Their gaiety was short-lived however when they heard a vehicle approaching.

Joan stepped forward to take a look. 'It's alright, it's one of my friends.'

'What is it, Jack? Everything alright?'

He jumped down from the vehicle, shaking his head. 'It's him…you know …He's refusing food. He keeps saying he's going to leave the island, get out and go home. I'm afraid he's going to make a run for it and if he's caught, we'll all be done for.'

'I'm sorry,' said Joan. 'That's what he was saying before. He kept trying to tell us he shouldn't be here anymore. He doesn't want to take food from us when we don't have enough for ourselves.'

'Well, I don't know what to do with him, Joan. He was alright at first, looking a lot better and helping me a bit in the yard. I don't know what's got into him, but I can't risk it. He'd be better off out of my place. I've got responsibilities and it's worrying my wife. Sorry, dear, he's got to go.' Jack turned away. 'I've got him in the back. I know you're up to your eyes, but you'll have to keep him here.'

Walking round, Jack opened the back of the van, and Ellen caught her breath as Lukasz scrambled out. He stood up tall and with his hands on his hips, taking deep breaths and blinking. But when he turned and caught sight of Ellen, his eyes burned into her, as if they were on fire.

A Sea of Barbed Wire

Chapter 35

On Monday morning both girls were at work, but Ellen didn't have her mind on the job. She had pleaded with her nan that they should take Lukasz back to their house, but Joan wouldn't hear of it. She wanted Lukasz to stay with her, to help her sort the house out, and said that it wasn't doing him much good being down in the cellar anyway. And she had insisted she would soon get him to eat again. Lucy kept glancing at Ellen quizzically and trying to make conversation:

'My baby's kickin' again, the little terror. It must be a boy; I can just picture him! I bet he has blonde hair an' blue eyes just like his daddy.' She waited for a response, but Ellen seemed miles away.

'OK, come on, what's up with you, Ellie? Something's happened. I know it has. I've never known you so quiet.'

'Sorry, I'm tired, that's all. I didn't sleep last night – hardly at all.' She smiled at her, hoping to sound convincing.

'You'll have to do better than that,' replied Lucy. 'We've known each other a long time. It's not the first time you've missed out on sleep. There's been a lot of bad stuff goin' on and you've hardly said a word to me all mornin'.' Saying this, she slammed a ball of dough down on the counter and faced her. With one eye on the corridor to make sure they were alone, she repeated in a whisper, 'Come on, Ellie, we're friends, aren't we? Haven't I trusted you with my worst secrets? No-one can be in more trouble than I am, let's face it!' She giggled and Ellen couldn't help but catch her smile.

'I'm worried sick, Lucy. I don't know what on earth to do.'
Her friend's expression changed because instantly she realised this must be a whopper of a secret.

'Don't tell me, you're pregnant! That's alright. We're in this together. Don't worry; Robert's such a lovely chap, he's bound to stand by you and –'

'No, no! I wish it was that simple. I know I shouldn't tell you, but I'll die if I can't tell someone. I'm fit to burst with it, but it's so dangerous. I don't know if I should tell you or anyone. It's deadly, Lucy, it really is.'

'Oh my God, Ellie, what on earth have you done?' cried Lucy, staring at her open-mouthed.

'Carry on with the kneading and I'll tell you while we work. You mustn't tell a soul – you must swear - promise me?'

'Of course! I ain't gonna breathe a word. Strike me down dead if I do!'

'Well, you see, we've been hiding a prisoner.' She glanced at Lucy uncertainly. 'Don't say anything till I've explained a bit more. One of those prisoners escaped and he made it to our back door asking for help, but then he collapsed. He was in a terrible state, horribly beaten up and his head was bleeding. We gave him some water and cleaned up his wounds a bit, but he was so weak we couldn't turn him away, you see.'

A Sea of Barbed Wire

For once in her life Lucy was quiet. She didn't say a word. Terror, like a pain, shot through Ellen as she waited for her reaction. She wasn't sure what she wanted her friend to say, perhaps a word to make her feel better, to reassure her – something. But Lucy said nothing.

Eventually to break the silence, Ellen said, 'I'm sorry. I should never have told you.'

A thousand thoughts appeared to flicker across Lucy's face.

'Bloody hell! I thought something was up with you, but honestly, Ellie! So, what's happened to him now?'

'We went on hiding him. Put him up in the attic first. He hardly had the strength to get up there that night. We were only going to let him stay until he got better, but then well, we couldn't just turn him out on the street, he wouldn't have lasted five minutes.' She glanced at Lucy to see how she was taking it and ploughed on. 'I know it's difficult for you to understand, but things just happen don't they. You don't mean them to happen and then suddenly ...'

'But why are you telling me now? You haven't still got him, have you?'

Ellen nodded. 'Yes, no, well, it's a long story but he's with my nan at the moment. He keeps saying he's going to get away, escape from the island and go back to find his family.'

Lucy chuckled bitterly. 'He'll be lucky. Where's he from, France?'

'Poland.'

'Poland?' She raised her eyebrows in amazement. 'How's he going to get there, swim?!' Her tone quickly became mocking.

Ellen began to feel uncomfortable. Immediately she knew it had been a mistake to tell her. For a moment, forgetting to breathe in the dread of what she had done, she thought she was going to faint. What a stupid thing to do, telling *her* of all people, and after all this time. She felt sick, realising she had betrayed Lukasz, betrayed her parents, her nan, and Robert - betrayed everyone. But she was in too deep to get out of it now. 'Lucy, please! You have to help me. You must swear you won't tell Franz. I'll help you all I can in getting Charlie back if you'll help me with Lukasz.'

'Is that his name, Lukasz? What's he like? I mean, is he handsome?' Her eyes danced mischievously. A typical question coming from her, but Ellen could have kicked herself because she blushed furiously and what was worse, Lucy noticed.

'Oh, I get it!' she giggled, cramming her mouth against her sleeve. 'You fancy him! Oooh, who would have thought it?!'

'No, it's not like that! Yes, he is good looking actually but that doesn't matter. I feel sorry for him. He's trapped and there's no way out unless there's an end to the war and everyone's free again.'

Lucy didn't look very convinced. 'Oh yeh? What does Robert say? Don't tell me he doesn't know!'

'Of course, I've told him. Strangely enough, Robert's in complete agreement with me about hiding him. He wasn't at first, he was worried that we would all get found out and arrested. But now he's so angry with it all. He criticises the Controlling Committee, the Germans, the War, everything. He's often complaining about how obedient everyone is and saying that more people should rebel. He says Guernsey people are acting like sheep, doing what they're told and submitting to any new rule the Germans care to throw at us.'

Lucy shrieked with laughter. 'Blimey! He's got it bad!'

'Ssshhh!' hissed Ellen, glancing over her shoulder in alarm. Whatever relief she had gained from sharing her secret with Lucy had been short-lived. It was reckless, stupid, and unnecessary to tell her, but now it was too late.

Left alone with their thoughts, the girls finished kneading one lot of dough and set about starting another batch while they wrapped those and put them aside to prove. When Lucy spoke again, Ellen thought she was mistaken in what she heard.

'What did you say?' she whispered, glancing about for signs of George or any other workers hanging around.

'I told you Franz would agree with your Robert, one hundred percent,' she repeated, sighing with a kind of exhaustion. 'It's all he talks about these days. Or rather, all he complains about – what his army is doin' and how awful it all is. I wouldn't be surprised if he stood up and told me he was goin' to join the other side, he's that fed-up!'

'You're joking!'

But Ellen could tell by the look on her face she wasn't joking. 'I'm afraid for him, Ellen. One of these days he's going to be overheard, or refuse to obey orders, or throw a punch at one of his officers and then it'll be the firing squad for him.' Unconsciously she placed a hand protectively over her baby bump. 'It will be the end of him, and me - the end of both of us. I can't bear to live without him now.'

Chapter 36

The following morning, even before they had taken their coats off, Lucy greeted Ellen with words she dreaded to hear.

'I've got something to tell you!' Saying this, Lucy cast her eyes around, appearing to enjoy every moment of the secret she was about to disclose. 'Franz said he can help you! He's come up with a plan to help your man escape the island. I knew he would. He's so clever!'

Ellen stared at her, completely thrown. 'You've told him? Oh, Lucy, you promised!'

'You need some help, right? If you don't want to find a way to save that chap, then forget it! I thought you'd be pleased.' She sniffed, looking very hurt and immediately turned away.

Out of her depth now, Ellen was aware of the dull headache, the foggy vagueness that stopped her being able to think clearly. The sleepless nights and lack of food was beginning to affect her ability to make decisions. But the most careless decision she had ever made was to open up to Lucy and now her whole world had been exposed. Somehow, she coped with Lucy's indignant reaction to her scolding, especially when she insisted Franz had a genuine interest in helping Lukasz escape.

A Sea of Barbed Wire

When she was walking to her nan's house after work later that day, she was so preoccupied with her thoughts it barely registered when on arriving at the house, Robert was working there. He was outside, up a ladder, fixing pieces of cardboard over some of the windows which had been broken by what was probably drunken clumsiness. She called up to him and he climbed down, wiping his hands on his trousers. He looked surprisingly well, probably because instead of being shut indoors at work in the bank he was working out in the fresh air. It had brought a colour to his cheeks; he looked younger and full of energy.

'I've taken a week off work,' he told her. 'About time. I haven't had time off for I don't know how long.' He kissed her fleetingly on the cheek.

'What a dreadful mess they made of Nan's lovely house. You're doing well, thanks Rob.'

'Until we can get some glass, this cardboard should help. Just be glad they haven't been and taken over your parents' house. That's what I fear, to find you being turned out and having nowhere to go. In The Grange and down Doyle Road, they've taken over a whole row of houses apparently, and pushed the residents out just because it was convenient for them. They've no thought for the people they're turning out on the street. There's one family I just heard about with three children and a new-born baby. They've given them twenty-four hours' notice to pack up and leave. I think they're going to relatives over St. Martin's way, but just as well they've got family who will take them in. Anyway, I'll get on with these windows and finish up, there's plenty more to do inside, including sweeping up all that broken glass upstairs.'

'I'll go and do that then if you like,' she replied and leaving him, she stepped indoors. There was definitely an atmosphere of work underway. The first person she saw was Lukasz. He had his sleeves rolled up and was washing down the paintwork.

'Ellie, you here! I wait for you. Are you okay? You not look well.'

She nodded and swallowed hard. 'I'm fine thanks, Lukasz. My goodness, you've been busy.'

The house certainly looked more liveable-in again. Some of the furniture was back where it belonged, the rug was again in place before the fireplace and there was a fire burning in the grate. It was more like her nan's old home again already.

'We make house better.'

'It does look nice, well done.'

'I like to help her. She good lady to me.'

Ellen nodded. 'Yes, my nan's very kind. She didn't deserve all this. Where is she though?'
He tossed his head towards the back of the house. 'She outside in garden.'

'Lukasz, did you eat anything today?'
He looked at her, thought for a moment, then shook his head. 'I alright. I have later.'

'Nan might make some soup, then we can all have some, eh?'

Ellen found her nan; she wasn't outside but in the kitchen washing down the shelves of the cupboards. 'These could do with a lick of white paint, but at least they'll be clean again. I need to get some food in.'

'Let me help you, Nan!' Ellen took off her coat and tied her hair back ready to do some work.

'Thank you dear, there's an old curtain there I've been tearing up for rags.'

Ellen began tearing the material. 'Robert's doing a good job with those broken windows, isn't he.'

'Yes, he insists on helping, he doesn't stop. He says he's taken time off work from the bank. It's very good of him.' She put down her cloth and looked close to tears. 'Ellie, love, I couldn't have coped with all this without you. Even if I don't say it much, I'm very grateful. Even Lukasz has been working tirelessly. I'm proud of him. Proud of you all.'

'He said how good you have been to him; he wants to help you.'

'But I'm worried about him, Ellie. I've told him to keep out of sight, but I can't persuade him to eat much at all. He says what I have I should eat myself.' Joan shrugged her shoulders, almost as if by his refusal of her food she felt rejected. 'We're all hungry and we don't have much, but I tell him we all have to eat.'

'He'll be alright, Nan. Don't worry about him. But if they come, if they see him here or in the garden, then …'

She nodded. 'Then we will all be finished. I know, dear. He keeps saying he wants to leave. He knows it's dangerous for him to be here, and he wants to get away. He told me he will go home, that he'll swim home. It's impossible, isn't it? He must know how far it is.'

Ellen shook her head. 'No, Nan. He doesn't know how far he is away from Poland or where we are. He thought this was England at first. All he knows is that he was put on a ship for a long time and after many days at sea he arrived here.'

Tearing off a strip, she plunged the rag into the bucket of water, wrung it out and got up on a chair to begin washing the shelves in the top cupboard. Her anxiety spurred her energy on, and silence fell on them as they worked. But Ellen's thoughts were clanging so loudly in her head she feared her nan could hear them. The weight she carried on her conscience was becoming unbearable. It was so vital she told her, yet so terrifying she could barely think. So she began, in a whisper, to explain.

'Nan, my friend at work, she knows someone who can help Lukasz get away.'

Joan looked at her as if she couldn't believe her ears. 'You mean you've told someone at work about Lukasz? How could you!'

'I didn't mean to tell her, but I just …'

'And she's told someone else already? Oh, Ellen!'

Joan stopped working and was fixing her with such an anxious stare. 'Heaven forbid! We'll all be in for it now if it gets out.'

'Nan, she's told her boyfriend. But she said he's not like the others, and I believe her. And he wants to help us.'

Joan stared at her. 'Have you taken leave of your senses, girl? Who is this boyfriend?'

'He's a German soldier. His name's Franz but hear me out, Nan. Franz hates the war, the army and how they treat the prisoners and slave workers. He said he can help Lukasz get away safely.'

Joan's shoulders sagged. She shrugged and seemed to age another few years on hearing this news. 'Huh! It's the first I've heard of a German soldier wanting to save lives. Whoever it is, don't trust him, Ellie. Listen to me: it'll be a trap. They pretend all kinds of things to get their way.'

'But Lucy's my best friend, Nan! I've known her a long time. Lucy wouldn't tell me something if it wasn't true.'

'Of course not, dear, but this soldier, this German she's taken up with, he could be tricking her. She'll be flattered by his attention, and he'll probably tell her anything she wants to hear, just to get his wicked way with her.'

'Actually, Nan, he's already got his wicked way with her. She's expecting his baby very soon. But he really does hate the army and all that Hitler stands for, honestly, I do believe her.'

Some footsteps could be heard approaching and Lukasz came into the kitchen. His chest was bare, having discarded his shirt, and Ellen was shocked by how thin he was, his ribs protruding and his face gaunt, his dark brooding eyes were in shadow, half hidden by the thick locks of his unkempt hair.

'I finish. I go outside now, chop wood for fire, yes?'

'Thank you, Lukasz. Go ahead but don't tire yourself and stay round the back of the house.'

When he had gone, Ellen whispered, 'He's so thin, Nan, I wish he would eat more. None of us have much but he has to eat something, or he'll die.'

'I've told him. I'm tired of telling him,' Joan said and shook her head. 'I wish your gran'pa was still alive, he would know what to do about all this. You know what Lukasz told me? That one day he'll just go, leave us, escape, and swim home. You know, he doesn't have a clue about how far it is or anything. As if he could swim to Poland! Or even England for that matter. It's ridiculous. He'll get blown to bits as soon as he steps onto the beach, even before he has a chance to reach the sea. But he won't listen to me. There are guards and searchlights at every point. He wouldn't stand a chance.'

'He doesn't understand though, Nan.'

'No, and where it's all going to end I don't know. But as for you telling your friend about him,' she paused and looked Ellen in the eye. 'It was the worst thing you could have done, but I'm sure you realise that now. You've put us all in grave danger. I thought you, of all people, would know better.'

'I'm sorry, it was stupid of me.'

Joan nodded. 'We all do stupid things, don't worry love.'

Chapter 37

Ellen left work late afternoon after another long day. Lucy was following close behind her. The chill sunlight was sharp as the sun was going down. They both blinked, squinting against the light. A tall figure was standing there in silhouette. The sun caught the edge of his rifle and that's when Ellen realised it was a German soldier. He stood to attention as if he was on duty.

'Oh, look, Franz is here!' whispered Lucy in delight and hurried up to him. Ellen walked hastily on, as quickly as she could, but Lucy called her back. 'Hey, wait Ellie! Franz has got something to tell you!'

She felt her knees go weak and she trembled as she gathered her coat tightly around herself protectively and retraced her steps. He was so tall, he peered down his long nose at her through his pale eyelashes and clicked his heels.

Lucy giggled. 'Don't look so worried, he doesn't bite you know!'

A few minutes later they were walking along together, Lucy pushing her bike and Franz walking alongside the two girls. Ellen felt self-conscious in his company, but Lucy was chattering away to him about her condition and what the nurse had said about her pregnancy.

'She says I should drink more full-cream milk and eat plenty of cheese and greens! Honestly, doesn't she know there's a war on!' Lucy was always joking about things, but Ellen knew what she was after: more supplies. Franz seemed happy to comply and answered:

'Of course, you shall have more. You are with child. I will see to it.'

Lucy glowed and stroked her bump of a tummy in satisfaction.

Franz glanced across at Ellen curiously. 'You have known my Lucy a long time, yes?'

'Since we were at school,' she replied, scanning the road ahead, desperately hoping no-one was coming along who would recognise her.

'You have enough to eat? Your family?'

'We manage,' Ellen said quickly. 'It's hard for everyone but we're OK.'

He nodded. He wasn't marching but dawdling with his rifle slung haphazardly across his shoulder and his gaze fixed on the ground most of the time. He raised his head and spoke directly to Ellen: 'You have a beautiful island. It is very quiet.'

'It used to be.' Ellen had replied without even looking at the soldier, but Lucy hooted with laughter. They came to the point where they had to part ways. With relief Ellen began to move away and said, 'Well, I'll see you tomorrow, Lucy. Bye!'

'Hang on! Franz had something to say to you.'

She paused reluctantly. 'What is it?' she mouthed, glancing behind her in case anyone was watching.

Franz came smartly towards her. 'We talk,' he said. 'We meet at Lucy's house tonight, seven o'clock, yes?'

A Sea of Barbed Wire

'No, no I can't come tonight. I'm seeing Robert.' She thought for a moment. 'Tomorrow night. I could come then.'

Franz nodded. 'If I'm off-duty, I come tomorrow.'

Lucy was standing by listening. 'See you in the mornin', Ellie. Off you go and see your Robert and …' she chuckled, 'behave yourself!'

Ellen hurried away. The sudden turn of events had frightened her, and she cursed herself for ever sharing her secret. Now she had to deal with the consequences, and she dreaded the prospect of owning up to her parents what she had done. If the war didn't end soon, and if Lukasz couldn't get away from Guernsey, how else were they all going to cope? The prospect of hiding him for much longer seemed increasingly dangerous. Was there no other solution?

*

The following night, with two hours to go before curfew, she walked to Lucy's cottage. She hadn't been there for a while but after a swift tap on the door and no-one responding, she let herself in and there, sitting in an armchair as relaxed as any man of the house would be, was Franz. He wasn't in uniform this time; he was dressed in a dark cotton shirt, open at the neck and as she entered, he stubbed out his cigarette and stood up to shake her hand.

'Hello Franz,' she said, feeling very uneasy. Lucy was nowhere to be seen.

'My girl is in the bath,' he explained, holding her gaze with his intense ice-blue eyes. 'I gave her some scented soap and she couldn't wait – apparently.' He raised his eyebrows at Ellen as if they understood each other.

It seemed funny being there in the sitting-room where Peter used to be before the war. Lucy's husband was an easy-going, likeable fellow, often sprawled out on the sofa, half-asleep and reeking of beer. It was all much tidier now. And she noted sadly there weren't any of Charlie's toys scattered around on the floor. Lucy must miss little Charlie dreadfully, thought Ellen, but she doesn't show it and now she hardly mentions him. Believing the attachment of motherhood runs deep, she supposed it wasn't easily conveyed, but Ellen couldn't help thinking it seemed as if the little boy had been forgotten.

At work that day she had quizzed Lucy about Franz. What was his background? What was his home life like? Was he married? Could he be trusted? To all these questions she answered willingly, painting a picture of him having such an idyllic childhood, such dependable parents, such loving brothers and sisters back home in Germany that even Ellen warmed to him. When he had been called up, he had told her they had all pleaded with him not to go, or to feign a physical incapacity. But she told Ellen with glowing eyes he was so brave, so proud of his fatherland that he felt he had to go. And then so soon he had regretted it.

Franz leant forward and spoke to her in a hushed voice. His German accent had the effect of making everything he said sound sharp, commanding and very specific.

'Whatever you might think of me, I want you to know that I only wear the German uniform to preserve

A Sea of Barbed Wire

my life. To speak out, to disobey, you understand, would be fatal. I have heard too much of the triumph achieved by the Third Reich, but it is not my way, the way of my father and grandfather. I salute Herr Hitler, but my heart is my own. He does not own it. I do not want to destroy your beautiful country. But ruin it they do with their concrete and barbed wire and mines. It is not in my nature to fight. When the war is over, and it will be over very soon I promise you,' he said, narrowing his eyes, 'I will tear the German army uniform from my back into shreds, stamp on it and burn it!' His eyes bore into her with fierce defiant passion. 'Not a word of this must you speak to a living soul!'

'No, no of course not,' she replied, flustered. She had hardly been given the chance not to agree and was so taken aback by this unexpected declaration, such an outpouring against the German Military Occupation, it was a shock. She had never expected to hear such words, least of all from a serving German soldier. How she wished Lucy would come and relieve her of this strange intensity.

But he went on: 'You have a friend in need, shall we say? I can advise you. All I can do is tell you what I know. For him to leave this island, it is impossible. People try and they get shot. Fishermen must take one of us with them as a chaperone. Three miles out from the coast, no more. They can row out so far and cast their nets, but then they must turn round and return. When they land their catch, we check the fish. Some of the fish we take to feed ourselves of course. But listen - at every point along the coast there is a guard with a machine gun. They look out to sea. They watch. Not often do they miss things, you understand? Sometimes I go myself with the fishermen. I carry a rifle of course, check their papers and observe their work. When we return to shore, I check the papers again, check in and weigh the fish. Your friend, your …er …special friend …he come with me to fish, yes? Does he know how to handle a boat?'

Ellen nodded reluctantly. 'He told me he does, that he used to go sea-fishing with his uncle.'

'Very well. I myself will go with him. I will check his papers and we will leave. But it would be more practical if he took with him a companion because with the fishermen, there are usually at least two of them. When we reach the distance allowed, I will leave the boat and swim to shore. I will tell the guards the fishing boat …it capsized …kaput …I will say I do not know what happened to the men.' Having stated his idea, Franz stared at her. His eyes bore no trace of emotion. 'This is my plan. What do you say?'

'But what will happen to my friend then?'

'Your friend, he can swim away like a fish!' Franz made a quick motion with his hand like a fish swimming through the water. He smiled but his eyes weren't smiling. 'No, when I leave them, they must continue to sail the boat on to England. When they get far enough out to sea, they can start the outboard motor, and all will be well.'

'It sounds a good plan,' said Ellen cautiously, hardly believing she was having such a conversation. 'But why would you risk your life to save our friend? We don't have any money to pay you.'

He scowled at her, and his eyes narrowed to a glint. 'I don't want your money! I hate this war! I loathe this army, this uniform, this occupation, pah!' He

A Sea of Barbed Wire

scoffed and his jaw jutted out in a menacing scowl. 'If I could murder Hitler with my bare hands I would! So, please understand, I will help your friend as if he is my own brother.'

The next day, Ellen could barely stir herself to go out again after work. She had arranged to meet Robert at her nan's house. That evening they hadn't planned to stop long at her nan's; they had tickets for a Christmas concert being put on in St. Martin's village hall.

True to his word, Robert was waiting for her and had his coat on when she arrived. As they walked down the path he held her hand, but Ellen felt distracted and nervous. She didn't want to spoil their evening by confiding in him about the plan Franz had put to her. But with this hanging over her she felt awkward and couldn't think what to talk about. They walked on in silence for several minutes. The hall wasn't far away and she longed to be there, to be enveloped in the magic of Christmas and forget all her worries.

He squeezed her hand. 'You're quiet my sweet. Tired, eh?'
Her heart raced. 'I've got something on my mind, Rob. After the concert, can we walk for a bit? I need to discuss something with you.'

'That sounds to me as if you'd be better talking about it now.' He stopped and faced her. 'We're going through a tough time, my sweet, but it won't always be like this. Sooner or later, we'll be free again.'

'Rob, I've done a terrible thing. I told Lucy about Lukasz. I don't know what came over me.'

He looked at her long and hard. 'I don't know what to say. You, of all people? Oh, Ellie!'

'I know. I'm sorry. There's more, it's a long story.'

He stared at her and she could see him swallow hard. 'Well, let's not talk about it now. We're going to a Christmas show and we're going to enjoy ourselves, aren't we! Right? Come on then!' He urged her forward and she, knowing neither Lukasz, her parents or her nan knew about the plan that Franz had devised, gave in and tried to put the whole thing out of her mind.

When they got there, it was a surprise to find the hall warm, buzzing with people and decorated with streamers and paper chains. Excitable chatter greeted them as the cast were milling about among the crowd already dressed in colourful costumes. 'Isn't it wonderful!' said Ellen. 'I wish we'd brought my nan with us. She would have really enjoyed it; they must have been working on it for months!' Robert smiled, looking relieved. The spirit of it all had banished the tension between them.

When a bell sounded everyone quietened down and took their seats. What followed was a kind of pantomime with short sketches, Christmas songs, dancing and magic tricks. Lights were low, candles flickered on the windowsills casting weird shadows on the blackout blinds. Such a change from the usual, the show promised to be a huge success, banishing all thoughts of the hardship outside. On stage first, a young girl dressed as an angel and accompanied by her music teacher on the piano, entered and curtsied.

While the first song was being performed, Ellen looked around and was fascinated to see the audience was comprised of a strange combination of people. Several German soldiers had taken the front seat, dressed in full uniform. When the song finished, they applauded loudly, entering into the spirit of it as merrily as everyone else. Half-way through the performance, clapping her hands and laughing, she turned to Robert to share her enjoyment only to catch him staring into space. She was horrified to see him preoccupied, lost in thought and not attending at all. The look on his face was one of terror.

Chapter 38

As Lukasz dug Joan's vegetable plot, he was always wary of any movement close by. The sound of distant gunfire made him nervous, and he expected soldiers to appear at any moment. The slightest rustle of wind in the bushes caused him to jump, as he imagined them coming towards him and shouting at him in their harsh staccato voices. It brought memories flooding back of those fearful times in his past. But working outside again, even though he felt exposed and vulnerable, it made him feel better. In the last few weeks, he had made steps towards reclaiming his relationship back with the land.

Out in the fresh air, digging and turning the soil, with the smell of horse manure nearby, the fragrance of pine needles and the tang of the salty sea-air, he was glad to have the company of a bird hopping about close to his feet as he dug, watching for the chance to grab a worm. With his thoughts constantly flashing back to the past, he raked the ground into a fine tilth and sowed cabbage seeds. Joan had been lucky to obtain the seeds. Local growers and her friends from neighbouring farms had struggled to get their hands on any but Jack had shared a few of his own with her.

Lukasz was used to the freezing temperatures of winter. The climate was mild by comparison to his

A Sea of Barbed Wire

home country and the physical work soon warmed him up; the old coat Joan had given him to wear was already cast off and hung on a nearby branch. It was her late husband's coat, he guessed, but she hadn't mentioned that. She didn't talk to him much, but what she said was honest and down to earth and he respected her for that. Joan had advised him not to think about the past, as whenever he did the desire for revenge would surge up in his heart. However, that dreadful day when the Nazis had come onto their farm was never far from his mind.

To quieten himself down he thought of Ellen. It wasn't often he saw her now, at least hardly ever when they were alone, and he missed her. When he closed his eyes he could see her face, and he remembered the flutter of passion and innocent blush on her cheek when he had kissed her. There was a connection between them which came alive whenever she was there, an unspoken bond; he had an instinct that she felt it too. He would go home, try to heal the violence of the past that haunted his memories. It was his duty to go back and reclaim his father's land, to find his poor mother and sister and honour his father's death.

So, while he threw all his remaining strength and energy into the land, he dreamt of the day he could return home. He even allowed himself to dream that he could take Ellen with him. At home he used to swim out to fetch his uncle's fishing boat in the estuary, and he could swim well against the tide. He was a strong swimmer, and he could hold his breath underwater for minutes at a time; of this too he had had years of practice as he used to dive to free the nets when they got trapped under the rocks. The sea was his friend.

Taking stock of things after the Germans had abandoned the house, the seed potatoes were missing, either eaten or stolen, the young cauliflower and brussels sprout plants had disappeared from the ground which was found to be churned up by their army vehicles. The stable where Joan's mare was kept had been turned into a dumping ground for their rusting machinery and rubbish. Although Joan had appeared to take it all in her stride, Lukasz knew she was hurt and he felt helpless to comfort her – all he could do was help to put the house back together. However, he considered that accepting food from her when she had such a meagre amount for herself was equal to cowardice in his eyes. He wouldn't take food from a baby, let alone from a widowed woman living on her own. He had never heard her complain, but he could see the sadness in her eyes. His own country had suffered enough from death and malnutrition in the past at the hands of the enemy who showed no mercy to the Polish people.

Revulsion at what had happened to his own family rose up inside him and fired his muscles with renewed energy. He could keep his hunger deep inside, reserve it for a time when there was food again, plentiful food, when he would be back home in the farmhouse kitchen with his mother.

*

When she arrived at her nan's house, Ellen took off her coat and went to look out of the kitchen window while Joan was making some oatmeal biscuits.

'Oh, my goodness, is that Lukasz out there, Nan? Isn't it a bit risky in daylight?'

A Sea of Barbed Wire

'The man's got to do something, love. No-one can see him from the road and the others are too far away to bother I should think. I can't keep him cooped up in the barn all day. Poor Lukasz. He dreams of going home and it has no basis in reality.'

'He can sail a boat apparently, Nan. Remember he told us he used to go fishing with his uncle? And he told me he's a strong swimmer, but he doesn't look very strong now, does he.' She paused, flicking her eyes across at Joan as if wondering whether to proceed. Taking a deep breath, she decided to go ahead. 'Look, don't be angry, Nan, but Lucy's boyfriend has come up with a plan to get him away.'

Joan nodded to herself. 'I see. So we're finished. The lot of us. This friend of yours has told her fancy German boyfriend about Lukasz and now you're telling me he's come up with a plan?' She turned to Ellen, flaming with sudden fury and desperation. 'Do you realise what you've done, Ellen? You've betrayed us all!'

'No, Nan! It's going to be alright,' she cried. 'Franz really wants to help. He was quite straight with me. Let him come here and then you can hear him for yourself. He's sincere and honest, really he is. Please believe me!'

'Sincere and honest? You really think so?' She raised her eyebrows and almost laughed.

'But he'll have to meet Lukasz first, of course,' added Ellen.

'Of course!' repeated Joan, shaking her head in despair. 'If only I could believe he's genuine. God knows there must be some truth, some path of righteousness out of this mess. I don't know, dear. Bless you, I trust your judgement and if you think he's a good man, whether he's a German or whatever he is, then let him come. But I warn you, I don't trust any German soldier and it could mean the beginning of the end for us.'

*

It was a solemn night for a meeting which was about to take place in Joan's house. It still smelt damp, of scrubbed floorboards and disinfectant and the furniture was sparse. But it was clean and tidy, although cold and rather empty. By the dim light of a candle, Ellen sat nervously beside Robert on wooden upright chairs, her parents sat on the sofa and Lukasz remained standing, hands in his pockets, eyes burning with apprehension. Joan walked about the room restlessly. Sitting apart from them, in a corner on his own was Joan's neighbouring farmer, her friend Jack. They barely spoke. All of them were listening for footsteps on the gravel – the expected arrival of Lucy and her boyfriend Franz. After fifteen minutes or so, it wasn't footsteps they heard so much as laughter; it was the sound of Lucy's girlish giggle that usually accompanied the time she spent with Franz. Joan went to open the door; a finger instinctively went to her lips and she fixed Ellen with a serious stare as she let them in.

Franz was dressed in the long blueish grey overcoat which most of the German soldiers wore and which had seen better days. Below his coat, Ellen saw the unmistakable leather of his highly polished jackboots.

'Ooh, let me introduce you,' cooed Lucy proudly, leaning back as she stood before them with a

A Sea of Barbed Wire

hand placed firmly on her hip protruding her abdomen to be even larger than ever under the candlelight.

Albert stood up and straightened his shoulders. 'Come on, girl, no need for formalities. Let's get straight down to business,' he said, putting on his most professional air. 'My daughter tells me you're prepared to help our friend here.' With a movement of his head, he indicated Lukasz who stood staring hard at Franz like a dog about to leap at a man's throat. The candle flickered in a slight draft. A flurry of grit sounded against the door and Joan looked up anxiously. Franz had a voice as sharp as a flick-knife and he rarely blinked. With a tall stature, he stood almost to attention, his gaze cool and expressionless.

'I'm willing to give your friend a chance, but I cannot promise we will succeed. The coast is highly monitored. However, I can arrange for the duty rota to fall to me on a particular day. My responsibility will simply be to see your friend on his way.' He looked directly at Lukasz for the first time. 'I'm told you can handle fishing nets and sail a boat?'

Lukasz didn't respond at first. He gazed at the soldier darkly, summing up the situation and looking at Ellen, perhaps for reassurance. 'I go many years with my uncle and my father to fish, yes.'

Franz nodded abruptly. 'Very well.'

Albert, ever the practical one, explained, 'You'll need to handle the boat on your own, lad. Can you do that?'

'I okay. I do it.'

The brief nature of his reply hadn't affected Franz who fired out the next question, this time towards Albert.

'Does he have the necessary papers?'

Joan spoke up. 'Wait a minute! What is the plan you have exactly? Sit down Franz, and you Lucy, and let's talk about this properly. How do we know we can trust you? Where will you head off from? I don't need to tell you the whole coast is mined and watched day and night.'

Franz looked around and perched himself on the edge of the armchair where Lucy had sat herself down. He put his arm around Lucy's shoulders and smiled at her.

'Listen. You see I'm a soldier? But under this uniform I'm a family man. You can trust me because what I say is from my heart.' Again, he smiled at Lucy. 'I am not what you think I am. I wear the uniform of a German soldier because, if I did not obey, they would stamp on me and grind my face into the dirt. If it were possible, I would help you Guernsey people, all of you, to escape this hell.'

Albert jumped to the defence. 'We don't want to escape, Sir. This is our island, and we live here. Why would we want to leave it so you lot can take over and claim it for yourselves?'

Franz looked down and picked a speck of something from his sleeve. 'But you like to escape the war, yes?'

Joan checked the gap in the blackout curtains. 'Don't we all want the war to end, Franz?' she said. 'You think by helping one poor man to escape it will ease your conscience?'

Franz shrugged. 'I don't believe in conscience. You think I follow Herr Hitler? I don't, I curse the man! If he was here now, I would throttle him with my bare hands!' He breathed in audibly and, for a moment a vivid colour rose on his cheeks. His eyes were like glass.

'So, what's your plan, Franz?' asked Joan, straight-faced, and preparing to listen to him.

'He cannot head for France. If discovered, he will be shot. It must be the English coast. I can advise your friend how to achieve this but that is all I can do. It is impossible, I would say, to leave the coast by any secret means; he must go at the appointed time, to leave with the other fisherman. He must have identity papers.' Franz turned to speak directly to Lukasz.

'You leave with the other fishing boats, and you take a soldier with you – that will be myself. I will check your papers. I will accompany you while you row three miles out, no more. Then you swim or take the boat further but then you are on your own.'

Lucy was motionless, gazing up at her hero like a child. Lukasz was leaning against the doorframe, nonchalantly scratching a mark off the paintwork with his fingernail thoughtfully. He didn't look at Franz.

'You not agree? You not come with me?' Suddenly Franz snapped his fingers. 'Stand up, man! When we get so far, I will leave you. I will leave the boat and swim back to shore. I'll tell the guards something happened: you jumped me, or the boat capsized …sank …kaput … I'll tell them I don't know what happened to the fisherman, he may be drowned. They won't argue with me.'

'But where will Lukasz go, once he's alone?' demanded Ellen suddenly, rising to her feet.

'He must find his way to England of course,' said Franz fiercely through his teeth. 'It won't be my concern.'

'It's too far to row all the way to England. It's a ridiculous plan,' Albert replied dismissively.

Franz stared at him as if he was stupid. 'When your friend gets out of earshot, he can start the outboard motor; it's simple.'

'Why would you do this, Franz? Risk your position to help this man?'

'Because I hate what I do, what I stand for, what Herr Hitler has done to my fatherland. He makes us poor and live like rats. We are the scourge of the earth! I loathe this war, always so hungry, always so far from my family! If I could leave and escape myself, I would.'

'Franz, you wouldn't go without me, would you!' cried Lucy. Just for a moment Ellen noticed that he glanced at her with some irritation.

Up to this point, Lukasz had said nothing further.

'Let's get down to business, shall we,' said Joan. 'Jack?' She turned to her friend as if they had prearranged something he was about to say. Jack stepped forward out of the shadows. He cleared his throat. 'My boat's moored up in Havelet Bay. I go out regularly, the Jerries are used to me. I'll go with you, Lukasz. Since my boy was evacuated, my wife has done nothing but worry and moan at me for sending him away. I'll go to England with you, lad, and find my son, make sure he's still alive. I'll get no peace otherwise. My wife has agreed.'

Franz nodded. 'You'll need papers.' He looked straight at Lukasz. 'You have papers? You have identity card?'

Ellen was fiddling with her cardigan buttons. She felt as if she was walking on the edge of a precipice. Could this really be happening?

'I not have papers. I not have money, but I have it here in my heart to be home!'

Tears were building in Ellen's eyes as she protested. 'It's too dangerous for him. Can't you see that? He doesn't know how far it is! Even if Jack's with him, what will happen to him when he does get to the coast of England?'

'He'll be with me, Ellie, love,' said Jack, suddenly stepping forward. 'I have relatives in Devon where my son's staying. They'll see Lukasz is okay.' Turning to Lukasz, he said, 'We'll head for a small cove close to Start Point, well away from the military ships and the busy defence traffic in The Solent. But we still haven't sorted out where you're going to get some ID papers.'

Joan spoke up. 'I've thought of that. My late husband's papers are still in the drawer. With a little adapting here and there, they should be acceptable.'

With a swift glance of uncertainty at Franz, Jack admitted he knew someone who could help with that.

Franz nodded slowly. 'It will be myself who checks the papers but see that they are in order. I can't be held responsible if they don't pass. So, I think our business here is done.' He moved towards the door and Lucy sprang to her feet. 'Wait for me, Franz!'

'I'll be in touch. When preparations are ready and the weather is fine, we will act.'

He clicked his heels before he turned and left, with Lucy fleeing after him.

Chapter 39

All day, Ellen couldn't take her mind off of Lukasz and what was going to occur. For over a week she had hardly seen him. Now, as the time drew near for his departure, she so desperately wanted to see him to say goodbye. After finishing work, she didn't return home. She went straight to her nan's house, tapped on the door and having no response she let herself into the kitchen. There was no-one about. Her nan must be out. If there was any chance of seeing Lukasz at all before he went, she had to find him, and quickly. But where would he be in the middle of the afternoon? If her nan wasn't at home to keep a lookout, surely he wouldn't be out working on the land in broad daylight? Her first thought was to try the stable. Since clearing it out and getting rid of the junk the Germans had piled up in there, her nan had been able to bring the mare back from the neighbouring farm. Lukasz was often in there these days, tending to the horse. At night he slept in the hayloft above, out of sight.

Walking across the farmyard towards the stable, she found it eerily quiet. There wasn't a single hen pecking around and the stable door stood ajar. The horse neighed, acknowledging her presence as she entered. Ellen stroked the mare's neck while she waited for her eyes to become accustomed to the dimness within.

Disappointment welled-up inside her. He wasn't there and she didn't know where else to look for him.

'Lukasz?' she whispered, moving her feet slightly on the straw scattered stone floor. Her heart leapt as she heard his voice, deep from within the hayloft above. 'I am here. I come down.'

He appeared above her, lowering a rope which was secured to one of the rafters. Climbing down the rope with ease, he landed beside her. 'Ellie! I want so much for you to come.'

'I had to see you. Tomorrow you'll leave here and I just -' She choked on the words.

He came towards her, put his arms around her and held her tight. She couldn't speak. Burying her face in his chest, her tears flowed unchecked while he held her. Perhaps it was only a few minutes, but it could have been an hour that they stood holding each other in the semi-darkness of the stable. There was no comfort in these last moments they had alone together other than knowing what they felt for each other. Maybe, just maybe it would be the beginning of a whole new adventure for Lukasz as he set off and left the island for good.

Finally as her tears subsided and she turned to look up into his face, he kissed her passionately on the lips, hugging her and murmuring her name. Time stood still.

When he released her, he began to speak in a low tone, barely audible. 'When I free, I not forget. The war, one day it be over. I go home, I find my sister, my mother. See they be safe. Then I come for you, I promise. We be together. We be like this: Ellie and Lukasz. Together.'

'Yes, if only that was possible!' she cried. 'But how long will it be before we're all free? Oh Lukasz, when you go tomorrow, be careful! I can't bear to think of it. I hope you'll be safe. Jack will look after you; you'll soon be safely in England.' She said nothing more, kissed him and went out of the door. Suddenly he went after her and hugged her. The future and what lay in store for them closed in around them in the chill of Winter.

'You not go, not yet. Stay with Lukasz!'

'I must. They'll be wondering where I am. Goodbye, Lukasz.' Placing her hand against his chest, where she could feel his heart beating, she whispered, 'Take my love with you, Lukasz. Keep it safe for me.' She cried softly, and leaving him, she saw a candle was burning in the kitchen window of the farmhouse – her nan must have returned home. But without disturbing her, she made her way quietly across the yard and soon reached the road. Within minutes she was on her way home in the gathering darkness. Every footstep she took, tore her further and further away from him and she could barely see for the tears. Tomorrow, if all went well, the ocean would be between them.

Night descended. The plan was in place, the details finalised and in a few hours Lukasz and Jack would be meeting Franz on the harbour. With so much at stake, Ellen tossed and turned half the night. Something wasn't right. At three o'clock, she got out of bed, pulled on some clothes and, shivering with the cold, crept downstairs and went straight out of the house. It was the curfew, and she was terrified of meeting anyone, least of all a soldier, but she just had to speak to Robert about something that was niggling her. Something Lucy had told her didn't quite add up. Robert was sensible and if there were any grounds for suspicion, he would know what to do.

Fortunately, she didn't meet a soul during the whole half hour it took her to walk to his place in town. Without waking anyone up she was able to get to the door of his apartment and with a few taps she received a gruff response.

'Who's there?'

'Rob, it's me!' she whispered. 'I'm so sorry but I must speak to you.'

After a bit of commotion inside, Robert appeared. He opened the door just a crack and peered out mournfully. He wasn't wearing his glasses, his hair was all over the place and his eyes looked puffy.

'Dear God, Ellie, what are you doing here in the middle of the night?'

When she was safely inside, his concern for her took over and he swept the eiderdown from his bed and wrapped it around her. 'You're shivering. What on earth are you doing coming out during the curfew? You could have been shot or anything could have happened to you. Now come on, tell me, my sweet, what's all this about?'

'Something's worrying me about tomorrow, something I remember Lucy telling me about Franz. It just doesn't make sense and it's only a few hours until they set off. I've got a horrible feeling Franz isn't the person he pretends to be. Supposing, just suppose he's been leading Lucy on all this time? Why is he risking everything to help Lukasz?'

'Perhaps it's what he says it is. He sounded pretty angry and dead against all the things the Germans are doing on the island. Well, you heard him, Ellie.'

'Yes, but Lucy told me a lot of them in his barracks hate the war too; they all want to get out of here and go home. Half of them never wanted to join up in the first place but they're not rebelling or plotting against the Occupying Forces. I'm scared, Rob, I'm worried for Lukasz and Jack. It could be a trap.'

'Ellie, darling, it's nearly four o'clock in the morning. They'll be leaving in two hours and all being well Lukasz will be on his way to England by daylight. It's too late to stop it now. We'll have to trust that everything will be alright.'

'But Rob, listen! Just as I was leaving work last night, Lucy was excited and showing off a bit, I suppose. Something she said made me think. She said, "Fancy, Franz doing that when he's so funny about water!" I didn't know what she meant and thought she was just teasing me but then while I was trying to go to sleep I suddenly remembered: Ages ago she told me that when he was a little boy, he had a cruel uncle who used to pretend to drown him in the sea. He kept holding him under until the very last minute until Franz was gasping for breath. He thought it was a joke. But he was only a little boy and it frightened him. Well it would, wouldn't it. Bit of a sick joke, don't you think?'

'But a lot of us have experiences as children that scare us, sweetheart. You can't go on a story like that to say he's set all this up and none of what he says is true.'

'I know, I know that Rob, but it reminded me of something else she told me ages ago. In the early days before they banned everyone from the beach, her and a bunch of local girls used to go down in the summer flirting around with the soldiers, sunbathing and swimming. Lucy told me Franz always refused to swim with the others. He always made some excuse, and she used to tease him that he was actually afraid of going in the water.'

Robert went quiet. 'Surely that can't be true.'

'Just suppose it's true though. Suppose he can't swim?'

'Where will Franz be now?' Robert checked his watch. It's just after four. I don't expect he'll be up yet.

'Probably he's at Lucy's house, fast asleep beside her, she replied.'

Grabbing his trousers from the chair, Robert began dressing and talking as he went. 'I'll go and challenge him. If they're sailing at six, by the time I get to Lucy's house they'll be up I bet.'

'But what are you going to say to him?' she pleaded.

'I'll think of something. But if he can't swim, how is he going to swim to shore? And I tell you what, if he's been tricking us all and deceiving Lucy, she needs to know.'

'But the curfew!'

'I can't worry about that. You stay here, I'll be back as soon as I can.'

'No, Rob, I'm coming with you!'

'And risk your life as well, no chance!'

'I have to Rob!'

With no time to argue, minutes later they were both creeping out of the door, their coats flying open as they went hurrying down a side street making as little noise as possible. The darkness gave the streets a moody presence as the night sky opened up above them in a void filled with stars. It was the darkest hour before dawn.

Chapter 40

The faintest glow of candlelight showed through cracks in the blackout curtains as Ellen and Robert approached Lucy's house. They were out of breath and desperately worried her neighbours would hear them. But relieved to see someone was up they went quickly to the door and tapped lightly. There was no response. Looking at each other, they both nodded, sure they could hear voices within - the chirpy voice of Lucy and the deep resonant response from Franz. They could also hear his belt buckles being fastened, the keys that hang from his uniform jangling, and his heavy jackboots on the stone floor declaring their official status in that tiny house. Robert tapped again and then - too impatient to wait - tried the door and it opened. Franz stood before them. He appeared to be just buttoning up his jacket when he came face to face with them both.

'Good morning, Sir!' said Robert. 'A word with you, please, before you leave, if you don't mind.' Always polite, Robert was a gentleman, even in the face of danger.

Unlike before, when he had been cordial, Franz was now very curt. His eyes narrowed.

'You dare to come here! You know I have a duty to perform.' He looked at his watch. 'So, what can I do for you?'

'I would like to check something. It's a delicate situation and I'm sure it's not true but there's one or two points I'm not clear about.'

'Not clear, you say? And what exactly are you "not clear" about? I don't have much time.' His icy gaze was like that of a snake.

Hearing voices, Lucy came hurrying through from the back room, wearing only her nightdress and holding her swelling abdomen protectively. It was apparent her time was very near.

'Oh, hello! What are you doing here?'

Ellen made a friendly gesture towards her, with a fleeting smile and quickly put her finger to her lips. Franz turned his cold eyes upon Robert and said quietly, 'So, you steal the last few minutes I have with my girl just to check a few things?' he asked, his sharp German accent spiking the atmosphere.

'I'll come straight to the point, Franz. I want you to give me your word that you'll carry out this task in good faith. We are in your debt. It's very admirable that you're prepared to put yourself in the gravest of danger to save our friend, a mere stranger to you, and I thank you.'

Franz regarded this formal speech soberly, with lowered lids. 'Why do you come here actually? You know the duty of a soldier is to serve. I do what I say I will do without question. I do not intend to fail. Do you challenge me?'

'No, no, I'm sure that what I've heard isn't true,' replied Robert, continuing offhandedly, 'that when you were a boy, an unfortunate experience at the hands of your uncle caused you to have a dreaded fear of water... that in fact you can't and could never swim.'

A Sea of Barbed Wire

Franz stared at Robert and his blue eyes cut through him, sharp as a razor. 'Who told you about that? It's a lie! It's a damned lie!'

Lucy hung onto his arm and looked up at Franz in adoration. 'You tell him, Franz! Of course, you can swim, can't you! You wouldn't be in the army if you couldn't!' But something appeared to fracture in Franz's brain. His blue eyes changed, the pupils became tiny and piercing. He threw off her grasp and faced Robert.

'What are you suggesting? Are you calling me a bloody coward?' Letting forth a torrent of rebukes in German, he grabbed Robert by the throat.

Lucy wailed, 'No Franz! Let him go! Rob didn't mean anything,' she pleaded. 'It was just a story we heard. It was nothing!'

'So!' he said, thrusting Robert away in disgust. 'You all talk together. You all gang up on me to trap me! You ask for my help and then you ridicule me. How dare you come here with your lies!' Before anyone knew what was happening, Ellen saw a flash and realised he had a knife. Stepping between them, she cried, 'Stop it!'

'Stay out of this, Ellie,' said Robert, moving protectively in front of her.

'Do you still dare to accuse me?' said Franz, fixing him with a long cold stare. Seconds later he lunged forward and thrust the knife into Robert's chest.

Time stood still.

Robert, gazing at Franz in genuine surprise, collapsed back into Ellen's arms and crumpled to the floor.

Lucy screamed. 'Franz! Oh my God, Franz, what have you done?'

'Halt den Mund!' he yelled, turning the blood-soaked knife towards her for a brief moment as if he was about to plunge it into her breast also. But cursing in German, he flung the knife down and marched towards the door. 'You can't keep your stupid mouth shut can you, girl! Damn you! Damn you all. Fools, all of you, bloody fools!' He stopped in the doorway, casting an eye over Robert's lifeless body where a stream of blood was seeping onto the floor. Beside him, covering face in her hands, was Ellen, whimpering in disbelief.

'Ha! You really believed I would risk my life to help your prisoner escape? Now I'll do my duty as a soldier of the Third Reich and make my report to the Commandant. You will all pay for this.'

He was out of the door. Lucy ran after him, crying and pleading. 'Franz, please Franz, wait! Don't tell them, please; please Franz!' He stopped and looked at her. Something seemed to be going through his mind as he stared at her for several seconds. And then he turned sharply and was gone.

Chaos ensued, with front-doors opening, shouting, yelling, and neighbours coming out of their homes, floundering in the darkness. Lucy stood still, completely at a loss as she saw Franz jump into his military vehicle and fire up the engine. Returning to the house, she found Ellen weeping over Robert's body.

'He's dead. Oh God! It's all my fault!' she wailed.

'It wasn't just you, it was all of us,' sobbed Ellen. 'We're all to blame. Poor Robert, I can't believe it. What can I do? What can I do? Help me, help me …'

But Lucy turned and fled from the house.

A close neighbour, followed by several others came rushing in through the open door and saw the tragedy that lay before them. The first, Harry, felt for a pulse, loosened Robert's collar and yelled:

'Telephone for an ambulance someone!'

Ellen still knelt beside Robert, shivering. She never took her eyes from his face which was as still and pale as the moon. Seeing Robert's thick rimmed glasses lying close by, she picked them up. There was a tinkling sound as the tiny fragments of broken glass went slipping through her fingers.

Chapter 41

It was three days before Christmas. Lukasz, accompanied by Jack, was waiting nervously on the harbour. Franz had arranged to meet them beside Jack's fishing boat at 6.15am. It was one of the blackest and bleakest of mornings, with just a glimmer of light showing on the horizon. As the curfew ended at 6 o'clock, more fishermen gradually began arriving, tending their nets, checking their boats in readiness. Each team of fishermen were preparing to set off with an armed soldier who would accompany them. Jack, with Lukasz by his side, waited patiently and expectantly for Franz to appear, growing more and more impatient and anxious by the minute.

The two men watched and waited as each boat was checked, boarded and pushed off from the harbour. By half-past six, however, Franz still hadn't appeared. Lukasz and Jack were still waiting for him on the harbour wall. They didn't speak. A few other fishermen were still gathered there, but most had already left. Those who remained were keeping themselves to themselves, hauling crab pots on board and setting them up with bait, untangling nets and filling their outboard motor engines with fuel. Seagulls whined in the distance, sounding like abandoned dogs, while Jack checked his equipment methodically, keeping himself busy and taking his time while keeping his eye on all the proceedings that went on around. Jack treated Lukasz with a certain detachment as if he accepted that they were both of other worlds but thrust together on a life-saving mission. The prospect of leaving Guernsey for what could be a very long time hadn't altered Jack's demeanour. He moved about with confidence and had stored some extra supplies for their journey under tarpaulins. He appeared to regard the Germans as fools, but his opinion of Franz himself he hadn't shared.

Guards stood sentry, solitary and watchful on each side of the jetty. It was as cold as a tomb. An arc from the searchlight scanned the harbour. The sentries on duty were watching like hawks for the slightest movement on surrounding cliffs, castle walls and rocks where no soul in their right mind would wander. Lukasz, seeing all these things and feeling the tension of tragic events from long ago, the blood pumped high in his veins, and he longed to be on his way.

With the false identity papers Joan had supplied him with tucked in the top pocket of his jacket, Lukasz sat motionless, staring at the gently moving tide which he hoped would soon carry him away. He longed for it to absorb him into its vastness and take him away to safety. He thought of Ellen and the new journey he was about to take, and something within him ached at the distance that he was putting between them.

An almost imperceptible lightening of the sky from black to slate grey within minutes revealed clouds slit open, torn across like a piece of silk to allow the first rays of sun through.

'He not come,' said Lukasz finally, under his breath.

'Ssh!' Jack dismissed any communication between them with a swift shake of the head.

But with sunrise came army activity and the sound of many footsteps marching towards the harbour. At the sound, the remaining fishermens' voices rose up in unison, murmuring in anticipation, and they moved about with more confidence, slinging ropes, and preparing for their day's work. They would be allowed to row three miles out and no further, casting nets, and probing the rocks and gullies for crabs and trawling the deep-sea currents for that precious food that once might have been selected as a delicacy but was now simply regarded as urgently needed food. They would bring back anything that was edible. If they returned to their families at dusk empty handed, if their crab pots produced nothing and their nets were filled with weed or torn and snagged, they would suffer the pain of hunger for another night.

Down by the harbour, several soldiers approached the group of fishermen, barking orders and shattering the peaceful scene, driving away the night with their cold reality. The fishermen were not much better than servants, prisoners in fact to their masters who would demand at least half their fish and leave them with the poorest of the catch, the tiddlers and the undersized shellfish. Jack and Lukasz were still waiting for Franz by Jack's boat. Their secret supplies of food and water for the journey were stowed away out of sight but their appetite was only for freedom.

Time went on. The other fishermen were gradually checked off, each boat preparing to leave and finally heading out to their three-mile limit, but Franz hadn't appeared. As the minutes passed, the two men grew more and more agitated. Finally, a German soldier, one they hadn't seen before, approached them and nodding to each of them, thrust out his hand, a gesture which Jack recognised as being a demand for their identity papers. Lukasz, instructed to obey every signal from Jack, followed and produced his own ID. With a cursory glance at each of their papers in turn, the soldier handed them back with a nod and indicated that they should proceed to board their boat. Following Jack, Lukasz climbed down the slippery lichen strewn steps and clambered into the boat. It rocked alarmingly until Lukasz adjusted his position and steadied it. Once aboard, Jack occupied himself sorting the nets and the soldier was about to climb down to join them when, out of the morning mist a figure came running. It was a woman. Every few yards she appeared to stop and catch her breath. And then her voice came ringing across the hollow harbour; it was a call shrill and desperate: 'Franz! Franz, wait!'

With her flimsy clothes flapping, she was nearing the boats and, in distress, was calling out with her little stifled screams which attracted the attention of those on the harbour wall. However, the soldier with them mumbled something in German which they assumed meant, "hysterical woman" because he shrugged and continued on down the steps. Lukasz caught hold of Jack's arm, looked into his eyes and stared into its depths. He had no need to speak. They had both heard and recognised her screams and the name she was calling. The question was left hanging unanswered in the air. Where was he? What were they going to do? Pitifully, the woman's cries continued to echo across the cold harbour in vain.

The soldier impatiently boarded the boat and with a sharp upwards motion of his head he ordered Jack to cast off. Jack uncoupled the rope while Lukasz took up the oars. At ease with rowing, Lukasz pushed off and they soon took up speed. Lukasz moved with an age-old rhythm which felt comfortable and familiar. Steadily and with purpose the boat slid away from the jetty out into the bleak black sea beyond. He was at peace with himself at last. The gentle rowing motion, the wash and suck of the oars, the mild knocking sound of wood against wood as the boat trembled and creaked under the strength of his arms, brought healing to his broken spirit.

The soldier stood up at the helm with his back to them, his gaze directed straight ahead. His rigid expression didn't alter, and his position didn't change other than he shifted his rifle to use as a prop to steady himself as the boat gathered momentum. They pulled further out to sea, and the wind and waves grew stronger. With the salty tang of the sea and the fishing nets, memories began to return, and Lukasz felt himself coming back to life. He heard his father's voice in his head, calm and reassuring, coming through to him with the movement of the oars as he put his shoulders to the task and heaved each stroke. The rising and plunging of their boat drove a path bravely through the waves.

He and Jack eyed each other behind the back of the solitary soldier who stood in silhouette against the brightening sky. Soon it would be daylight. They were impatient, hungry for their freedom, for the open sea, to set their course for the English coast. Like a carved monument to victory and dominance, the soldier still hadn't turned round. At any moment he might turn and

A Sea of Barbed Wire

say that this was far enough, that they were within the three-mile limit, and they must stop and cast their nets.

More memories. Lukasz heard his father's shout of warning as the Nazis tore onto their farmland, and his sister's screams as she was dragged away. His mother's cries of terror. Then the gunshots and his father falling and the sight of his shattered forehead. And then another memory broke through that Lukasz had been fighting off ever since it had happened. Out of the swirling depths of his mind came the final memory, monstrous in its vividness. Irena, his sweet sister being pushed savagely up against the wall of the house by the brute of a soldier. Her clothes being ripped off. Her innocent body being ravaged. And her screams.

He came back to reality with a jolt. Jack put a firm hand on his shoulder and nodded at their soldier. 'We've got to do something,' he hissed in his ear. Lukasz saw the broad back of the German soldier and the memory of the soldier bearing down on Irena fired up in his veins. In an instant he stood up and swung the oar with such a force of revenge at the soldier's head it caught him and felled him with one massive blow. Without a single word passing between them, they knew what to do. Dead or alive, with an almighty effort, they heaved his body up and over the side, casting his rifle out after him.

They watched in silence as the bulk of him floated briefly and lifelessly before succumbing to the waves. Gradually the fabric of the German's uniform took on water and became submerged, sinking lower and disappearing into the depths. As the soldier sank, a healing balm soothed the ugly memories of the past. Both men watched the surface for several minutes until there was no sign that anything had occurred. The dark sea lapped against the boat impatiently. It was hard to believe, but suddenly they were on their own. Taking it in turns, they rowed until they were well away from the three-mile limit and out of sight of land. Moving confidently towards the stern of the boat, Jack pulled the cord, and the outboard motor sprang into life. They were, at last, on their way to England.

*

The innocent face of Lucy staring after Franz as he had left the house hurt him so unexpectedly that for a moment he felt completely confused. Within seconds he found himself feeling loyal neither to his regiment nor to his love for the local girl who was expecting his child. Whimpering helplessly, he clambered into his vehicle in tears, and hearing Lucy's piercing screams, he accidentally jammed his hand in the door. The pain was excruciating. It seared up his arm and brought him a sobering sense of the reality of what he had done. But it was too late. There was no way back. Suddenly he was a young boy again, weeping in his mother's lap. Tucking his broken hand inside his jacket, Franz fired up the ignition and drove off blindly at speed down the road. He was revving the engine cruelly, driving without lights, the wheels throwing up dirt and gravel as he went. But after driving for several minutes, he skidded to a halt again, and sat totally still in the driver's seat, staring straight ahead of him into the darkness. Minutes later he started up again, turned the vehicle round and sped off in the opposite direction, hurtling through the narrow lanes without lights, oblivious to everything. Eventually

A Sea of Barbed Wire

he found himself driving along the coast road, going further and further away from the town.

Coming to Port Soif, where the coastal path was all but sealed off with barbed wire and the beach heavily mined, he drove off the road, his vehicle lurching crazily across the uneven ground. It hit a rock and came to a standstill. Flinging open the door, and leaving the engine running, he headed straight for the sea. The sea that he hated with every breath of his body. Muttering to himself incoherently as his jackboots crunched on the shingle, and ignoring the red and black warning signs, "Achtung!" and "Minen!" he kept on. His eyes were fixed on the sea that had stolen his courage when he was a small boy. The sea owed him a final favour. The tide was high and the roar of the waves overpowered him. Gasping as the freezing water hit his thighs and seeped into his boots, Franz felt the strength and the rush of the waves against his body and he shut his eyes tightly as he ploughed into the depths. Suddenly an explosion went up. It shattered the silence, throwing Franz, seawater, rocks and gravel high into the air.

When the scene eventually settled again, and several German soldiers trained their binoculars across the beach, all that was visible were the gentle waves lapping over a still dark shape on the waterline. Dawn was just breaking; a glimmer of light transformed the scene with colours and shadows. There was the distant sound of a vehicle engine ticking over and the soft mewing of seagulls. But Franz, his pain, his love and betrayal, were no more.

Chapter 42

A few hours had passed by and it was about 9.30am. Ellen was sitting by the fire drinking tea. She had been taken in and cared for by Lucy's neighbours, Harry and his wife Olive. They spoke little, each afraid of speculating on what might happen to them. Hardly noticeable at first, they became aware of a faint tapping sound on the door. Harry got up with a grim expression and went to see who it was. They heard him ask someone to come in quickly and the door closed. Lucy appeared, wrapped in a shawl and as pale as death. She was blue around the eyes and shivering uncontrollably. When she caught sight of Ellen she rushed to her, weeping. What she needed was comfort, protection, forgiveness, but she said nothing and simply sat huddled close to Ellen like a frightened child.

'Has Franz gone?' asked Ellen quietly.

Lucy nodded without replying.

'But do you think he'll really send the soldiers for us, Lucy?'

'I don't know, he might!' she cried. 'And I don't know what to do!'

Olive handed her a cup of hot tea. 'Don't worry. Drink this, love, it'll warm you up, eh? Not much else any of us can do right now.'

But as Lucy sat there, trembling and holding her cup, she very quietly began to groan. Ellen noticed it first and put an arm around her, 'You've had a terrible shock, don't worry. Try to forget it and drink your tea. You can't do anything by worrying.'

'But poor Robert, I'm so sorry! I never …I never thought Franz would - '

'He's in the hospital, Lucy. They said he's lost a lot of blood, but the doctor thinks he should recover.'

Lucy looked incredulous. 'So Franz didn't –'

'No, he probably meant to, but he didn't kill him.'

'Oh! I can't believe it! That's such a relief!' She moaned again, but this time she put down her tea and pressed her hands against her tummy, gasping. 'My baby! I think my baby's coming! But it's too soon, Ellie, it's too soon!'

*

It was late afternoon now and events of the previous night had retreated into the shadows like a haunting nightmare. Olive, Harry's wife, went to telephone the hospital for a third time. When she came back into the room, she looked straight at Ellen.

'Well, my dear, they said your Robert's doing well and he's comfortable.' She looked at her husband. 'Thanks to you, Harry love! You acted quickly and stemmed the flow of blood, so he stands a good chance. We'll telephone again in a little while, eh?' She stroked Ellen's hair and smoothed it back from her tear-stained face. 'And would you like to know how your friend Lucy is?'

Ellen nodded. She was too emotional, too worked up to even speak.

'Baby arrived safely an hour ago and mum and baby are both well!'
All Ellen could do was sigh, close her eyes and whisper,
'Thank God.'

The following afternoon, in the quietness of the hospital ward, Ellen had been sitting by Robert's bedside for an hour. Sometimes his eyelids flickered, and she whispered his name. Sometimes his breathing faltered, and she ran for the nurse, only to be told he was okay and sleeping peacefully. 'He's probably dreaming, dear. They do, you know, it's the painkillers.'

It was late in the day when he eventually opened his eyes. He murmured 'Ellie?'

'I'm here. Rob, how are you feeling?'

He peered around the ward, trying to locate where he was but when he started to move, he winced in pain. 'What happened? I had the most dreadful dream. What time is it?'

But before she could answer, he was asleep again.

Presently, a nurse came down the ward.

'Are you alright, lovey? Here, I've brought you a hot cuppa and some biscuits – yes, biscuits! Aren't we the lucky ones!' Checking Robert's pulse, she adjusted his bedclothes, took his temperature, and scribbled a few figures on the chart.

'He's doing well, your young man, eh? We'll soon have him up and about again. Come on then, young Robert, are you going to wake up for your sweetheart here?'

A Sea of Barbed Wire

He opened his eyes, startled, and looked around. 'Oh, I was dreaming again!' His gaze fell on Ellen and he smiled faintly, peering around the room.

'Where's my glasses? Can you find my glasses for me? I can't see a thing!'

'They're broken I'm afraid. We'll try to get you another pair, don't worry.'

'I'll have to get back to work, Ellie. They need me at the bank. I wonder, if you wouldn't mind, if you could telephone …'

Before she could assure him that it was all taken care of, he was asleep again. She smiled, kissed his cheek and left him to rest.

Following the signs to the maternity ward, Ellen heard the plaintive voice of a new-born baby. On the far side, in a bed by the window, she saw Lucy sitting propped up by pillows. The baby responsible for the crying lay in her arms, its tiny face screwed up in agitation and its miniature hands stretched out and grabbing at the air.

'How sweet! Just look at him!'

'It's a girl, Ellie,' she said flatly. Lucy looked so small and pale in the bed, almost a child herself. 'She wasn't meant to come yet either, not for another month or so!'

'It was the shock, Lucy, it was bound to affect you.'

But her friend's eyes kept flicking nervously across the ward to the other mothers. She seemed afraid of something. Sitting down on a chair beside the bed, Ellen was wary of her nervousness and chose her words carefully.

'She's beautiful. Just look at her lovely blue eyes.'

'They all hate me in here. No-one speaks to me an' I want to go home.'

'Of course they don't hate you, Lucy. You're just feeling sensitive right now. Take no notice, you'll soon be out of here.'

'I suppose they know about Franz, they're callin' me a Jerry bag,' she said, sniffing.

'Well, they don't know half of what you've suffered. You've been through so much. But look at your baby, how pretty she is!' she said, gazing at the tiny baby in amazement. Then she looked down the ward to where three other new mothers had visitors huddled round them. Some of them were talking in hushed tones and occasionally glancing in their direction and they weren't smiling. How lonely Lucy must feel. But there was something she had to ask her, and she wasn't looking forward to it. 'Have you heard anything? I mean, do you know what happened to Franz?'

Lucy nodded and looked her straight in the eye. 'One of his German soldier mates came to see me. It was very early this mornin', still dark. He didn't want to be seen I suppose. They wouldn't allow him on the ward.' Her eyes shifted, dull and lifeless. 'Anyway, he scribbled this note. Matron gave it to me.' Saying this, she took a small scrap of paper from under her pillow.

Ellen read the scrawl that announced, in the briefest of words, the death of his comrade Franz by suicide. There were no condolences, no details.

'Goodness, I'm so sorry, Lucy...I had no idea.'

'Sorry? Why should *you* be sorry? I'm the one who should be sorry! There's Robert lying in bed, fighting for his life because of him and…' Unable to finish her sentence, she examined the tiny baby's fingers who had ceased crying and was now suckling contentedly at her breast.

'Robert's recovering well. Don't worry, they say he'll be okay.'

'But you were right, Ellie. Franz was a bastard after all. Just like all the others. What a coward. He didn't deserve to have a beautiful little daughter like this – and I don't either actually.'

'Don't say that! You've been through a lot, we all have. It's this war, this dreadful hideous war. And look at her! She can't be blamed for who her father was, the poor little lamb!'

Lucy was struggling to cope, wiping her nose on her sleeve. 'How is Robert though, really? Tell me!'

'He's talking a bit and he's in a lot of pain of course, and very weak, but it could have been much worse.'

'I really thought Franz had murdered him, you know, and it was all my fault.'

'No, of course it wasn't your fault! Don't think that. And the doctors say as long as they can get hold of enough penicillin to keep fighting off any infection Robert will recover and be as good as new. Poor old Robert, when he met me he didn't know what he was letting himself in for, did he!' she said and smiled.

'What about...' She glanced down the ward before whispering, 'What about Lukasz, did he manage to get away alright?'

Just hearing his name was enough. Ellen's smile vanished and her eyes filled with tears.

'I don't know!' she replied softly. 'That's the awful thing. I don't know if I'll ever hear what became of him and if they ever made it. Nan told me Jack hasn't returned home to his farm and so far, no-one's heard from him. As far as we know the Germans haven't started out on a mad search or made any new threats. No-one's heard anything but who knows? They could both be on the run somewhere, still on the island, hiding somewhere, waiting for it all to blow over. I'm scared, Lucy. Everyone's so secretive, we don't know who we can trust anymore.'

The fearful scenarios that haunted her sprung into her mind with renewed clarity, of Lukasz being shot or visions of his body being washed up on some remote beach. Visualising such a scene was more than she could bear. She held the tears back, but they came like rocks in her throat. 'Oh Lucy! What if he was discovered and they shot him dead? I might never know!'

'Come on, don't even think that! He's probably in England by now, safe an' sound. But we're still in danger too, aren't we? What if they've searched the room where Franz was staying and found out something? The soldiers could still come for us.' Suddenly aware that they were still in the ward and ought to keep their voices down, Ellen put her finger to her lips.

'Let's not think about it. Come on, look after your little daughter and just worry about her for now. Try to forget all about the other night, okay?'

'I wish I could! I wonder what made Franz change his mind though. He swore he was goin' to report us as he went stormin' out the door. Somethin' must have happened. And they say he took his own life? What an idiot!'

Attempting to make light of the situation failed her and she gave a sudden bitter laugh. 'I really loved him, you know, Ellie. I really loved him!' she cried, almost losing her hold on the tiny baby in her arms. Ellen gently took the baby girl from her and cradled her.

'I really believe you did, Lucy, and I think he loved you too. You looked so happy when you were together. It just all went wrong for you both.'

Lucy's tears subsided. She pulled herself together and smiled weakly at the sight of Ellen rocking the baby to sleep. 'You're looking very comfortable, look at you! Perhaps you'll have one of your own one day, eh? Perhaps you and Robert will end up getting hitched!' She sniffed, blew her nose and looked a lot more cheerful.

But Ellen was shaking her head. 'I don't think I can marry Rob, Lucy. Even if he ever asks me again.'

'It's Lukasz, isn't it.'

'I'm afraid so.'

She left Lucy, walked out of the hospital and tried her hardest to imagine where Lukasz was and what he was doing. That indescribable rush of love had been torn away from her. But he couldn't have stayed on the island. Sooner or later, he would have been discovered. She just hoped that he had made it, that he was free. Oh, how she hoped he was free! Something special had been there between them which she had never experienced before, and she cherished it. Lucy had lost her true love but held her lover's baby in her arms. Ellen realised she had nothing of Lukasz to keep. She longed for him, but he couldn't have stayed. Wherever he was she hoped he carried her love with him in his heart. As she walked out of the hospital that day and breathed in the wild sea air, she had the strangest sensation that somewhere out there Lukasz was thinking of her. Despite all that had gone before, her optimism returned.

*

Several months later, spring was in the air when Ellen got home from work one afternoon. There had been no end to the speculation about what had happened to the two men who they could only hope had set off as planned to escape to England. When she saw her mother standing at the open door waiting for her, the sight made her stomach turn over in fear.

'What's happened, Mum? It's not Nan, is it?'

'No, it's okay, love. It's not bad news. Your nan's in there. Don't worry.'

Staring at her mother's curious smile, Ellen rushed past her. They were all so used to whispering, and talking in hushed tones, it had become second nature to them. In the sitting-room, she found her nan sitting on the settee.

'Ellie, love! I've got something to tell you. Jack's wife came to see me this morning. She's finally received a Red Cross letter from Jack.' She winked at her.

'From Jack! That means he's alright, they made it! What did it say, Nan?' cried Ellen.

'Not much, love. Remember, they're only allowed to write twenty-five words, and the Germans scrutinise everything, but ...' She chuckled. 'He's safe, they both are. That's the main thing. Come and sit down here with me.' Joan patted the seat beside her. Ellen did so, her eyes never leaving her nan's face.

A Sea of Barbed Wire

'Jack's message said something like they were keeping well, they were working hard together on the farm and he said *the lad was eating again.*'

Ellen couldn't hold back any longer. 'Do you think he meant Lukasz?' Joan nodded, smiling and gazing at her curiously. 'I'd bet my last slice of bread that's what he meant.'

'So they made it, Nan! Oh, I'm so relieved!' She burst into tears and sat weeping with joy for several minutes. When she had recovered herself a little she said, 'I couldn't say anything before, but …' Looking up with a tear-stained face, she whispered, 'I'm in love with Lukasz. I'm sorry, I should've told you before.'

Joan put her arm around her shoulders and hugged her. 'I already knew, love,' she replied. 'I think we all knew there was something special between you two. Isn't that right, Meg?'

Meg nodded. 'Yes, as much as we all tried to warn you, Ellie. But what about Robert? He almost died trying to protect you, remember.'

'He knows how I feel about Lukasz, Mum. I had to tell him. But we're still good friends. He told me the other day he just keeps hoping that one day I'll forget about Lukasz and …' She smiled sadly. 'Poor Robert. Poor dear Robert! He deserves better than that but what can I do? At least he's back at work now and almost back to his old self.'

'But will you forget Lukasz, Ellie?' asked Joan.

'No, Nan. I don't think I ever will. He promised me he would come back for me one day and I believe him.' Saying this, her thoughts spiralled away to when she was with him last, how he had promised so fervently to return and held her in his arms so lovingly. She would wait, however long it took, however long the war went on, she knew she couldn't help but would wait for him. The future spread out before her with renewed hope. The Red Cross message from Jack confirmed all that she had been feeling all along; that Lukasz was alive and free. One day she knew they would be together again. Like the sun coming out from behind the clouds, her spirits lifted. She felt strong enough to face the future now, whatever that might hold.

A Sea of Barbed Wire

Dear Reader,

I hope you have enjoyed reading **A Sea of Barbed Wire**. Perhaps you have even grown fond of some of the characters. When I've finished writing a book, I'm often reluctant to let my characters go because I become so involved in their lives; they are like friends and I miss them!

Let me tell you that I have begun working on a sequel. I intend to revisit their lives after the Channel Islands have been liberated by the Allies. Evacuees are returning home, and Guernsey people are reclaiming their land and their freedom. But the island has been damaged, and many houses are in a state of disrepair. The beaches are heavily mined and sealed off with barbed wire and the coastline is scarred by ugly concrete bunkers, so there is much work to be done. Many challenges lie ahead.

If you have enjoyed reading this novel, please leave a review on Amazon and if you have any comments or questions, you are welcome to contact me via my website where you will find my email address and links to social media. I am always pleased to hear from my readers. Also keep an eye out on my website for further news and updates: https://theresaleflem.com/

Thank you so much.

Theresa Le Flem

A Sea of Barbed Wire
Acknowledgements

My heartfelt thanks to the Guernsey people who lived through those years of hardship and recorded their stories. I often feel I'm trespassing on well-trodden paths that others have journeyed down and who, quite understandably, sometimes would prefer not to remember. Memories are sometimes best left where they lie, particularly recollections of troubled times, so I'm very grateful to have the opportunity to read memoirs by, for example, June Money, as well as the excellent diary by the Rev. Douglas Ord. I have had several conversations with June Money who even welcomed my questions with tea and cake! Thank you, June.

I give my sincere thanks to Dr. Gilly Carr, of Cambridge University, for her well-informed friendly advice, her expertise, and her encouragement during the writing process. Thank you, Gilly. Your emails always give me a boost and your comments often sparked new ideas when my imagination was flagging.

A special thank you to Sally Woolland who agreed to be the first to read the manuscript from beginning to end and who, on finishing it, gave such a positive response. As she was reading it, she described to me the suspense she endured as events unfolded. She told me it thrilled her, and she became so attached to the characters she worried about their safety! This is what all novelists hope to achieve. Her response encouraged me so much. Thank you, Sally.

Thank you to the staff of The Priaulx Library and the Guille-Allès Library in St. Peter Port for their helpful advice during the time I was researching for this novel.

I would like to mark my appreciation for the help received from Richard Heaume, owner of the German Occupation Museum. This is a place which offered me the unique experience of stepping back in time. On entering the museum, it always sends a chill up my spine. Richard kindly responded to my request for some original German barbed wire which I wanted to photograph in order to create the design for the book cover. He magically produced a length of fragile barbed wire which was still intact if somewhat rusty. It was just what I needed.

I would also like to mention the Rev. Peter Lane for reading and checking the chapter containing German dialogue. Thank you, Peter.

Finally, my most grateful thanks go to my husband Graham for his confidence in me, his patience when I spent hours at the computer totally unaware of the time, for driving me around to hunt out various German bunkers – which he tells me was not exactly his choice of a day out – and for putting up with Guernsey history books piled up in every room. Graham, your encouragement, support, and gentle persuasion for me to complete and publish this book means the world to me.

A Sea of Barbed Wire